She stilled and
The bird had landed
a leftover biscuit on one of the plates. Andrew silently edged nearer to the bird, then swiftly lowered the lid on top of it. A great flapping of wings sounded from underneath. Andrew managed to slide the top over to the edge of the table. Placing the tray underneath, he neatly trapped the bird inside.

Grinning triumphantly, he turned to show Miss Whittingham. From behind her came a deep "woof," and the giant furry body of Fergus leapt up, knocking Miss Whittingham to the side, and landed directly against his chest. Andrew overbalanced, falling backward onto his rear end, arms flailing. The bird escaped his trap and flew calmly out the window. Andrew shoved at Fergus ineffectually, trapped under more than one hundred pounds of wolfhound, the dog's large paws pinning him to the ground.

"Fergus, off," cried Miss Whittingham. Fergus immediately got up and returned to her side. Andrew lay there a few moments, staring at the ceiling, and tried to figure out why every time he encountered this woman calamity ensued. At the sound of muffled laughter, he sat up to face Miss Whittingham. She had also been knocked to the floor in Fergus' frenzy to capture the bird. She sat across the rug from him, wild wisps of hair escaping from her bun, her face alight with laughter. Her eyes sparkled. She laughed so hard she gasped for breath between giggles. He had never seen such a beautiful sight. His breath caught in his throat. Why hadn't he noticed before how breathtaking she was?

Thief of My Heart

by

Karla Kratovil

Hearts of Stoneleigh Manor, Book 2

This is a work of fiction. Names, characters, places, and incidents are either the product of the author's imagination or are used fictitiously, and any resemblance to actual persons living or dead, business establishments, events, or locales, is entirely coincidental.

Thief of My Heart

Contact Information: info@thewildrosepress.com

Cover Art by *Diana Carlile*

The Wild Rose Press, Inc.
PO Box 708
Adams Basin, NY 14410-0708
Visit us at www.thewildrosepress.com

Publishing History
First Tea Rose Edition, 2020
Trade Paperback ISBN 978-1-5092-3191-1
Digital ISBN 978-1-5092-3192-8

Hearts of Stoneleigh Manor, Book 2
Published in the United States of America

Dedication

To my mom and dad,
who always believe I can accomplish anything.

Chapter 1

Andrew Henry Langdon, Duke of Gilchrest, lay staring up at the velvet canopy of his large four-post bed. The room was dark, cool, and perfect for sleeping. But as usual, he lay wide awake, unable to quiet the constant rumble of his thoughts. A soft rustle came from the curtains which hung in front of the french doors. Then a shadow slid into the room. It walked along the carpet soundlessly. One hand ran over the back of a leather wing chair then along the edge of his washbasin as it wandered across the room.

Andrew lay still, tense, waiting for the man to wander closer to the bed, and ready to seize the culprit who dared violate his home. Dear God, what if the man had entered into his sons' room or his sister's? The muscles in his shoulders bunched as the silhouette paused not three feet away. In one fluid motion, he vaulted out of the bed and grabbed hold of a thin arm. He pinned the man against the nearest wall and pushed one forearm against his throat.

"You should have picked a house where the owner sleeps more soundly, young man. You dare to steal into the ducal mansion?"

He looked down at the shadowed, dirty face of a lad who couldn't be more than a boy of fourteen based on the slight frame. Wide dark eyes met his from under a tattered cap before the boy began to struggle. Andrew flattened his body against the writhing youth, pinning him more firmly against the wall.

This was no boy. His body pressed against a pair of soft breasts. He removed his arm off her throat. Her baggy jacket hung open, and he reached inside to run a hand from the curve of her breast down over a small waist and gently flared hips. The shock of his discovery burned through him. Andrew stepped back, releasing her arm.

Pale moonlight peeked out from behind the clouds, and he could see the thief flash him a wide grin. Then she stood on tiptoe, brushing a featherlight kiss across his lips. Before he could even blink, she disappeared out the french doors. Andrew stood rooted in place for several moments. Gathering his wits, he raced out to the balcony, his eyes scanning across the lawn.

The moon had disappeared back behind the clouds, and it was hard to see anything on such a dark night. He leaned forward against the cold wrought iron of his balcony. Yes, there he glimpsed a small dark form disappear through the hedges at the bottom of the garden. How did she get down there so quickly? He peered over the balustrade, curious how she had managed to climb up to the second floor. A cool breeze danced across his skin, reminding him he was naked, and he went back inside.

He sank onto the side of the bed, and he ran a hand down over his face to clear the last vestiges of astonishment from his brain. Maybe he was dreaming? What in the hell was a woman, dressed like a boy, doing creeping into his room in the middle of the night?

He should ring for Holmes. Have his butler call the constable. Andrew sighed, his deep inhale turning into a yawn. What he really wanted was to head downstairs and get himself a brandy to take the edge off the shock. But no, he'd recently given up spirits in an effort to put his life back on track. So instead, he lay back down on the bed and closed his eyes.

He yawned again, his jaw cracking with the effort. He tugged at the sheet, pulling it over him. Tomorrow morning would be soon enough to call the constable, to put a man to watch the perimeter of the house. He would be practical in the morning. Then he attempted to quiet his mind and force himself to sleep.

****

Five blocks away, Emma Whittingham climbed the great oak outside her own window and scrambled into her bedroom. She ripped the cap off her head and flung it across the room. What a disaster tonight had been. Not only had she not acquired the piece she wanted, but she had been bloody caught sneaking around the Duke of Gilchrest's bedchamber in the middle of the night!

Fergus let out a low woof from his spot in the corner. He got up, stretching his long legs before coming over to greet her. Emma gave his enormous head a soft scratch, bending down to give him a kiss on his wet snout. She went over to sit at her vanity and began pulling pins from her neatly coiled hair. When the duke grabbed her, she'd looked up into his face and seen such fierceness etched into his features. Her breath had escaped in one great whoosh when the hard length of his body pressed against hers. The heat he exuded surprised her.

She looked at her reflection in the vanity's mirror, even now her faced flushed pink at the memory. It had almost made her laugh out loud when he had dropped back so quickly, and with such a look of astonishment on his face.

Emma walked over to splash her face with water from the basin. Taking the washcloth, she scrubbed the soot from her face. The kiss had been pure folly, but she hadn't been able to resist. When would she ever again be so near to such a gorgeous specimen of masculinity, let alone kiss one? She should be upset he figured out she was a woman. Pretending to be an adolescent boy helped to protect her real identity. But she couldn't be sorry about the way his hand felt skimming down her curves. She trembled a bit, remembering.

Emma pulled off her coat, shirt, and pants, stowing them in their spot in the false bottom of her wardrobe. She threw a nightgown over her head and sat back down at the vanity. Picking up her brush, she started to brush through her long golden-brown hair. She frowned at her reflection. Tonight she had lost her opportunity to steal the necklace.

A picture of the Duchess of Gilchrest's ruby necklace rose in her mind. The duchess had worn it at Lady Cummings' party just last month. It had taken Emma's breath away with its beauty. The necklace was made up of dozens of rubies clustered together to create flowers that flowed down vines of gold filigree. The centerpiece was a collection of rubies and diamonds assembled to form a fiery sunburst which had sparkled every time the duchess laughed at her companion's witty repartee.

Now the duke would be on high alert. It would be too risky to go back in. She gave a loud snort of frustration. The family was supposed to be out of town.

What a foolish mistake to trust secondhand information from that imbecile Johnny Gates. She should have done her own reconnaissance, then she wouldn't have ended up in the wrong damn bedroom. She set her brush down with a thunk. She would just have to choose another mark. Lord knew there were plenty of rich households in Mayfair that could afford to lose a bauble or two.

"Come on, Fergus, time for bed." She climbed under the covers. Fergus, obedient as always, jumped up and settled himself at the foot of her bed, covering her feet with his warmth.

Chapter 2

The next morning, Emma awoke to the gleeful voices of the hellions. Her brothers jumped up and down on her bed.

"Emma! Emma, wake up!"

She groaned and pulled the covers up over her head in an attempt to muffle the sound of their cheerfulness. To no avail.

"Emma, today is Tuesday. Tuesday is market day, hooray!" She still did not move. The twins loved market day because Lucy always took them to the park while Emma shopped with Mrs. Fenway, their housekeeper.

"What time is it?" Emma mumbled from beneath the covers.

"We don't know." They continued to bounce on her bed.

"Its seven o'clock," said a sleepy voice from the door.

Emma popped her head from under the covers to see her sister leaning against the doorjamb in her nightgown, eyes still heavy with sleep. Lucy was closest to her in age, at twenty. Even first thing in the morning, Lucy's hair managed to look artfully tousled. Her long blonde locks fell in perfect waves around an oval face with big cornflower blue eyes and delicate features.

"Why can't you two bounce around your own beds? Why must you wake us all with your cacophony?" Lucy said.

"It's marketing day!" As if that explained everything.

Emma looked at Fergus who had taken refuge at the top of the bed. "Some guard dog you are." Fergus gave her a bland look and drooled on her pillow. Emma sighed and sat up, pushing her hair away from her face.

"All right, you lot, go downstairs and bother Mrs. Fenway for some breakfast. Leave me to get dressed, or we will never get to the market." The twins jumped down in unison and scurried out of the room at top speed for the kitchen.

She lay back down against her pillow with a sigh. Lucy came over and sat down on the section of the bed where the twins had just vacated.

Leaning back against the bedpost, she said, "Late night? Did you get what you were looking for?"

"No, I did not. I ran into some trouble." Seeing her sister's worried face, she said, "Nothing I couldn't get out of, but I wasn't able to get the necklace."

"Emma, perhaps this is a sign you should stop. You have been lucky so far not to have been caught. The season is starting, and I will find a husband, someone who will take care of us all. There is no reason for you to keep risking yourself in this manner."

Emma admired her sister's confident attitude, but Lucy had no idea the amount of debts Emma had been painstakingly paying off. Nor did she understand the money it took to feed them all, to keep just the skeleton staff, not to mention the expenses of the social season. Modiste bills, the draper, the hat maker…

Lucy understood money was tight, but not to what extent. Emma preferred to shield her from the harsh reality of the financial hardship their father had left them. She was the oldest. The responsibility lay with her to keep the family together and to take care of them.

"I'm sure you will land a fine titled gentleman. You will be the most sought-after debutant of the season." She leaned over and gave her sister a hug. "Don't worry about me. You know how much I love the thrill of the hunt. I will just have to find another bauble to lift from its unsuspecting owner." She grinned at her sister, hoping Lucy wouldn't ask her any more details about last night. "Have you made your list for market day? You know I would forget half the things we need without your list."

"Yes, I worked on it last night with Mrs. Fenway. I will go wake Margie and Abby," she said, referring to their two younger sisters. "Get dressed, and we will meet you downstairs for breakfast." Lucy scooted off the bed and sailed out of the room.

Instead of getting up to get dressed for the day, Emma snuggled back into the covers. She turned away from Fergus' rancid breath. Five more minutes. She yelped when something hit against her shoulder.

"Get up lazy bones and get dressed!" Lucy shouted from the doorway.

Emma rolled over and grabbed the slipper that had hit her. She hurled it back at her sister. "Fine!" Grumbling, she climbed out of bed and grudgingly started her day.

When Emma entered the breakfast room, she found all five of her siblings seated and eating. She paused in surprise at the scene. Normally, in the morning

Margaret and Abigail sat together behind the morning paper or latest scandal rag, their plates of food untouched. At fourteen and twelve they were captivated by the goings-on of society.

The twins, Max and Will, were a rambunctious six years old. Their normal routine included running around the table, with their toast in hand, in an endless game of tag. She could rarely get them to sit down long enough to eat, let alone to teach them any proper table manners. Emma had given up on taming them last year after she had to let their nurse go, due to a need to tighten the household budget. They were sweet-natured boys, albeit a little wild. Lucy was the only one who she could have a decent conversation with across the breakfast table.

Emma went to the sideboard to serve herself some eggs and toast. She could hear giggling behind her, but it abruptly stopped as she turned around. Giving the table a stern look, she sat down and reached for her tea.

Lucy broke the silence. "Emma, I think you should take the boys to the park today, and I will go to the market with Mrs. Fenway. I have several things I need in addition to the household list."

"We will join you, Lucy," Margie said with far too much enthusiasm. Abby nodded her head along with her sister.

"What do you need? Remember the budget is tight as we get ready for your first season."

Lucy's gaze dropped to her plate, and she bit her lower lip as she tried to come up with what it was she needed. She was a terrible liar. Unfortunately, the younger girls were excellent fibbers. They jumped in to save her.

"She needs new writing paper and new hair clips to match that lovely blue gown we ordered. These are things a lady must pick out for herself you know," Abby said.

"And you two, why are you so excited to go marketing?" Emma eyed them. "Are you planning on being a help or a hindrance?"

"We'll be a help. We promise." Abby and Margie gave her their best angelic expressions. Not that Emma was fooled, and she was just about to say so when Lucy cut in—

"Emma, just let it be. Your birthday is in three days. Take the boys to the park and leave us to our shopping."

Emma frowned. She had hoped everyone would forget her birthday. There was nothing celebratory about her turning twenty-five. She was unmarried and living a scandalous double life whilst mothering her five younger siblings. Not exactly how she had pictured her life turning out. She glanced around the table at the smiling faces of her brothers and sisters and sighed in defeat.

"All right, boys, gather your dogs, and let's get ready for the park." Max and Will jumped up and raced to the kitchen. No doubt they would whip the dogs into a frenzy before they even had them all leashed. She finished her eggs quickly and along with Fergus headed toward the kitchen.

Last Christmas their uncle had decided what all the children needed was each their own dog. He had showed up Christmas morning with much fanfare and five big boxes. Fergus had not been enthusiastic about having five new dogs in the house and neither had

Emma. It was just like Uncle Charles to show up with some grand gesture and then leave her to figure out all the details.

"All right, boys, each of you leash your pups, and I will take Lord Pettigrew." She attached the lead to Abigail's little beagle. Turning to Fergus, she said, "Don't give me that sad face. You know you have to wear the leash in the park." Fergus would never wander from Emma's side, but he made the other patrons in the park nervous with his large size and grizzled face. She kept him on the lead for appearance's sake.

They all left through the back entrance, walking through the small garden and out to the alley which led to the mews. As they gained the park, Emma let the boys run ahead with their dogs to burn off some energy. She kept an eye out, walking at a more leisurely pace behind them, letting Fergus and Lord Pettigrew sniff around at their leisure.

After she lost sight of the boys around a corner, a loud frenzy of barking broke out. Uh-oh. She hurried around the corner and saw four little boys and four dogs all in a tangle of arms, legs, and furry tails. A tall gentleman with dark hair appeared. He let out an ear-piercing whistle, and all four dogs paused, looking toward him.

"Sit!" he said. Dogs and boys all sat down in the middle of the path at his command.

She winced, instantly recognizing the Duke of Gilchrest. He was the last person she wanted to happen upon in the park. This morning his broad shoulders were covered in a superfine coat of dark blue. His long legs, encased in perfectly fitted breeches, led down into a pair of polished hessians. His dark hair framed a face dominated by a long nose and strong jaw. A face which currently held a rather thunderous expression. Oh dear. Emma hurried forward.

"I am so sorry, Your Grace! Max, Will, please stand up and calmly untangle your dogs."

****

What a damn mess! The Duke of Gilchrest looked at the young woman whose commanding tone galvanized her two sons to untangle themselves and their corgis from Andrew's two sons. Her expression was one of barely contained mirth.

"Well, I still don't know how you do it, but I wish I could have you around all the time to bring order to my unruly family. Even little boys sit at your command." She covered her mouth with one hand; her brown eyes danced with laughter. Her eyes were fanned by lush dark lashes and sat in a beautiful oval face with a small pert nose and peaches and cream complexion. Her golden-brown hair was piled high on her head, and a little blue bonnet sat atop at a jaunty angle. He narrowed his gaze on her face. "Have we met?"

"Yes, I am afraid we have. Earlier this summer you and your brother had to save a young woman from my throng of dogs. You have quite an impressive whistle. You had all the dogs' attention then too. How unfortunate we keep meeting under the same chaotic circumstances."

"Yes! I remember. Poor Vivian nearly toppled into the pond." He smiled thinking about his sister-in-law's clumsiness. She had probably been to blame for getting tangled in the dogs' leads. "You do seem to travel with a lot of dogs. Mrs…?"

"Miss Emmaline Whittingham. And these two are

my brothers, Max and William." The two little boys bowed, and their sister beamed at them.

"Duke of Gilchrest." He tipped his hat. "These are my sons, Grayson and Tyler."

"It's very nice to meet you, Miss Whittingham." Grayson executed a perfect bow. "Egads, that is the biggest dog I have ever seen!"

Andrew gave his son a frown. "That's not polite, Grayson." Although he could hardly blame him, an enormous dog sat next to Miss Whittingham. Her delicate hand lay atop his massive head. The dog stared at them with wise gray eyes, and a large drop of drool dangled from the corner of his mouth.

"This is Fergus. He is an Irish wolfhound. He found me one day in trouble with some scoundrels trying to rob me, and we have been together ever since. He is very gentle with children but most protective of me," Miss Whittingham explained.

"He is a gentle giant," Max said, throwing his arms around Fergus' neck. The dog turned his head and licked the boy's face.

"Were you set upon by thieves? Certainly not here in Mayfair I hope," Andrew asked.

"I was on Bond Street." Miss Whittingham replied, her gaze on the dog as she scratched Fergus behind the ears.

How strange that a young gentlewoman would be wandering along Bond Street by herself with no footman to protect her. And really, she just adopted an oversized dog from the street? What sort of family allowed their daughter to come home with an eighty-pound stray? He shook his head. Just as he was about to politely make their excuses, he glanced over at the four boys. They were exchanging stories about their pets. Grayson's small hands waved in the air as he described his hound running through the kitchen garden, long ears flapping and a scullery maid chasing the dog with her broom. Laughter rang out from the other three boys as Grayson finished his story. He hadn't seen a smile like that on Grayson's face for months. And Tyler, usually so quiet, chatted like a magpie to Max and William.

Looking again at Miss Whittingham and her beast of a dog, he silently sighed. "We were just heading to the great meadow to throw balls for the dogs. Would you all care to join us?"

Miss Whittingham's eyes widened as she looked up at him. Her polite "No, thank you," was drowned out by a chorus of "Yes!" from the boys. En masse, the children and dogs raced ahead down the path. Miss Whittingham frowned as she watched her brothers race ahead.

"Shall we?" He gestured for her to precede him.

Taking the leashes in hand, she started down the path, and he fell in next to her as they walked past a row of blueberry bushes.

Andrew had never been comfortable making small talk, especially with women. Despite growing up with a younger sister, he always felt rather awkward with the fairer sex. When he was a young man, girls had simply left him tongue-tied and feeling oafish. Never any type of lothario, he had allowed his parents to arrange a match, and married right out of university. He had quickly learned how manipulative and confusing women could be. His wife had often accused him of not understanding her at all.

Since his wife's death last winter, Andrew had

been almost a total social recluse. But earlier this summer, he decided to focus on getting himself and his children out of the house and back into some semblance of regular life. His list of goals included the boys making friends with other children their age. Taking a deep breath, he resigned himself to making conversation with the lady.

As they arrived at the great meadow, Andrew pulled several balls from his coat pockets and threw them out to the boys. He spotted a bench nearby. Gesturing to it, he again said, “Shall we?”

Miss Whittingham looked up at him strangely but, nodding her head, went over and sat down on the bench.

Andrew floundered for something to say which wasn’t “Shall we?” lest she think him a total idiot. “How many dogs do you own? I remember there being quite a few tangled around my sister-in-law.”

“There are actually six dogs in all.” Miss Whittingham sighed.

Andrew raised both eyebrows.

“You see, I have five younger brothers and sisters. My uncle dotes on all the children, and he thought it would make terrific Christmas gifts if each could have their own puppy.” She gave him a wry look. “They all loved him dearly for the gift, but he does not have to live with the menagerie. I had banned all the dogs to the mews. Lucy and Margaret have trained their little dogs sufficiently that they now can reside in the house. But Lord Pettigrew here and the boys’ pups are still too high-spirited to have the run of the house. So here we are trying to exercise off some energy.”

“Lord Pettigrew?” Andrew had to smile.

"Yes, Abigail has a flair for the dramatic. I think Lord Pettigrew is some gothic novel hero."

"And your parents don't mind having six dogs running around?"

"My father passed away four years ago only a year after my mother died birthing the twins. I am afraid the whole crazy bunch are mine to care for these days." A look of sadness crept into her eyes, and Andrew had the sudden urge to pull her to him and offer some comfort.

"I know well the burden of responsibilities. What of your uncle? Didn't he receive guardianship of the children?"

"He is the black sheep of the family, and my father and he were estranged. Yes, he is the guardian for us, but he only pops in every once in a while to see we are all right and then disappears again on his many adventures." She waved a hand around. Her lips set in a tight line.

Andrew frowned in disapproval. What sort of man didn't take his responsibilities seriously? Black sheep or not.

Miss Whittingham seemed to regret her words. "Oh, he is a dear. He stayed for almost a year after Father passed. He just can't be in one place for too long, I guess." Then she abruptly stood and called out to her brothers. "Max, Will, come on. We best keep going on our adventures today. Fergus and Lord Pettigrew need to exercise as well. Remember I promised we would go look at the tall ships?" She turned back to him and gave a small curtsy. "Thank you for being so understanding today, Your Grace. I hope next time we meet under more civilized circumstances."

Andrew tipped his hat. "Thank you for letting your

brothers entertain my sons for a while. We have just returned to town, and I hoped that the boys would find some friends."

"Boys, say goodbye." After perfunctory goodbyes were said, Miss Whittingham hurried away with her brothers in tow.

Andrew stared after her for a moment. Talking with her had been less of a chore than he first assumed. Six dogs…he chuckled. For such a young woman—he wouldn't guess she was more than three and twenty—she had quite a lot of responsibility upon her lovely shoulders. What a shame this uncle she mentioned had left her high and dry to care for all the children. The man should be ashamed of himself for shirking his duties as guardian.

Andrew sat down on the bench as his boys threw the ball for their pups once again. Glancing down, he spied a blue reticule. She must have forgotten it in her haste to leave their conversation. He picked up the small beaded purse, turning it over in his hand. He smiled. This could be the perfect opportunity for him to find out more about the lovely Miss Whittingham.

****

Emma berated herself as she and the boys continued on their walk through the park. How could you sit and chat with the Duke of Gilchrest like it was an everyday occurrence? The duke that you ogled last night in his bedroom!

Although, after her initial fear that he would recognize her had been set aside, she had rather liked him. He was quiet and a bit reserved, but she saw genuine interest in his eyes as he asked her questions about her family. And like a fool, she kept talking, telling him her whole sad family history. Ugh! She shouldn't call attention to herself in any way. Lucy's first big ball was a week from today, and Emma didn't want even a breath of scandal to mar her sister's chances of finding a good husband. Emma's secret life could ruin her sibling's chance at a decent match.

Fergus paused to sniff under a holly bush, pulling her to a full stop. She tugged the lead to get him moving again, but to no avail. Her efforts no match against one hundred pounds of dog. Once Fergus caught a scent, there was no deterring him until he had investigated thoroughly.

Emma smiled, remembering how they had met. She hadn't lied to the duke, but she hadn't told the whole truth either. She had, in fact, been behind a shop on Bond Street, shimmying down the trellis. When she hit the bottom, two thugs surrounded her, wanting the bag of trinkets she had just stolen fair and square. When she refused to take the bag off, one of the men produced a knife and backed her up against the wall. Truly worried at that point, she began to panic. But then Fergus had leapt out of the shadows, closing his big jaws down on the knife-wielding man's arm. The thug's friend took one look at Fergus and ran away down the alley.

Releasing the man's arm, Fergus then stepped in between them, growling. The man hightailed it after his friend without a backward glance. Afraid the dog would turn and attack her next, Emma held very still, watching the dog carefully as the ruffians ran away. Once the men were out of sight, Fergus simply sat down, tongue panting. She had cautiously held out her hand for him to sniff, and he licked it, giving a sad low whine. How had such an unusual dog ended up on the streets of London? "Thank you, kind sir." She gave the dog a small bow and turned to leave. But Fergus followed her home. After getting a good look at his too thin frame and big sad eyes, she had decided to keep him. That had been three years ago.

"Emma, come on! Look, I can see the sails already!" Will's excited voice called out from up ahead.

She focused her attention back to the boys. Her brothers and sisters were the main reason she had embraced her nighttime adventures. Her life had not unfolded as she had planned, but she'd be damned sure her siblings would receive a better chance for a happy future.

Chapter 3

That afternoon, Andrew sat behind his big maple desk, dictating replies to various correspondence to his secretary, Holmes. Andrew diligently took care of estate business each day at one o'clock. Even after his wife's death, when he spent his nights drowning his regrets in liquor, he had still always spent his afternoons with Holmes, paying attention to the hundreds of details involved in running the dukedom. His father had left him with numerous mortgaged properties and declining estates. The old man had let things run themselves with very little oversight. Andrew spent the last five years since his father's passing investing back into the properties, paying off debts, and making changes that had been revenue generating. He was damn proud of what he had been able to accomplish.

"Will that be all, Your Grace?" Holmes asked as he tucked his spectacles into his front breast pocket.

"Actually, one more thing. Holmes, what do you know about a Miss Whittingham? Who is her father?"

"Hmm. Whittingham. I believe that was the surname for Viscount Newton, deceased a few years back. Well known for his bad luck at the tables and his love of drink. I don't know anything about the family."

Sitting back in his chair, Andrew considered the information. "Find out what you can about the family, specifically about an uncle, I don't know his name. Discreetly please, and get back to me."

"Of course, Your Grace."

"And will you send in Rhodes please?"

"Yes, Your Grace."

What was he going to do about his mystery intruder last night? When he woke up this morning, he almost believed he dreamt the incident. He hadn't called for the constable simply because it all sounded fantastical. A woman sneaking into his room in the middle of the night. He could only imagine the chuckles that statement would receive.

"Your Grace, how can I be of help?" Andrew's butler, Rhodes, entered the room.

"Ah yes, I have heard disconcerting rumors at the club of an increase in thefts in and around Mayfair. I would like you to assign one of the footmen to be on guard at night around the grounds and perimeter of the house. We can't be too safe with the family back in residence."

"Yes, sir. I will assign someone immediately."

"No need to alarm the household. I am just taking precautions."

"Yes, Your Grace."

Andrew turned back to his desk with the intent of reading through a lengthy letter from his land steward at Stoneleigh. But his thoughts continued to return to a pair of brandy-colored eyes filled with humor. He glanced over at the blue reticule sitting on the far corner of his desk. Curiosity got the better of him, and reaching for it, he popped the little purse open. Inside were a few coins, a handkerchief, and a pair of well-worn gloves. Feeling disappointed there were not any clues to help him learn more about Miss Whittingham, he closed the little bag.

As he was about to stuff it in his drawer, something sharp dug into his palm. Opening it back up, he dumped out the contents, and feeling around inside, he again felt the sharp object. He spied a small pocket sewn into the lining of the purse and reached in with two fingers to pull out a ring with a ruby of enormous proportions. The ruby was a marquise cut and set high on a gold band encrusted with small diamonds.

She certainly would miss a ring of this value. He took another look at the beautiful ring. The ruby flashed like fire in the sunlight. Andrew shook his head at the size of the jewel. He couldn't imagine why she would be carrying around such a ring; it seemed too ostentatious for a young woman her age. He returned it back to the purse and closed the clasp carefully. He would go around tomorrow and return the reticule to her.

****

"Emma, my girl, how is my favorite niece?"

Emma let out a soft sigh and set down her quill on the desk. The household budget would have to wait. It had been a difficult couple of days. The last person she felt like dealing with was Charles Whittingham. She pasted a smile on her face and greeted her uncle.

"Uncle Charles, how good to see you."

He looked, as always, impeccably put together. His tall thin frame was elegantly dressed in black breeches and a jacket the color of dark eggplant. The cravat at his throat, a crisp white, was in sharp contrast to his black waistcoat. A bright gold watch and fob glittered against the black backdrop. He had a long face with a prominent nose and dark-winged eyebrows. With a dramatic bow, he doffed his beaver hat.

"Won't you sit down? Can I offer you tea?" she said.

"No thank you, darling. I will just collect what you have for me and be on my way."

Her uncle handled the selling of any pieces Emma acquired in order to protect her identity. Charles had a fence to which he sold all her items, a man he had worked with for many years.

"Are you sure? It's no trouble, and I'm sure the children would like to see you. I can call them to join us."

"I have several appointments this morning. I am in town with my dear Lady Worchester, and she has plans for us to have lunch and do some shopping." Charles moved his walking stick back and forth between his hands, a sign she recognized as impatience. The lion's head, which set atop the cane, reminded her of the first time she had seen Charles.

When Emma's father died, she had been not quite twenty. She met Charles for the first time when he arrived for the reading of the will. She hadn't even known her father had another brother. The two men had not spoken in twenty-five years.

During the reading, it had become depressingly obvious to both of them there was nothing of value to inherit beyond the title itself. Emma had been dumbstruck at the sheer amount of debt her father owed. He had gambled away her and Lucy's dowries, the house in town was mortgaged, and he had accrued a mountain of personal debts.

By contrast, Charles had not seemed surprised at

the state of affairs. The expression on his face told her he was not happy becoming guardian to six new relations. He had pulled aside the solicitor, and a hushed but heated discussion ensued for several minutes. Then with his face like a thundercloud, he made to leave, grabbing his walking stick. As he passed her chair, Emma reached out desperately for his hand, and looking up at him with her tearstained face, she had just clung to him, this stranger. She'd needed someone, anyone, to help her understand this mess.

Charles stayed with them for almost a year. He had been the only person willing to speak to her as an adult and lay out the truth of their circumstances. He was honest with her about himself and his own precarious financial situation. Emma struggled to flesh out her options for supporting her siblings. In the end, Charles taught her what he knew best, how to be a thief.

Charles had once been one of the very best thieves in England and the continent. He taught Emma everything she knew about burglary. But larceny was a young man's game. Now that he was older, he had found an alternative occupation as a cicisbeo. His current mark was a twice-widowed lady whose wealthy husbands had left her very rich and very lonely. Charles explained to Emma he rather liked being a kept man of leisure, his only duties to see to the pleasure of his current amore.

Emma would forever be grateful to him for helping her to find a way to support her family, but Charles could be such a trial sometimes. His flair for the dramatic was legendary, and even though she knew he had grown to love them all, he couldn't be counted on in a pinch. He moved around often, always on to the next place, the next amore.

"I haven't the items I said I would have." Emma slumped into a wingback chair by the fireplace. "It's been a bad week."

"What's happened?" Charles wandered to the fireplace, leaning one elbow against the marble.

"I stole a beautiful ruby ring, and somehow I have misplaced the reticule in which it was kept. I have torn apart the house but cannot find it anywhere. Even worse, two nights ago I attempted a job at a house I thought was empty but instead was caught red-handed."

"What! How did you escape?"

Emma explained the events at the ducal mansion to him.

"Good girl, the element of surprise is always your best friend. Do you think he would be able to identify you?"

"No, it was dark, and I had my face covered in soot. I ran into him yesterday in the park with the boys, quite by accident. There was not even a flicker of recognition."

"Well, that's something anyway. If you are caught stealing from a peer of the realm, you would surely hang. As much as I admire your initiative, you should not hit such a high-profile target. It's too dangerous!" He frowned.

The reprimand stung her pride. "I thought they were all still in the country. The house had been dark for weeks. Uncle, if you only could have seen this necklace. It is so beautiful. A festoon necklace of rubies arranged to create a red river of gleaming flowers. I was dazzled by it. I just had to try." Emma pinched the bridge of her nose. That necklace could have paid off the remainder of their mortgage of which she had been so fastidiously chipping away. She knew she would never own a necklace such as that, but she might have worn it for a bit around her bedroom just to feel its glory lying around her throat.

"Your failure to have any pieces for me today is a disappointment." His frown deepened, making Emma squirm in her seat. "Fortunately, I do have another lead for you. I was playing cards with a Mr. and Mrs. Hopwood at a party the other night. They are in town spending all their lovely coal mining money. Mrs. Hopwood was wearing the most divine bracelet. Diamonds and black onyx. She and Mr. Hopwood are staying in apartments at the Royal Arms Hotel until next week when they return north. It would be an easy job, and while not as lucrative as the duchess' necklace, it would bring in a good price."

He came over, patted Emma's shoulder, and gave her a brief kiss on the cheek. "Send around a note when you have something for me." Placing his hat on his head, he saluted her with the top of his walking stick and left.

Emma leaned back in her chair. She supposed it would make for an easy job. She had been in and out of the Royal Arms Hotel many times. It was a busy hotel; no one would notice an extra maid bustling about. Feeling a bit better at the prospect of a new challenge, she went to find out what mischief her brothers and sisters were up to. The house was entirely too quiet.

Chapter 4

Lady Caroline Langdon glanced up as her brother Andrew entered the breakfast room.

"Good morning, Mother. Caroline." He greeted them, leaning down to give their mother a kiss on the cheek.

"Good morning, Andrew, how did you sleep last night?"

"Well, thank you." His rote response made her roll her eyes.

Andrew never slept well anymore. He used to drink brandy all night in his study before stumbling off to bed or passing out on the sofa. But in the months since he had given up the bottle, he hadn't slept it seemed at all. These days she often heard him roaming down the hallway past her room in the middle of the night, going where she didn't know.

Caroline filled her plate with eggs and toast from the buffet table while Andrew poured himself a cup of tea.

"Caroline, are you familiar with a Miss Whittingham?" He took a sip of tea.

Caroline sat down across from him. "No, I don't think so. Why do you ask?"

"Yesterday, the boys and I literally ran into Miss Whittingham, her brothers, and all their dogs in Hyde Park. She and I chatted while the boys, who are all of an age, played with the dogs."

Caroline exchanged a surprised look with her mother. Andrew had socialized with a stranger in the park? That did not sound like her brother.

He took a bite of toast. "She left her reticule sitting on the bench. I would like to return it, but I don't want to show up on her doorstep by myself. Would you be willing to come with me?"

Again, Caroline and her mother glanced at each other. Andrew could have the item returned by a footman easily enough. "Yes, I am free this morning. How about eleven?"

"Excellent." He stood, and taking his toast with him, he quit the room.

Caroline turned to her mother. "He is still not eating much, is he?"

"Never at breakfast anyway," she replied. "He is not sleeping well either, no matter what he says. I can see the dark circles under his eyes clear as day. What he needs is a wife to care for him. He certainly doesn't listen to me."

"Mother, let him be. He needs to heal in his own time. Look what we are doing today, visiting a Miss Whittingham. Maybe there is hope yet. I'll let you know what happens." She winked at her mother and dug into her eggs.

Caroline met her brother at the front door at eleven, and they headed outside into a perfect fall day. The air was crisp, the sky blue. A few leaves swirled around the walkway as they walked along.

"You don't mind walking? It's not too far," Andrew asked.

"Not at all it's perfect weather for walking,"

Caroline replied. She was pleased to have time to question her brother further about the mysterious dog lady. "So tell me more about your encounter in the park."

"Miss Whittingham's younger brothers came careening around the bend, and all four boys and all four dogs got tangled up together. It was quite the disaster, but Miss Whittingham could not stop giggling behind her hand. She somehow made the whole debacle seem funny." Andrew smiled, and Caroline's heart warmed at the rare sight.

"She owns this ridiculously enormous dog. Who would have such a large animal in the city?" He held up the little blue purse. "She left this on the park bench. When I lifted it, I felt something protruding, and well…look at this ring which was in one of the pockets. Why would she carry such an expensive piece of jewelry around Hyde Park?"

The ring he showed her was a sizable ruby set high in a thick gold band. "That is an impressive stone, although I must say it's a bit grandiose for a young lady." She put her arm through her brother's. "Let's go find out more about your Miss Whittingham. You always did love a good puzzle."

****

Was that it? Was it the reason he couldn't stop thinking about her? Was she a puzzle he must solve before he could set her firmly out of his mind? They turned the corner. "This should be the street." Andrew pulled a small scrap of paper Holmes had given him with the Whittingham's address. "It's number four."

They came to a stop in front of a fine old house of good size. Pleasingly symmetrical, the windows gleamed in the mid-morning sunshine. But as they entered through the wrought iron gate, they had to brush past overgrown shrubbery to make their way up the walkway. Ivy grew wild up the sides of the brick walls and covered the bell pull. As he knocked at the front door, a loud scream pealed out from inside the house. He looked over at Caroline, who raised her eyebrows. Andrew pounded his fist against the door. After a few moments there was still no response. A loud crash came from inside and wild barking. Andrew grabbed the door handle, thinking he would have to force the door open, but the knob turned easily in his hand, and he flung the door open wide.

A pack of dogs, all different sizes, raced through the foyer, followed by a pack of children. Finally, Miss Whittingham careened around the corner, her stocking feet sliding across the marble tiles. Spotting Caroline and him in the hallway, she came to sudden halt.

"Close the door, before they all get loose!"

Andrew pulled Caroline into the house and slammed the front door shut.

"Are you all right? We heard someone scream," Andrew asked.

Miss Whittingham took a deep breath and blew a stray piece of hair out from her eyes. Before she could answer, a bird flew right past him, and the whole pack of dogs and children came running back out of the room they had just ran into.

"Get him!"

"He's too fast!"

Andrew quickly deduced the situation. "Everyone halt," he shouted. Then he let loose a sharp whistle, which had all the dogs stopping in their tracks.

"Sit," he commanded.

The dogs all immediately sat, and all four children looked up in surprise at the two guests. The children were draped in bedsheets and had crowns of ivy in their hair. Andrew could not for the life of him come up with an explanation as to why.

"Thank goodness for that whistle! You really must teach me how to do that someday," Miss Whittingham said, relief etched into her features. Just then the rogue bird flew back through the foyer, circling above their heads before disappearing down the hallway. The dogs all began to bark again.

"Everyone grab hold of a dog, for goodness' sake!" Emma ordered her siblings. "I will take care of the bird." She hurried down the hallway, a broom grasped in her hands.

Andrew grabbed up a small, fluffy, white dog and thrust it at Caroline. "Hold this one." He strode off after Miss Whittingham, finding her in what looked to be the breakfast room. The bird flapped around the chandelier, and Miss Whittingham batted at it with her broom.

She froze as he entered the room. Lowering the broom, she shrugged her shoulders. "I hoped to chase it out that open window."

Andrew looked around and saw a large silver serving tray with a lid. "Let's be still and see if it will set itself down somewhere I can capture it." Walking over, he grabbed up the tray and lid.

"Brilliant!" Miss Whittingham said. They waited patiently for the badly frightened bird to settle down. "It was my sister," she said, "who screamed, I mean. We were watching the children put on a play, and the bird flew in the window and landed right atop Lucy's blonde curls." Her lips twitched in amusement, and Andrew found himself grinning at the picture she described. "I would have been able to shoo it out the window easily enough if the boys hadn't thought it was a grand idea to send the dogs after it while I was getting the broom from the kitchen."

She stilled and slowly nodded her head to the left. The bird had landed on the table. It picked delicately at a leftover biscuit on one of the plates. Andrew silently edged nearer to the bird, then swiftly lowered the lid on top of it. A great flapping of wings sounded from underneath. Andrew managed to slide the top over to the edge of the table. Placing the tray underneath, he neatly trapped the bird inside.

Grinning triumphantly, he turned to show Miss Whittingham. From behind her came a deep "woof," and the giant furry body of Fergus leapt up, knocking Miss Whittingham to the side, and landed directly against his chest. Andrew overbalanced, falling backward onto his rear end, arms flailing. The bird escaped his trap and flew calmly out the window. Andrew shoved at Fergus ineffectually, trapped under more than one hundred pounds of wolfhound. The dog's large paws pinned him to the ground.

"Fergus, off," cried Miss Whittingham. Fergus immediately got up and returned to her side. Andrew lay there a few moments, staring at the ceiling, and tried to figure out why every time he encountered this woman calamity ensued. At the sound of muffled laughter, he sat up to face Miss Whittingham. She had also been knocked to the floor in Fergus' frenzy to capture the bird. She sat across the rug from him, wild wisps of hair escaping from her bun, her face alight with laughter. Her eyes sparkled. She laughed so hard she gasped for breath between giggles. He had never seen such a beautiful sight. His breath caught in his throat. Why hadn't he noticed before how breathtaking she was?

Tears of laughter rolled down her face. "You…you looked like some mad…" She inhaled much needed air. "Some mad magician making a bird appear from a breakfast plate. Ta-da!" She burst into fresh giggles. Her mirth was infectious, and Andrew found himself laughing as well. The laughter felt so good he found he couldn't stop, and he fell onto his back, chuckling like mad. A high-pitched yip of a dog rang out. Turning his head, he found a crowd of shocked faces staring at them from the doorway.

He scrambled up. Giving a hand down to Miss Whittingham, he helped her to her feet. Her face flushed red, and she straightened her skirts. She declared, "The bird has escaped back into the great outdoors through the window. All is well."

****

Emma clapped her hands together as she struggled to banish her embarrassment. "Well, I think that is all the drama I can endure for one day. Boys, you take the dogs back outside to the garden. And all of you change out of your costumes and go see Mrs. Fenway about having something to eat before you have to get back to your studies. I need to go see how poor Lucy is faring after her traumatic experience with the bird." The children dispersed, and Emma was left staring at a tall, striking young lady with dark hair and bright blue eyes. The duke quickly stepped in and introduced them.

"Miss Whittingham, this is my sister, Lady

Caroline Langdon."

"It's so lovely to meet you, Lady Caroline." Emma sketched a quick curtsy. "Here, let me show you both to the morning room." She headed down the hallway, hoping they wouldn't look into any of the open doorways. Most of the rooms were bare; all the furnishings had been sold in order to keep the household budget afloat. She kept the morning room for receiving guests, and the library was where the family gathered most often. Lud! She must look a disaster. Why was it every time she saw the duke, he caught her in the middle of some catastrophe?

"Please have a seat. I will just go look in on my sister and order some tea for us." Emma backed out of the room to hurry down to the kitchen. All the younger children were seated around the table, eating figs and buttered bread. Lucy was there also, still looking a bit shaken. Emma paced back and forth across the room.

"Mrs. Fenway, can you put together some tea for guests? Use the best china we have left, please. Do we have any of those biscuits we baked this morning?"

"What guests?" Lucy straightened in her chair.

"The duke and some other lady," Max said with his mouth full of bread.

"Did he say a duke?" Lucy stood up with a look of alarm on her face.

"Yes, the one we ran into yesterday in the park. The Duke of Gilchrest. He is here with his sister. Lord Almighty! What are they doing here?" Emma took a slow breath through her nose. She looked over at Lucy, who stared at her openmouthed.

"You met a duke, conversed with one in the park yesterday, and didn't tell me?" Lucy exclaimed.

"I never thought we would see him again. Certainly not in my foyer as I ran through like a madwoman chasing a bird with a broom."

"Oh no. Truly?" Lucy came over and grabbed both of Emma's hands. "Look at me. This is what is going to happen. We are both going to rush upstairs to repair our appearance very quickly. Then we will go greet our guests." Lucy gave her a shake, then said over her shoulder, "Mrs. Fenway, can you please deliver the tea tray to the morning room when it is ready?"

"Yes, ma'am."

Emma forced herself to snap out of her embarrassed stupor. Then they dashed up the back staircase.

****

"Please excuse us for coming by unannounced. Gilchrest found your reticule and wanted to return it to you," Lady Caroline said.

"Yes, in all the excitement I almost forgot about it." The duke pulled her small blue purse from his coat pocket. "You left it on the bench at the park."

She took the reticule with shaking hands. It was the one which held the ruby ring. Hallelujah.

"Thank you so much. I have been looking everywhere for this," she said, a bit breathless. "It is my favorite one." Emma surreptitiously felt for the ring and, finding its shape inside, let out a quiet sigh of relief.

Lady Caroline turned to Lucy and asked conversationally, "Have we met? You look familiar."

Lucy's eyes widened as she stared at the duke's sister. She shook her head.

"This will be my sister's first season out in

society," Emma interjected.

"Yes, I am quite excited." Recovering her manners, Lucy poured tea for their guests. "Sugar?"

"Yes, please. This will be my third season. Up until now I have been avoiding having to choose a husband, but I have promised my mother to be serious this year. I am happy to lend you any advice." She took a sip of tea. "Will you both be going to Lady Landsdowne's soiree on Saturday? She always kicks off the season with her own personal flair." Lady Caroline smiled so warmly it was hard not to smile back at her.

"We would appreciate any knowledge you can impart about the social season, as our own mother passed away many years ago before I even had my first season," Emma replied.

"Oh, I am so sorry to hear that. You both must come over and meet my mother. We shall help you both formulate a plan of attack for the season," Lady Caroline announced.

Emma was shocked to have someone so high up in society offer her friendship so easily. "This season is really for Lucy. At five and twenty, I am firmly on the shelf. I will simply be acting as Lucy's chaperone."

The duke frowned at her remarks. Perhaps he was not so happy his sister was inviting them over.

"We should go, Caroline. We don't want to monopolize their afternoon." The duke stood up and held out his hand for his sister. "Thank you for tea. As always, it has been entertaining." He gave her a genuine smile which made the corners of his blue-gray eyes wrinkle attractively. She returned his smile automatically, puzzled to why he had seemed annoyed just a few moments before.

She showed them to the front door, and after the farewells she leaned back against the wood. She and Lucy glanced at each other. Had they just been invited to meet the Duchess of Gilchrest and receive advice about navigating the social season?

Lucy grinned at her. "Did that conversation just happen, or am I still upstairs in bed dreaming?"

Emma grimaced. "Lucy, fate is a strange and tricky thing." She pulled Lucy back into the morning room and closed the door. She sucked a deep breath. "The necklace I was after the other night, when I was caught sneaking into the bedroom, was the Duchess of Gilchrest's necklace!"

Lucy gasped. "The duchess caught you sneaking into her room?"

"No, it wasn't her room, it was the duke's room, and he is the one who caught me." She crumpled onto the sofa, putting her head into her hands. How had she managed to get herself into this sticky situation?

"But he obviously didn't recognize you, right?" Lucy asked.

"I don't believe so, but that's why I was never going to tell you I ran into him. I planned to avoid him at all costs. It should have been easy to do. But now we will be visiting the very lady I was going to rob. This is all too much."

Lucy sat down next to her. "You must quit now while you still can. We will find another way to carry on. It's too risky. I know you are the older sister, but you must heed me! No more jobs." Lucy looked like a disapproving angel, her scowl out of place on her beautiful face.

Emma nodded her head and said, "Yes, you're

right."

But the truth was she had no intention of quitting. What Lucy didn't understand was when Emma was out scrambling across rooftops and slipping into darkened houses, she never felt so alive and free. She enjoyed flouting society's rules, the ones which made it impossible for a gently bred woman to earn a living for herself without selling her body.

She could have gone into service; she wasn't too proud for that. But what of the children? They deserved a chance to keep their place in society; Max was heir to the viscountcy, for heaven's sake. No, she was the master of her own destiny; she would care for her responsibilities how she chose. There was risk, yes, but she would be more careful how she chose her marks. No more society ladies. She would stick to wealthy merchants and expensive paramours.

Chapter 5

Emma made her way through the busy kitchens at the Royal Arms Hotel. Not a soul took notice of her in her maid's uniform, which consisted of a simple black dress and crisp white apron. Her hair was pulled back in a tight bun and covered in a white cap. She kept her eyes cast downward as she headed up the back stairs with a small basket, hooked over her arm, containing rags and extra candles. The Hopwoods were staying in apartments on the third floor. Emma idled slowly down the hallway, pretending to clean and check the sconces. Mr. and Mrs. Hopwood had exited the hotel thirty minutes ago, but she needed to make sure the room was empty. Moments later, just as she expected, the Hopwood's maid came out of the suite, no doubt heading downstairs for her own dinner.

She returned the woman's polite "good evening" as the older lady passed by and kept her eyes on the glass sconce she cleaned with her rag. The minute the woman turned the corner, Emma pulled the tools she needed from her basket. She made quick work of the lock to Mr. and Mrs. Hopwood's rooms. Once inside she had no trouble finding Mrs. Hopwood's jewelry.

In the large armoire she found a felt-lined wooden box which held what she sought. Emma shook her head. Rich people were so careless with their valuables. She pulled out the onyx and diamond bracelet and found a matching pair of earrings. The lady owned more than just the one set, but Emma stopped herself from taking any more pieces. Often one or two missing items are just assumed lost, but to clean out the whole box would immediately raise the alarm.

She did not waste any more time in the suite. She peeked out the door to make sure the hallway was clear. Slipping out, she gathered her basket to head down the hall. A clicking of heels on the front stairs caused her to freeze. She turned to a wall sconce once again, pretending to change the candle. As a well-dressed couple made their way past her, she quickly dropped into a deep curtsy, head bowed. Whew! To guests of the hotel, she knew from experience, all the help looked the same to them. She replaced the candle and hurried down to the back stairway. At the bottom, she turned left and entered a broom closet where she had stashed her boy's clothing. Making quick work of changing clothes, she emerged swinging the basket and whistling. She left the hotel through a back door designated for deliveries.

The cool night air filled her lungs. She allowed herself a wide grin as she walked down the street away from the hotel with the loose-limbed gait of a young man. This was exactly the kind of easy job she had needed to gain her confidence back after last week's close call at the duke's house. Exhilaration coursed through her veins. The inherent risk of being somewhere she should not always made her feel this way. It had been quite a day. She was too restless to go home to bed, so she turned down Gloucester Street heading toward the tall spire of St. Stephen's Church.

Soon Emma sat atop the roof of St. Stephen's, her

back leaning against the smooth stone wall of the bell tower. Tonight was dark, thanks to clouds covering the moon. A breeze tickled the back of her neck below her cap. Patches of inky black sky and stars bright as diamonds emerged here and there between the gray haze of the clouds. This was her favorite spot. This was where she came to breathe and to brood.

Today, she was five and twenty.

She'd spent her birthday with her family. They took her out for ice cream in Vauxhall Gardens. Then they flew kites. Later after luncheon, Margie and Abby brought out the enormous cake they'd made. The boys washed all the dogs so they could be presentable and join in on the celebration. The children sang silly songs and stuffed themselves with cake.

Uncle Charles had come to her birthday luncheon bearing a large bouquet of flowers. He told her the Hopwoods would be at a dinner party that evening at a mutual acquaintance of his. He shared, with a meaningful look her way, the couple always liked to stay and play cards late into the night.

Lucy presented her with a beautiful gown of emerald damask. When she protested at the expense, Lucy smiled and said she had her own ways to find an extra penny or two. Emma sighed. The dress was gorgeous, but it wasn't a dress for a chaperone. That was a dress for gaining attention. Her role was to blend in, to keep watch.

At twenty-five, her chance for marriage and family were long passed. She had been engaged once. But her schoolgirl dreams of a dashing Prince Charming had been shattered by the reality of the cruel man her father selected for her to marry. Thankfully, fate stepped in to change her circumstances. She'd promised to never see her sisters put into a similar situation. These days she took care of herself and those who counted on her. Counting on a man to sweep in and take care of everything was just a silly fairy tale.

Emma ran her fingers over the uneven surface of the onyx and diamond bracelet. It was her birthday, and all day she had smiled and done what everyone else wanted her to do, including stealing this bracelet. She stuffed it back into her pocket. What did she want? Did she even know anymore?

Her thoughts drifted to the memory of the duke's naked form sprawled out on his great big bed. She grinned. Right now, what she wanted was to see him again. He would surely be fast asleep by now. He wouldn't even know she was there. Her decision made, she stood up and nimbly leapt over the short wall. She scooted past the bell, descending the ladder to the alcove below. Anticipation warmed her belly. She would be careful not to wake him. She'd just go peek in on him and see how he was sleeping tonight.

The walk over was quickly done by the back alleys. Past sleeping horses and dark carriage houses. She shimmied up the back wall to Gilchrest House's gardens. Pausing at the top, she scanned the grounds and the house. All the windows were dark and the gardens empty. She silently landed in the soft grass. A soft snore broke the silence as she approached the west wing. Frozen in place, she peered around a bush. She spotted a footman dressed in Gilchrest livery, slumped against the wall, sound asleep. She rolled her eyes and slipped past him. Turning the corner, she counted the windows. Fourth in from the left—that was his.

Climbing slowly, careful to not make a sound, Emma slipped over the balcony railing and tried the handle on the french door. It turned easily. Anticipation fluttered in her belly as she pulled the glass door open. She slipped inside, closing the curtains behind her. The dark outline of a chair stood nearby and next to it a small table. She took a seat in the overstuffed chair, tucking her feet under her. Facing the sleeping man on the bed, she let her eyes adjust to the dark room.

Like earlier in the week, he slept sprawled on his stomach, only half covered by the blankets. One arm up above his head and the other hanging down over the edge. It was too dark to make out his features, but she remembered his square jaw and wide mouth. His dark hair usually trimmed short and neat would probably be mussed from sleeping.

What would it be like to run a finger across those lips? To sink into his kiss, and feel his body pressed against hers. Entranced by the idea, she rose and crept across the carpet, drawn to him. What would it have been like to have had a man like this as her husband? A warm body to sleep next to in the night. Someone with which to share her worries and burdens. Her heart ached with the possibilities. Emma reached out a hand and brushed a lock of hair from his brow before she even realized what she was doing.

A large hand captured her wrist, startling her back into reality.

****

Andrew sat up lightning quick, swinging his legs over the edge of the bed. Moving his hands to her waist, he held the woman in place between his knees. Just like the other night, it was so dark the woman's features were shadowed.

"I thought you were a figment of my imagination last time." Andrew gentled his hold on her, not wanting to scare her. "Who are you? Why are you here?"

His mystery woman said nothing. Instead she reached out a hand, and her fingers lightly skimmed the hair over his ear. Then they trailed gently down his cheek. He narrowed his eyes, straining to discern more than just her shadowed shape. One delicate fingertip danced across his lips, and his eyes closed at the pleasure the featherlight touch sent through his body.

In the dark his other senses were heightened. A hum of pleasure escaped her lips as her fingers glided over his bare shoulders. Her curious hands set his body aflame, but he forced himself to stay immobile, unwilling to break the spell.

She cupped the sides of his face, and the brush of her lips against his was whisper soft. Then again. This time when she pressed her lips more firmly to his, he kissed her back. His tongue darted out to taste her honeyed lips. She let out that soft hum of pleasure again. She changed the angle of their kiss, sinking in deeper. He wrapped one arm around her waist, bringing her closer. The kiss escalated from exploratory to hot and needy.

Andrew slid his other hand up, cupping her breast. He found it was the perfect handful. He brushed a thumb across her nipple through the cotton of her shirt and found it tight and hard. She gasped and broke away. Stepping out of his arms, she stumbled backward a few steps.

His eyes popped open. "Wait!"

He reached out for her, but she stepped back

farther, and then she disappeared through the velvet curtains leading out to the balcony. Andrew didn't bother to give chase. Shock at what just transpired kept him rooted to the bed. He fell back against the mattress and sucked in a deep breath. Dear God, he needed a drink.

****

Emma raced home at full speed. She had never felt so alive. She knew she had taken an enormous risk tonight, but the reward had been worth it. That man was sinfully sexy. Even though she could never really have him, tonight had been wonderful. She would tuck away the memory of that searing kiss to pull out in the future when she was feeling sad or lonely. Her heart beat a wild rhythm in her chest. Her birthday had turned out to be rather better than she expected after all.

Chapter 6

Emma fussed with her hair, pushing a clip in to secure wayward strands. Her hair was straight as a pin, and little wisps of brown hair were always escaping the confines of her coiffure. Maybe she should hire a lady's maid. Just for the season.

She frowned at her reflection. If she didn't pay off the last payment for Hertford Manor, she could manage it. Hertford would still be a neglected rundown manor in January. Soon enough for her to own it outright. The manor house was her own modest dream, a place of her own out in the countryside where she could breathe deeply and plant a garden. She hoped to be able to bring the children out there for the summer next year. Remove them from the stench of summer of the city.

Lucy popped her head around the door. "Are you ready?"

"Yes, I suppose so."

Lucy came into the room. "How do I look?" She turned to show off her light blue dress with a dark blue stripped spencer jacket. "Respectable enough to meet a duchess?"

"Definitely. You look lovely. How about me?" Emma had donned a dove gray dress with a yellow jacket trimmed in gray velvet.

"You look very fetching in yellow, Emma."

"All right then, let's get going. We should be able

to walk there without too much trouble. It's not far."

They were greeted at the door to the duke's house by a butler and shown to a bright airy morning room. Lady Caroline breezed into the room, followed by an older version of herself. Tall and willowy, the duchess exuded elegance. Sharp gray eyes were framed by dark eyebrows and high cheekbones. A serene smile stretched across her face as her daughter rushed forward to greet them.

"Hello! I am so glad you could come. Mother, may I present to you Miss Whittingham and her sister Miss Lucy Whittingham. This is my mother, the Duchess of Gilchrest."

Emma and Lucy both curtsied. "It's a pleasure to meet you," Emma managed, a bit in awe.

"Please sit down. We have tea ordered. So Caroline tells me this is your first season, Miss Lucy, and that your parents are both deceased. Who was your father, Miss Whittingham?" the duchess asked politely.

"Our father was Viscount Newton. He died four years ago after a long illness of the lungs." The well-practiced lie rolled off her tongue easily. "Our brother Maximillian, his heir, is only just turned six. I am raising all of them, with Lucy's help of course." Emma took a sip of her tea. She hoped that would put their curiosity to rest.

"All of them?" the duchess inquired.

"I have five siblings: Lucy, Margaret, Abigail, Max, and his twin brother, William. We have quite the full house and sometimes a wild one as Lady Caroline can attest to."

Lady Caroline smiled. "They also have a pack of lovely exuberant dogs."

Emma's cheeks heated. "Each of us has their own dog, a gift from our uncle. He thought it a fantastic present for the children. Although, he does not live with us, so he doesn't understand what chaos can ensue with six dogs in the house."

"Oh dear." The duchess' eyes widened. "Miss Whittingham, I do admire you for managing such a large household at such a young age."

"Thank you, ma'am. I do wish I could whistle like the duke can. That piercing whistle always manages to command the dogs' attention, the children too, for that matter. I quite admire the way everyone stops and pays attention to him."

Lady Caroline and her mother exchanged a look of surprise. Lady Caroline turned to Lucy. "So are you excited for Lady Lansdowne's ball on Saturday evening? You did say you were going, didn't you?"

In fact, they had received an invitation to the ball just yesterday quite out of the blue. Emma had her suspicions as to whom arranged for them to be invited.

"Yes, we are. I'm feeling rather nervous, though," Lucy said.

"Don't be. I will be happy to introduce you to the right people. In fact, after I met you the other day, Mother and I discussed your situation. Because you don't have your parents to watch out for you, Mother would be more than happy to sponsor you this season."

Emma and Lucy both gasped in response. Lucy recovered her voice first. "Thank you, Your Grace! I am honored to have your support."

"You're welcome. Caroline has taken a liking to you both, and she has excellent judgment," the duchess said.

There was a crash from the hall and a very loud "Ow!" followed by a deep voice.

"All right, my love?"

Lady Caroline grabbed her mother's hand. Her voice rang out in excitement. "The lovebirds are back! Excuse me, please." She jumped up and hurried out of the room.

"My apologies for Caroline's abrupt behavior." The duchess wore an indulgent smile. "Her brother was recently married to her best friend. The two have been on their honeymoon, and it seems they have just returned. They are two of her favorite people in the world."

"Perhaps we should go then," Emma said.

"No, please stay. We can all have tea together. You will enjoy meeting Vivian. She is of an age with you. Why don't you both go out onto the terrace and enjoy the fine fall weather? Through those doors. We will meet you outside shortly." The duchess rose and swept out of the room.

Emma and Lucy, following the duchess' orders, exited through the french doors to the terrace beyond. The gardens were exquisite. Laid out in a formal style, with low hedges in neat squares surrounding garden beds of roses. Large oak trees stood guard toward the bottom, along the tall wall which separated the property from the lane beyond. To the left of the rose gardens was a small orchard and to the right, a lovely little pond which gleamed in the sun. You could almost forget you were in the city looking out at the extensive grounds of the ducal mansion.

Lucy let out a small cry of dismay. Emma turned from the view. "What's happened?"

"Oh dear, look. I've brushed up against that gooseberry bush there and gotten something all on my skirt. I will have to go in and see if I can find a servant. Perhaps if I can brush it off immediately, it won't stain."

"All right, see if you can fix it. I will wait out here for the others."

After fifteen minutes of waiting, Emma became bored. She stepped down the low flat stairs of the terrace to wander around the gardens. As she strolled through the roses admiring the many varieties, a thwacking sound rang out. Her curiosity piqued, she followed the intermittent thwacks into the orchard. Dappled sunlight fell through the bare branches, creating patterns of light on the grass floor. Not too far in she saw a shed with a thatch roof. In front sat a rough-hewn bench.

Thwack. On the other side of the shed, amidst a pile of logs was the duke. Emma stopped short. He stood, shirtless, facing the opposite direction from where she approached. The duke raised an axe overhead and with one great motion split a log neatly down the middle. Her mouth fell open, and her feet felt rooted to the ground. With each chop of his ax, the muscles in his shoulders and back flexed and bunched. His broad shoulders gleamed with sweat, and the hair at his nape was damp with it as well. His breeches fit him like a second skin and gave her an excellent view of his tight buttocks. Warmth spread through her as she remembered how the muscles in his arms had felt smooth and hard under her hands last night.

He turned to reach for another log and spied her. Emma flushed, embarrassed to be caught ogling him.

“Oh, pardon me, Your Grace.” She took a step back, her hand fluttering at her throat. “I was just walking through the gardens, and I could not identify the strange sound coming from this direction.”

The duke walked over to the bench, grabbed his shirt, and pulled it over his head.

She should turn and walk away. But her mouth wouldn’t listen to her brain, and she continued her effort to explain. “Lucy and I are visiting with your mother and sister. We were interrupted by your brother and sister-in-law arriving, and your mother sent us out to the terrace to enjoy the nice day, but Lucy got something on her skirt and had to go back into the house to clean it, and…” She petered off. Oh dear, this situation was so inappropriate.

“Well, has your curiosity been satisfied?” One eyebrow rose as he casually tucked his shirt back into place. He reached for his waistcoat next.

Indeed, it had. She knew she should go back to the terrace, but again her mouth had its own ideas. “May I ask why you are out here chopping wood? Don’t you have someone to do that for you?”

“It is restorative,” he replied.

Restorative? Chopping wood?

At her questioning look he elaborated. “It was my brother’s idea.” He ran a hand through his hair as though attempting to fix it into some semblance of order. “After my wife died, I was drowning myself in drink. My brother helped me to sober up before it could become a permanent bad habit. It was he who suggested I use physical exercise to work out my emotions. Riding my horse, swimming, long walks, chopping wood.” He gestured to the axe. “There aren’t many places to be alone outdoors in London. Which is why I am hiding out here in the orchard."

Her eyes widened. She was stunned at the personal information he had just confided to her. "I'm sorry I intruded into your solitude."

One side of his mouth tipped up in a self-deprecating smile. "Sometimes I need to be interrupted. Too much brooding isn't good."

Emma sat down on the bench while he slipped on his jacket. "I admire your efforts to keep from drinking in excess. It is something my own father was never able to accomplish. His drunkenness had a profound effect on our family." She stared out into the trees blindly as memories of her father washed over her. "It's what led to his death, in fact."

The duke settled next to her. "I'm sorry to hear that. I know my own children were the driving force which helped me to pull out from my misery. I did not want to let them down."

"If only that had been true for my father. Although alcohol had been ruling his life for years. My mother's death pulled my father deeper into his downward spiral. He didn't even see us anymore."

They sat on the bench for a few minutes in silence. Her hands, clasped tightly together, were covered by one of his larger ones. He rubbed a circle with his thumb along the back of one until her fingers relaxed their vise grip on each other. His quiet understanding filled the space between them. Unsettled, she said, "I should get back."

He smiled and stood up. "May I walk you back?" He offered his arm, and they headed out of the orchard.

"So the lovebirds have returned."

"That's just what your sister said."

"Yes, well, it is heartening to know people do marry for love occasionally. Caroline and I are pleased to see them happy, but they are rather disgustingly sweet with each other."

They arrived back on the terrace just as the rest of his family came out through the doors with Lucy in tow.

"Andrew! Look who has returned from their honeymoon," Caroline exclaimed.

Tea was served, and Emma enjoyed meeting Lord and Lady Langdon. Vivian, as she had insisted they call her, was a vibrant lady short in stature but large in personality. Her husband, Lord Langdon, was reserved and quiet. He was tall and broad shouldered like the duke, and he had the same long straight nose and square jaw as his brother. But he had gray eyes instead of the duke's intense blue. He held his wife's hand in his while they all conversed.

Although the company was entertaining, Emma couldn't help feeling awkward about her conversation with the duke. After her foolish behavior last night, she had told herself firmly to avoid the man. Now, not even twenty-four hours later, she'd sat alone with him revealing family secrets. This wouldn't do at all. As soon as it was polite, she thanked her hosts, and she and Lucy took their leave.

Chapter 7

Andrew sat outside on the terrace with his brother in companionable silence. The ladies had gone inside to discuss tomorrow night's ball. His thoughts wandered to a certain lady who always managed to catch him off guard. Today most of all. She discovered him half undressed and doing manual labor in the orchard. Then he had gazed into her warm brown eyes and confessed his weakness for drink as easily as if he were talking about the weather. He shook his head. What must she think of him?

He reached for his glass of hot cider. This was what he got for fostering friendships for his sister. After his initial meeting with Miss Whittingham, he had recognized she and her sister were in way above their heads going into the social season without a sponsor. And Caroline had been so mopey lately with Vivian and Jack getting married. It had seemed like a good plan to encourage their friendship. That was until Miss Whittingham began wandering around his orchard, catching him unawares.

He had needed to expend some energy after last night. His mystery woman had appeared, seduced him with her kisses, and then run away like a frightened doe. What game was she playing with him? His desire for her had pulsed in his veins all night after her visit. By morning he had been wound up tighter than a pocket watch. When would she show up again? Or had he frightened her away with his ardor? His late wife, Lydia, had always said he was far too carnal, too rough handed for her. Their marriage bed had been one of many facets of their relationship in which they had been entirely incompatible.

Jack interrupted his thoughts. “So Miss Whittingham seemed quite nice.”

“To which one do you refer? They are both quite nice,” Andrew replied.

“The one who couldn’t stop laughing at the story Vivian was telling. About the time Vivi spilled wine on Waverly, and he almost cried at the stain on his sleeve. The younger sister seemed a bit appalled, but the elder sister could not stifle her giggles. I wonder if she knows Waverly?”

Jack’s wife, Vivian, had quite an eventful first season, making all sorts of mistakes which would have cowed a normal debutante. But Vivian possessed the unusual ability to laugh at herself. Along with a mouth that often landed her trouble, and a spine made of steel. She was one of Andrew’s very favorite people.

“Perhaps, but Miss Whittingham often laughs at difficult situations. She sees humor when most would see disaster. She even made me laugh the other day.” He smiled, thinking about the bird escapade.

“That is a rare talent indeed,” Jack teased. “She is quite lovely, not as beautiful as her sister perhaps.”

“Her sister? I suppose she is all right if you like the standard blonde debutante. But Miss Whittingham’s eyes are like liquid chocolate. They are filled with humor and intelligence. Her hair is the exact shade of melted caramel, and she is tall enough she would fit right up against you…" Andrew broke off as he looked over at his brother's smirking face. He cleared his throat. "Yes, well, she is far lovelier than her sister."

He must be in trouble; he was describing a perfectly respectable lady like he would a delicious dessert. Maybe it was time he found himself a mistress. He had been living like a monk for more than a year now. His mystery woman had managed to resuscitate all his baser instincts in just one steamy encounter. Andrew took a gulp of cider.

"So how was the trip?" Andrew asked Jack. "Still planning to stay and watch over Caro for the season? Or will you turn tail and disappear to the Caribbean with your bride?"

His brother owned a lucrative shipping company based out of the Port of Nassau. After many years of being estranged, Jack had returned to England earlier this year, with a promise he would make an effort to be part of the family again.

Andrew had been in a bad way. He blamed himself for his wife's death, and the alcohol had been a way to drown those feelings of guilt. Jack helped him to realize how stuck he was in the past. His brother's support and his responsibility to his children pulled him from the mire of self-recrimination. He hoped Jack would stay in England a while longer. He needed his steady presence in his life.

"As tempting as that scenario may be, I am staying on like I promised. Vivian is quite determined to meddle and find Caroline a husband. I am sure it will lead to utter disaster." Jack raised his mug of cider in toast. "A lady who can make my brother smile again? I may have to do some meddling myself."

Andrew sent him a warning frown, quickly changing his mind about the merits of having little brothers around.

****

Every window in the Lansdowne's Mayfair mansion was lit, it seemed. The house positively pulsed with energy. Andrew escorted his mother and sister up the stairs where they were received by their hosts and announced. His brother and sister-in-law came up right behind them. Andrew took a moment to assess the room. It was the usual crush of people. Being tall came in handy as he scanned the room looking for the Whittingham sisters.

"There they are, Mother. By the refreshment table. Shall we go join them?"

"Yes," his mother replied. "You and Jack must dance with Miss Lucy. It will pique the interest of other gentleman if they see her dancing."

"Certainly," Andrew replied.

"And her sister as well," Caroline piped in from his other side. "There is no reason she should sit on the sidelines. I don't care for all that nonsense about being on the shelf. She is a lovely woman. Don't you think so, Andrew?"

"Certainly," he said again, noncommittally. He wasn't fool enough to admit his interest in Miss Whittingham in front of his mother and sister. He expertly weaved them through the crowd. Stopping here and there to greet other guests. They finally reached where Miss Whittingham and her sister were standing.

Miss Whittingham looked breathtaking tonight in an evening gown of emerald green, her dress shimmering in the candlelight. Green ribbon wove through her hair, and a pair of simple gold earrings hung from her ears, accentuating her lovely neck. The only thing missing was a necklace to showcase the neckline of her dress. Odd she would be wearing such simple jewelry considering the ostentatious ring she had been carrying around earlier in the week.

He gave a small bow. “Good evening, ladies. You both look lovely this evening.”

“Good evening, Your Grace.” The Misses Whittingham executed curtsies.

“We are so glad to have found you. It is quite a crush, although it always is,” Caroline exclaimed.

“May I put my name in your dance card?” Andrew looked right at Miss Whittingham.

“Yes, of course.”

Jack stepped up. “Miss Lucy, may have a dance on your card?” She blushed and handed him her card. Then both Andrew and Jack traded cards and signed the other lady’s card as well. As everyone chatted, Andrew leaned in closer to Miss Whittingham.

“You look exquisite tonight.”

“Thank you, Your Grace. And thank you for arranging for us to be invited tonight.”

Andrew didn’t bother to deny it; he just nodded his head. “You both deserve to get off on the right foot.”

“May I remind you I am just here to be Lucy’s chaperone? I’ve no intentions to hunt for a husband.” She straightened her shoulders, disapproval wrinkling her brow.

Andrew chuckled softly. “Your dress says otherwise.” The orchestra started the music, and Andrew turned to Lucy. “I believe this my dance.” He held out a hand and guided Miss Lucy onto the dance floor.

As he twirled Miss Lucy through the reel, he spotted Beau Harrington across the dance floor. Every muscle in his body tensed. He had been a fool to think Harrington would stay permanently out of the social scene. After Lydia's death, Andrew spent months blaming himself. Staring at the man, he clearly saw that Harrington had been the reason Lydia had come running back to London. The reason she had gotten the fever and died. If Harrington hadn't been seducing his wife, she might still be alive.

"Your Grace, you're hurting my hand," Miss Lucy said.

Andrew immediately softened his grip on her hand. "I am so sorry, Miss Lucy." He managed a tight smile.

"You seem distracted, my lord. I don't think you've heard a word I said. Are you all right?" She looked up at him quizzically.

Andrew mentally shook himself. The manners bred into him since childhood kicked in. He attempted to smile more naturally. "No, all is well. How are you enjoying the ball so far?"

"Very much. All these glittering dresses twirling around like mad. The beautiful house and the sparkling chandeliers, it is just how I imagined."

The music stopped, and they clapped politely.

A voice from behind them called out, "Lord Gilchrest!"

Andrew turned to find their hostess, Lady Lansdowne.

"I am so glad you could come tonight," she gushed. "Does this mean you are out of mourning, Your Grace? Will you be joining in on this year's season?" Her eyes twinkled with curiosity.

Standing beside her was Beau Harrington. Andrew kept his focus on his hostess. "I am simply here to support my sister during her season. May I introduce you to Miss Lucy Whittingham? Miss Whittingham, our hostess, Lady Lansdowne, and Mr. Harrington."

Lucy Whittingham curtsied prettily. "It's so nice to meet you both."

"Ah yes, Miss Whittingham. Was your father Viscount Newton?" Lady Lansdowne asked.

"Indeed. He passed away four years ago. The Duchess of Gilchrest has kindly offered to sponsor me this season in my debut."

Andrew turned to Mr. Harrington. "Mr. Harrington, I didn't know you were in London again. Hasn't your company been travelling the continent?"

In fact, Harrington had, in an effort at self-preservation, no doubt, disappeared after Lydia's death. Andrew had his whereabouts looked into, and hearing he was out of the country, had put him firmly out of his mind.

"Yes, we have been. But we are putting together a new play. *Macbeth*. I am here gathering fresh talent."

"I do so love Shakespeare," Lady Lansdowne interjected. "You always put on a brilliant production, Mr. Harrington."

"I wonder if you will give as generously to the playhouse this year as you have in the past, Your Grace? Your wife always did support the arts." Harrington smirked.

Andrew gave him a look meant to freeze even the most emboldened man. If Harrington hadn't just been dancing with their hostess, he would have given the man the cut direct instead of standing here making inane small talk with the piece of shit. "I will be reassessing to which establishments I will donate money to this year. Please excuse us."

Turning, he took Lucy's arm and delivered her back to her sister. "Thank you, Miss Lucy, for the dance. I hope you enjoy the rest of your evening."

Then he turned on his heel to go in search of a drink.

****

Lucy threaded her arm through Emma's. "Emma, while we were dancing, it became apparent the duke is very upset about something." Keeping her voice low, her sister murmured, "At first I thought it was something I said. Then after the dance was finished, we spoke with Lady Lansdowne and her partner, a man named Mr. Harrington. He made the duke quite angry. Do you see him over there? The very handsome man in the outlandish chartreuse suit."

Emma had indeed noticed the duke's face, looking like a thundercloud when escorting Lucy off the dance floor. "How can that man dress so flamboyantly and get away with it, I wonder?" Mr. Harrington had copious amounts of lace flowing from his cuffs and at his throat. He even had a ridiculous gold monocle which he kept raising to his eye and waving around for effect as he spoke with the ladies surrounding him."

"He is the owner of a theatre troupe and is quite famous. Although the duke definitely did not like him, of that I am sure," Lucy replied.

"Perhaps I should find the duke and see if he is all right?" Emma bit her lower lip, wondering if the duke would even care to talk to her. She couldn't leave Lucy unchaperoned; she would have to wait for an opportunity to talk to him later.

Her opportunity came about twenty minutes later when Lady Caroline and Lady Langdon approached.

“Ladies, I want to introduce you to some of my friends. Let’s take a walk around the ballroom,” Lady Caroline said.

“If you’ll excuse me. I’m in need of the retiring room. Take Lucy around, and I will catch up with you shortly,” Emma fibbed.

She exited the ballroom, thinking to find the duke in the drawing room where the gentlemen were playing cards. She dared not go inside, but perhaps she could get a peek in. Or find his brother, Lord Langdon, and have him check on the duke. But first she had to find the drawing room.

She headed down a hallway and at the end found herself facing a choice, left or right. The loud, raucous laughter of several gentleman came from behind her. Not wanting to be caught out wandering the hallways alone, she darted around the corner to the right. The voices grew louder. *Drat*, they were coming her way. She tried the first door she came to and slipped into the room.

Closing the door softly behind her, she turned to find the object of her search. The duke sat on a couch, his profile lit by the fire blazing in the fireplace. He leaned forward, his elbows on his knees and his fingers laced tightly. Even from across the room, she could feel the tension rolling off him in waves. So deep in his thoughts he didn’t notice her, his expression looked forlorn. On the low table in front of him was a tumbler of brandy.

****

"I thought you weren't drinking anymore."

Devil be, what was she doing here? He'd heard the door open and close but hoped the intruder would have the grace to exit when they saw the room was occupied. No such luck, here she was intruding into his solitude…again.

"I am not drinking it. I am just contemplating drinking it." He stared into the amber liquid.

"Then why are you here alone, contemplating drinking a glass of brandy?"

Miss Whittingham moved closer to him. As he lifted his head to look at her, her deep brown eyes widened with concern. *Damn*, he ran a hand over his face, trying to wipe away his thoughts of the past. This was why he went off to seethe by himself. He didn't need beautiful ladies regarding him with worried expressions; he got enough of that at home.

She came to stand between him and the sofa table. Reaching out a hand, she brushed her fingers through the hair at his brow. Her gentle touch undid him. Closing his eyes, he took in a deep breath, and his hands came up to rest on her waist. When he opened his eyes, the sense of déjà vu was acute. Her hand brushing though his hair, her standing above him, the shadows playing across her face.

Then she broke the spell by stepping out his reach. She settled herself on the chair to his left. "Do you want to talk about it?"

Andrew leaned back against the couch and sighed. Surprisingly, he found he did want to talk about it. "My wife died last January from a terrible fever. She had left us at Stoneleigh, my country seat in Kent, to return to the city, and that is where she got sick."

"I am so sorry. Do you miss her terribly?"

He should. He knew he should miss his wife. That would be the proper response. "She was coming back to London to be with her lover, Beau Harrington. He was the one who wrote me when she became sick. By the time I arrived at Gilchrest House, she was already gone." Andrew risked a look at Miss Whittingham to gauge her reaction. She looked appalled, her mouth forming a small O.

"We did not have a happy marriage. It was a marriage arranged by our parents. Lydia was manipulative, demanding, and more often than not unhappy. When she died, I spent many months blaming myself. You see, we had fought. I let her go back to London by herself because I was just so tired of the yelling and the tears. I wanted to be rid of her and enjoy the holiday with the boys." He closed his eyes again, the old feeling of guilt rearing its ugly head. "I should have insisted she stay, tried harder to work it out. She would still be alive, and the boys would not be grieving for their mother."

Emma came to sit next to him on the sofa. "It was not your fault. Her own selfishness was the cause of her death."

He opened his eyes to look at her. "My brother said much the same thing to me this past summer. Seeing Harrington tonight brought back all of the old feelings of anger and guilt. I wanted to kill him, there on the dance floor, just wrap my hands around his neck and squeeze." He shook his head. "She made a fool of me. The saddest part is I am sure he wasn't the only lover she had taken over the years."

He stared into the fire for several moments. Then he confessed the worst of it. "I feel guilty that I am glad she is gone. She was the mother of my children for God's sake, but I don't feel sad. I feel relieved I don't have her in my life anymore."

Emma tugged on his arm until he faced her again. "Betrayal is a hard pill to swallow. You deserve to move on with your life and reach for happiness."

She brushed the back of her knuckles across his cheek, the move so intimate it stole his breath. As he gazed into the liquid warmth of her eyes, he found himself believing her quiet statement. Happiness. How long had it been since he thought about what made him happy? He cupped one side of her face with his hand. Kissing those soft ruby lips would make him happy. He leaned in to kiss her, but she pulled back.

"I believe you owe me a dance, Your Grace. Perhaps we should return to the party."

He blinked. Yes, return to the party. What was he thinking? Taking advantage of her kindness by trying to kiss her. He smiled in an effort to put her back at ease. "I think it's time you stopped 'your gracing' me. My name is Andrew. Considering how much information of a personal nature you know about me, Your Grace seems a bit formal."

"But I couldn't. It wouldn't be proper at all!"

He sighed. That was true enough. "Then call me Gilchrest. That's what my friends call me. Aren't we friends, Emmaline?" he said, pointedly using her Christian name.

"All right…Gilchrest then." He liked the way his name sounded rolling off her lips, sort of soft and breathy. One corner of her mouth tilted up. "Emma.

Everyone calls me Emma."

"Emma, yes, that suits you." He brushed one finger down her cheek. "Let's get back to the ballroom." Andrew stood and led her out of the room, leaving behind the full glass of brandy and much of his sordid past.

****

Andrew let Emma go into the ballroom first. He backtracked down the hall to enter from a different doorway. As he walked in, he was met by the rumble of several deep voices talking nearby. The four men stood in a semicircle, facing out to the dance floor. A glass of brandy in each man's hand, they kept an eye on the room. No doubt waiting for something scandal worthy to occur and brighten a rather dull evening.

Lord Persil asked the group, "How many burglaries have there been?"

Andrew joined them. "Good evening, gentlemen." He gave each a small nod of greeting. Lord Lansdowne stood among them.

"Ah, Your Grace. We were just talking about an article Fenwick read in this morning's paper. Apparently, London has a cat burglar on the loose. One of the apartments at the Royal Arm Hotel was robbed two nights ago."

"Though according to the paper, it is not only this robbery." Lord Fenwick's Adam's apple bobbed up and down excitedly. "There have been several reports of thefts in and around West London over the past year. According to the article, it is always jewelry which is taken."

"Well, lads, keep your wives' jewelry locked away properly. The Royal Arms Hotel is right here in

Mayfair. That's too close for my comfort," Lansdowne said.

Andrew's breath caught in his throat. This thief must be his mystery woman. Why else would she have been sneaking into his home in the dead of night? When she visited him two nights ago, had she just robbed the Royal Arms Hotel? Her purpose had not seemed to be robbery that night. He remembered vividly the feel of her hands running along his body, her lips warm and inviting. Was seduction part of her ploy?

The strains of the minuet were beginning. "Excuse me, I must go find my partner for this set." He walked away, mind buzzing.

He spotted Emma through the crowd and wound his way to her. He needed to forget about his mysterious thief and focus on getting to know this very real woman better. A beautiful woman who made him laugh and had the uncanny ability to pull all his secrets from him. No less a mystery than the thief. There was much more to her than her role as beleaguered but doting sister. He couldn't put his finger on what, but it was going to be a pleasure finding out.

Chapter 8

Emma felt rather than saw the duke approach, her senses finely tuned to him.

Caroline said, "Gilchrest, there you are! Where have you been?"

He ignored his sister entirely and smiled at Emma. "Miss Whittingham, I believe this is my dance." He held out his arm.

Emma smiled in return and let Gilchrest lead her out onto the dance floor. Facing her, he placed his right palm against hers. The melody began, and turning clockwise, eyes locked, they started to dance. She shouldn't be here dancing with the duke. She was a fraud, a thief in lady's clothing. But tonight, she felt elegant and beautiful in her shimmering green dress. He saw her that way. She would hold on to this feeling for as long as it lasted.

Gilchrest stiffened suddenly. As they twirled, she caught sight of the man in the chartreuse suit. Harrington. "Do you want to leave the dance floor?" she asked quietly.

His hand tightened on her waist. "And miss having an opportunity to have you in my arms? Absolutely not."

A blush warmed her cheeks at his comment. She peeked over his shoulder at Harrington. He was dancing with a lady in a scandalously low-cut dress of dark blue velvet. As Harrington laughed at something the lady said, his monocle fell from his eye, disappearing into her ample décolletage. The lady gasped, but they both continued dancing with the gold chain attached to the monocle like a delicate bridge between them. Emma burst into a fit of giggles over the absurd picture it made. The duke looked down at her with an eyebrow raised in question.

"Oh dear, that awful Mr. Harrington just lost his ridiculous monocle right down his dance partner's dress." Emma giggled again. "The woman doesn't want to reach down into her dress on the dance floor to retrieve it, no doubt, so they are just dancing around with the little gold chain from his waist coat swinging between them."

She snorted, very unladylike, trying to suppress another laugh. Gilchrest twirled them in a tight circle so he could try to see what she was describing. A rumble of laughter erupted from his chest. Hearing it made her laugh even harder, and their chuckling caused many of the couples dancing nearby to look over at them in surprise. Which just made them laugh even more. He maneuvered them to the side of the dance floor, and they stumbled out of the crowd hand in hand.

"Goodness, Andrew! You two are making a scene."

Emma's head snapped up. The Duchess of Gilchrest stared at the two of them as if they had grown two heads. Emma sobered. Straightening her shoulders, she put what she hoped was a serene expression on her face. She glanced sideways at Gilchrest, who was also trying to compose himself.

"Ah-ahem." The duke's ears reddened. "Sorry,

once we got started laughing, it seemed impossible to stop." He smiled over at Emma, and she couldn't help but grin back.

The duchess' eyes twinkled. She gave her son a small pat on the cheek. "Well, it's certainly nice to see your smile again."

****

Later that night, Emma lay in her bed wide awake, her thoughts on the duke. He'd asked her to call him Andrew. As outrageous as that was, she liked thinking about him as Andrew. The duke was someone above her station with whom she would never dream of being friends, but Andrew was a man who laughed with her. He was a man who rescued her from unruly dogs and errant birds. A man who slept restlessly and battled his own demons just as she did.

Was he truly all right after his encounter with Harrington tonight? Perhaps she should go check on him, just to make sure he wasn't brooding into a glass of brandy. She sat up in bed and swung her legs over the edge.

No! What was she thinking? She flung herself back onto the mattress. What if he was brooding with a bottle of brandy? Andrew didn't need her coming in through the window to rescue him. Emma chewed her bottom lip. She did want to see him, though.

Ten minutes later, she climbed out of bed, disgusted with her own indecision. She retrieved her pants, jacket, and man's shirt from the wardrobe. Her real life bound her to society's rules, to her responsibilities to her family. But the night belonged to her. Within its darkness she was brave and fearless. She took what she wanted. And right now, she wanted to see him.

She stayed in the shadows as she passed down the lane behind the houses on Kent Street. Emma breathed in the crisp night air. A waxing moon in the sky showed a sliver of light. She turned the corner to St. Georges Avenue and was soon near Gilchrest House. A horse whinnied from the mews behind the ducal mansion. She froze in place, listening for sounds of any stable hands still awake. The night continued to be silent. She climbed the wall and leapt to the ground. As she made her way through the gardens, she ran a hand through a bed of lavender, letting loose the delicate fragrance. Standing under his window, she had a moment of indecision. A picture of him rose in her mind. It featured his dark blue eyes and a wide generous mouth turned up in laughter. She began to climb.

Emma slipped into his room, pulling the curtains tightly behind her, shutting out the faint moonlight. She turned to look toward the bed, letting her eyes adjust. Andrew lay sleeping, his shadowed form motionless on his back. She curled up in a wingback chair close to the door, just wanting to be near him without interrupting his slumber.

"You know, you should really quit before you are discovered."

Emma startled at the sound of his deep voice. Did the man never sleep?

He sat up with a rustle of linens. "You have made the papers. Tonight there was talk at the ball about a jewel thief loose in London. Was it you who robbed the Royal Arms Hotel?"

Emma gasped. Had the burglary made the news? With all the talk of the Lansdowne Ball from Lucy over breakfast, she hadn't even read the paper this morning. Oh dear, the last thing she needed was to garner any attention from the Magistrate's office.

"Why are you here?" His voice growled, rough and demanding. "Do you plan to rob me? Is that what you were doing here the first night I caught you sneaking into my room?"

Too many questions she dared not answer. She got up, quickly crossed to him, and placed a finger across his lips. *Please stop asking questions I can't answer*, she silently pleaded. But touching him was a mistake. His lips were warm and soft, his scent a spicy mix of bergamot and cedar. She knew she shouldn't be here, but he had become a beacon in the stormy sea of her life. The smell and feel of him enticed her to take dangerous risks, just to be near to him.

****

"What are you doing here?" Andrew asked again to the dark figure before him. Damn it, he needed to light a candle! He started to rise, but her hands pressed on his shoulders, pushing him back onto the mattress. Then her mouth was on his, hot and demanding. He snaked an arm around her waist. She wasn't getting away tonight.

He needn't have worried. She climbed up into his lap so she sat straddling him, her breasts pressed up against his chest. He wrapped his other arm around her to cradle the back of her head. When his hand met the band of her cap, he tore it off in one swift move and flung it across the room. She pulled back in surprise. A long braid tumbled down her back. He ran his fingers down the length of the silky rope of hair. She made a small hum in the back of her throat and captured his mouth again.

This time he would try not to frighten her; he would let her take the lead. Their tongues clashed again and again, exploring, tasting. Pushing the jacket off her shoulders, he slowly tugged it down and off. He broke the kiss to bury his nose at her throat, drinking in her fresh clean scent. She was intoxicating. Was he mad? Who was this siren?

Her hands were busy exploring his shoulders and back. His erection hardened in response to her attentions. He grabbed hold of her derriere to pull her tighter against him, rubbing her along his length. She gasped. Then she mimicked his movement with her hips, and he lost his mind.

In one quick move he had her beneath him. Andrew murmured against her mouth, “Is this what you want? Because if not, you need to tell me now before we go any further.” He raised himself up above her, waiting for some response. Her hand reached up to pull his head down, pressing her soft lips against his. He would take that as a yes and thank God.

He reached down and pulled her shirt from the waistband of her breeches. She raised her hands up overhead, and in one swift move he had the shirt off and tossed it to the floor. He ran a hand down her neck, his fingers trailing down to circle one of her breasts, circling slowly until he reached the tight peak of her nipple. He bent over and flicked his tongue gently across it. Receiving a gratifying hum of pleasure from her, he repeated the gesture with the other breast. They were perfect soft globes of smooth skin covering heated flesh. He lavished them with attention, taking each one in turn into his mouth, sucking and licking. She writhed underneath him with muffled moans of pleasure. He was determined to make it as difficult as possible for her to stay silent.

He moved himself down farther, trailing kisses from her breastbone down to the taut plane of her belly. She giggled. Pausing, he experimentally ran his tongue along her ribcage. She giggled again, and he froze. No…it couldn't be.

"Ticklish, are we, darling?" He nuzzled the spot under her ribcage once more, running his tongue across her skin until she laughed out loud. He reared up onto his arms above her; his eyes strained against the inky darkness, trying to decipher her features. He definitely knew that laugh.

Before he could utter another word, she wrapped a leg around his flank and rolled them both again. Now she sat on top of him. She ruthlessly took his mouth prisoner. Her tongue dove in, and her hands ran rampant over his chest. Then one inquisitive hand reached down and found his cock. Wrapping her fingers around him, she gave it a squeeze, and he forgot everything but the feel of her body against his.

He unbuttoned her trousers, sliding them down over her hips in a flash. But they got stuck at the knees, and he had to flip her onto her back once again in order to get the pants the rest of the way off. In the process of untangling her legs from the wretched garment, her foot came up and whacked him in the side of head. He sat back on his haunches, rubbing his temple. Damn it! Then he fumbled to find the pants at the ankles. With one vicious tug, they joined the rest of her clothes on the floor.

She climbed back on top of him, and guiding him

to her entrance, she sheathed him in one slow stroke. He threw his head back with a groan of pleasure, his fingers digging into her hips. She was so tight. So wet. He lifted her up a little and then plunged in again. She moaned and seized his mouth, kissing him with abandon. He drove himself into her again and again.

She gripped his shoulders for balance. Her hair fell around them like a fragrant silky curtain. This woman was a mystery and a revelation. She would surely incinerate him with the passion she let loose. But had he ever felt this alive? He wanted to hear her cry out in pleasure, to feel her fall apart in his arms. Thrusting a hand into her hair, he arched her back so that he could take one pebble-hard nipple into his mouth. At his slow hard pull on her breast, she tightened up around him like a vice as she reached her crisis. He drove his hips in and out, climbing right to the edge of his own orgasm. Then he pulled out and spilled his seed against her stomach, holding her closely against him as his own pleasure rolled through him.

"Who are you?" he murmured into her hair. In response she buried her face into his neck, placing a kiss at his racing pulse.

After he could catch his breath, he laid her gently onto the bed, tucking her next to him. She snuggled against his chest and wrapped one arm and one leg around him. He sighed deeply. This woman, whoever she was, felt just right. He yawned, totally content. And he slept.

****

Emma looked over at Andrew as he snored softly. The soft gray light of pre-dawn seeped in around the curtains while she quietly dressed. His face looked tranquil in sleep. Her heart squeezed tight in her chest. The last few hours had been amazing. It far surpassed her one other adolescent experience with lovemaking. Her fingers itched to reach out and brush an errant hair from his brow. Instead she rested her fingers on her lips. It was time for Cinderella to go home.

She dared not come to him at night anymore. There had been a moment in which she thought she had given herself away. Too close. She must be practical for her family's sake. Quickly placing her cap onto her head, she bundled her hair up into it and pulled it low over her face. She slipped out to the balcony and made her way home.

Chapter 9

Andrew woke up with the midmorning sun streaming in the window. Sitting up, he blinked, surprised he had slept so late. He was not surprised to find himself alone. Cursing, he glanced around the room for any signs his mystery lover had been there with him the night before.

Was he mad to think it had been Emma?

Lying back down, he threw an arm over his eyes to block out the sunshine. He recognized that laugh; he was sure of it. He'd heard Emma laugh and giggle enough over the last few weeks.

A jewel thief, though? Impossible!

Although…she had that enormous ruby ring hidden in her purse. He frowned at the ceiling. No…he must find out more about Emma before jumping to any conclusions. His thoughts were like a runaway carriage careening wildly through his brain. He tried to reconcile all he knew about the lovely Miss Whittingham. She was a lady who always found humor in calamity. A lady who listened to his darkest memories without judgement. A lady who bravely shouldered the responsibly of raising five younger siblings. She was…a jewel thief who climbed into his room at night to seduce him with her passionate kisses?

A brief knock sounded at his door, and his valet, Winston, came bustling into the room. As usual, his dark brown hair was oiled back neatly, his uniform pressed and starched, and his white gloves pristine.

"Your Grace, your mother requests your presence at luncheon. Shall we get you dressed and shaved?"

Winston disappeared into the dressing room without waiting for Andrew to reply. Extremely efficient and extremely bossy, Winston had been with Andrew for the past five years. From what Andrew knew from Rhodes, Winston previously worked for a gentleman who had mistreated him. No one on the man's staff had mourned when the gentleman was thrown from his horse and trampled to death. Winston had shown up at Gilchrest House the very next day with his references and his trunk.

Andrew still wasn't sure how Winston convinced Rhodes to give him a trial period. But he had been relieved to rid himself of the ancient man who'd been his father's valet. Poor old Hobbs moved slower than molasses, and Andrew often found him propped up in a chair asleep in the dressing room.

He raised his arm off his eyes, calling out to Winston. "I don't think I am up for an interrogation by my mother today. Tell her I am ill, or I am hungover."

Winston popped his balding head out of the dressing room. "Are you hungover, sir?"

"No…in fact I am not. You know I am avoiding spirits."

Winston raised one bushy eyebrow. "Are you ill, sir?"

"Oh, fine! Get me dressed." Andrew grumbled in surrender. "You'd think a grown man could lie in his own bed in his own house and stew if he wants to." He climbed out of bed and headed for the washbasin. "I am still the duke, am I not?" Splashing his face, he started his morning ablutions.

****

Emma woke up just a few hours after falling exhausted into her bed. Someone tickled the bottom of her foot. She tugged the foot back under the covers and pulled the blankets up over her head, trying to ignore the loud whispers coming from the foot of her bed.

"Emma, please wake up." Abby's cheerful voice chirped. "Mrs. Fenway said we should let you and Lucy sleep this morning because you were both out late last night, but we are busting at the seams to know all the details about the ball!"

"It is almost half past eight in the morning," Margie said with exasperation.

Half past eight? That was letting her sleep in? Well, hang them both. Couldn't she have one morning to sleep in late? What she wanted was to go over every exquisite detail of last night in her head while she lolled about in bed. *Ha! Not likely.* Emma peeked out at Fergus, who was curled up in the corner. "Fergus. Get rid of them please."

Fergus rambled over to the girls and gave each of them a lick across the cheek. Margie and Abby both giggled and scratched his giant head.

"Traitor," Emma mumbled from beneath the covers. And then a bit louder, "If you two go fetch me a cup of tea from Mrs. Fenway, I will tell you about the ball."

"Right away, Emma." The girls scrambled off the bed and hurried out the door.

Emma sighed and folded the covers down. This would give her at least twenty minutes more of peace.

But as she lay there with the morning light pouring into the room, she couldn't get back to sleep. Daylight meant the return of her normal life and duties. She sat up, pushing the hair from her face. Fergus jumped up on the bed next to her, putting his head in her lap.

"Oh Fergus, last night was wonderful," she whispered. "I don't feel guilty at all, even if it makes me a woman of loose morals. Don't worry, I won't go back. He is the duke, and I am just a slightly used viscount's daughter, but oh, it was one delicious stolen night." She sighed again, hugging Fergus' shaggy neck. He gazed up at her with total understanding. He was the best confidant a girl could have.

"Emma, Emma!" The boys raced into the room in their nightshirts and bare feet. "Are we going to the park today?"

They climbed in next to her, their little bodies snuggling under her arms. She kissed each of them on the head. Her real life wasn't so bad. There were plenty of worries, but there were plenty of rewards as well.

"Yes, today we planned to sail our paper boats on the pond and have a picnic."

"Hurray!"

"Now get dressed and go downstairs for some breakfast."

The boys raced out only to be replaced within ten minutes by her sisters, back with the tea and their questions. Lucy wandered in as well and was more than happy to tell the girls all about the evening while Emma quietly enjoyed her drink.

"Everyone was dressed to the nines. I have never seen so many jewels in one place! Some of the ladies even had jewels sewn onto their dresses. And the gentlemen all looked fine in their suits. The Duke of Gilchrest and Lord Langdon both danced with me, and afterward my dance card filled. My feet are aching this morning, but it was so grand!" She lay back on the bed.

"And you, Emma, did you dance with many a fine gentleman too?" Margie asked.

"Well, not nearly as many as Lucy. But I did have fun in spite of myself." Emma grinned at her younger sisters.

Lucy turned her head toward her. "Where did you get off to last night?"

Emma's heart raced. "I don't know what you mean. I didn't go anywhere." She looked down into her tea.

"At the ball, in the middle of the evening, I was looking for you but couldn't find you anywhere. Then you mysteriously appeared right at my elbow."

"Oh, at the ball. Yes, well, I got a little lost trying to find the retiring room that's all."

Abby bounced on the bed trying to recapture Lucy's attention. "So did you dance with anyone who you could fall madly in love with?"

"No, pet, not yet." Lucy sat up and patted Abby's hand. "I don't think you can fall in love with someone in the course of one dance. Marriage is a very serious business. You have to keep your wits about you when choosing a husband." Over Abby's head she gave Emma a wink. "Come on, let's all go get dressed and leave Emma to her tea."

After the girls left her room, Emma leaned back against pillows, contemplating what Lucy just said. Can you fall in love with someone over the course of one dance? At fifteen she would have said yes, but experience had taught her that knowing someone, the true person, took time. And you can't risk your heart after just one dance.

She had indeed fallen in love with a boy while dancing. Mathew Linford had been the pastor's son at the parish church in the county where her family spent the summer when she was seventeen. He'd been so handsome and friendly toward her at a time when she had felt hopelessly tall and awkward. He asked her to dance at Mrs. Denbigh's party, the first social event Emma had been allowed to go to by her parents. He had been attentive, and she had quite fallen in love with him that night.

When Mathew came walking by their house, on the way to and from his own, he would stop to lean on the fence in front and wait for her to come out and say hello. Then one day, a week or so after the party, when her parents were out visiting some neighbors, Matthew came by and convinced her to take a walk with him. They meandered arm in arm through the tall grasses around the lake. Matthew led her to a small fishing cabin, and with his sweet words and gentle kisses she willingly gave him her virginity.

The whole experience had been less than exciting. In fact, it had been rather painful and over quickly. Afterward, she expected soft words and promises about their future, but Matthew had buttoned up his pants and tucked his shirt back in with quiet efficiency. He bent over to take her chin in one hand. "That was fun, love. Now don't worry, I won't tell anyone, and you won't tell anyone, and no one will get into trouble." He gave her a swift kiss. "I will see you soon. I promise."

She had not seen him again. The very next day,

unbeknownst to her, he left for London. At church on Sunday, she learned his father had been able to acquire him a commission in the Royal Navy, the date of his departure set months ago. Devastated, Emma had cried in her room every night for two weeks. The initial sharp pain of betrayal transformed into a ball of fear that she could be with child. When her courses came a week later, she sent up a prayer of thanks. She then firmly set aside her fleeting feelings of infatuation for Matthew and with them the wide-eyed trust of her youth.

Emma drained the last of her tea, pulling her thoughts back to the present. She thought about her dance with Andrew last night and the laughter in his eyes. If she were looking for a husband, which she definitely was not, having a man she could laugh with would be at the top of her list. Emma chuckled. A man would need to have a sense of humor to put up with her crazy house full of children and dogs. No, she was doing all right taking care of things herself, heart intact, and only one minor lapse in judgement. Today was a new day with no mistakes. Emma got out of bed to get dressed.

****

At Gilchrest House, Andrew came downstairs with the reluctance of a man facing the firing squad. All he wanted to do was hole up in his study and try to decide what he was going to do about Emma Whittingham. The longer he was awake, the more doubt crept in that he was wrong about the identity of his mystery lover.

What had happened to his predicable well-ordered life that he would even be contemplating the identity of a woman who came and seduced him in the middle of the night? A woman who was most likely a thief. A woman who was possibly a viscount's daughter?

Andrew walked into the breakfast room to find his family already eating. "Good afternoon, everyone. Jack, is that you behind there?"

Jack pulled the paper down away from his face to greet him. "Just trying to ignore the endless discussion of last night's event."

Vivian pinched her husband's arm. Jack grimaced. "I was there. I don't need a recap of the evening's entertainments." He snapped the paper back up and continued to read.

Andrew smiled and sat at his place at the head of the table. A footman came over at once to pour him tea. "So what are you ladies discussing? Or should I say whom are you discussing?"

"In fact, we were talking about Miss Lucy Whittingham," Caroline said. "I couldn't be prouder of her debut. She appeared to have had a grand time."

"I agree," his mother said as she spread lemon curd on her toast. "We will have to find out who will come to call on her today. But I did see her dance with one man who I think would be a perfect match, Lord Davenport."

"Yes! Why didn't I think of that?" Caroline agreed. "He is just the sort of gentleman who would make a good match for a quiet girl like Lucy."

"I think we should have a dinner party and invite them both along with a few others. Let them have an opportunity to talk for longer than a turn around the dance floor."

Jack pulled his paper down, a frown on his face. "You're going to invite who to dinner?"

"Lord Davenport." Vivian patted his arm. "They

want to match him up with Lucy Whittingham. Don't scowl, he is a perfectly nice man." She gave him a stern look. "You will have to be on your best behavior."

Which made Jack's scowl deepen. Lord Davenport had been courting Vivian earlier this year, much to Jack's ire. Even though Vivian had turned down Lord Davenport's proposal of marriage, the man was still not Jack's favorite person.

Andrew agreed with the idea for the match. Davenport was a good chap and an old friend of his from university. He had recently inherited his title and was looking for a wife.

"Oh dear, do you think he would decline to come because of his embarrassment over Vivi's refusal?" Caroline asked the table at large. Then she turned toward him. "Andrew, would you invite him? He'd be more likely to say yes."

"Yes, I suppose I can without too much difficulty. I often see him at White's. Just let me know the details when you decide." Andrew ignored the frown his brother threw in his direction. Jack shouldn't hold a grudge. He'd won the lady in the end and was disgustingly happy. Andrew took a bite of toast, hmm…his favorite, raspberry jam.

"Andrew," said his mother. "You looked like you were actually having fun last night. I don't know the last time I've heard you laugh out loud in the past year. Was it something Miss Whittingham said?"

Andrew thought about Emma's contagious humor. How she had tried to hold back her laughter and failed miserably. "Yes, Mother, it was something she said."

"I have heard him laughing recently." Caroline smiled at him smugly. "Last time it was he and Miss

Whittingham on the floor of her breakfast room, roaring with laughter about some bird or something."

Andrew gave her his best ducal glower, the one that froze most men in their tracks. Unfortunately, Caroline was not most men. She bit into her toast, her eyes filled mischief.

"Tangled on the floor with an unmarried miss, I didn't think you had in you, Mr. Lord and Manor." Jack smirked, happy to add to his discomfort. Vivian held her napkin to cover her mouth, but it didn't stop the giggle that burst out.

"We weren't tangled together. Her behemoth of a dog had just knocked me on my ass." A loud huff of indignation came from next to him. "Sorry, Mother."

Rhodes entered the room, saving Andrew from any further explanations. "Your Grace, Mr. Holmes is here waiting for you in your study."

"Thank you, Rhodes." Andrew poured himself another cup of tea. "Excuse me." He gave his brother and sister another withering look and walked out of the room.

"Holmes, what can I do for you?" Andrew asked his man of business as he settled himself into his leather desk chair, relieved to be away from the questioning looks of his family.

"Your Grace, you asked me to inform you when I found out any more information about a Miss Whittingham and her family."

"Holmes, you have impeccable timing as usual. Please sit down and tell me what you found out."

"Well, sir, Miss Whittingham is indeed the daughter of the late Viscount Newton. He died four years ago. His wife died the year previous, giving birth to his heir, a Maximillian Whittingham." Holmes looked up from his notes. "The word is there were twins, which can often complicate the birth." Andrew nodded his head. He knew all this already, but he waited for Holmes to continue.

Holmes shuffled his papers. "The viscount was well known for being an inveterate gambler. He was banned from several establishments because of the extent of his debts. At the time of his death, all that was left of his estate was the entailed property in Lincolnshire. Everything else had been mortgaged or sold.

"There was a Charles Whittingham assigned guardianship of the children. He is the youngest brother and was estranged from his family. The second son died in the war with the Colonies. My guess is the estranged brother received guardianship in default as the closest male relative. He was not living in England at the time of his brother's death. No one seems to know anything about this uncle. Perhaps he has some self-made income which keeps the family afloat?"

Holmes adjusted his spectacles and flipped to a new page. "According to the bank, the house in town was paid off last year. I was able to find out that they keep a very small staff, just a housekeeper and one maid. The maid was very willing to talk to me for a few extra shillings. Most of the staff was let go shortly after the viscount's death. She said the strangest thing. The household has five dogs and one wolf." He frowned at his notes like he still couldn't believe that last piece of information.

"It's an Irish wolfhound. Her dog, I mean," Andrew clarified, and Holmes' expression cleared.

"That makes more sense, I guess."

"Anything more?" Andrew asked.

"Just that Miss Emmaline Whittingham was engaged to be married four years ago before her father's death to the Marquis Longwood. Her fiancé died in an accident before they could marry. That's all I was able to find out, Your Grace."

"Thank you, Holmes." Andrew's chest tightened at that last bit of information. The Marquis Longwood had been a womanizer and general right bastard. In fact, Andrew's own valet had come from Longwood's household right after the man died. To think of his Emma being shackled to a man like that made Andrew's stomach turn.

"That will be all, Holmes. I will see you tomorrow at our regular time."

After Holmes exited the room, Andrew leaned back in his chair and took a bracing sip of his tea. What did he know about Miss Whittingham? Emma's financial situation was most likely precarious. Perhaps this dog-gifting uncle of hers helped to keep the family in their Mayfair house. Although not well enough to keep up the house or to staff it properly. As the eldest, Emma took on all the responsibilities of keeping the family together it seemed. Did she keep her family well-dressed during the season by stealing and selling jewelry? Where would a viscount's daughter even learn such a thing? This woman was a confounded puzzle for sure.

There was a knock at the door, and at Andrew's "enter," his two sons came rushing into the room.

"Father, it's the perfect day to fly kites, just windy enough." Grayson came to a stop, breathless with excitement, in front of his desk.

"We made our own, Father. Look, mine is blue." Tyler held up his homemade kite for inspection.

Andrew smiled. "Come here, let me have a closer look at those." He scooped the five-year-old Tyler up onto his lap and examined his kite carefully. "It looks like she would fly. Good job. And yours, Grayson. What a nice long tail you've put on it."

Grayson beamed at him. "I helped Tyler with his, just a bit."

"As you should. It's your responsibility as the older brother to help your little brother."

"I am the little brother." Tyler snuggled against Andrew's chest. "Will you take us to the park? Nanny Fischer is awful at flying kites. She always gets the string all tangled."

He looked down at his son, and for the thousandth time in the last year he was thankful he had the two of them in his life. "Absolutely, shall we take a picnic?"

"Yes!" chorused the boys.

"Grayson, why don't you ring for Mr. Rhodes."

Rhodes arrived a few minutes later. "Rhodes, can you please tell Mrs. Blume to pack a picnic lunch for myself and the boys. And tell Nanny Fischer I will be taking the boys to the park."

"Yes, Your Grace."

He turned back to the boys. "Now, who would like to play a game of tiddlywinks while we wait for our lunch to be packed?"

Chapter 10

It seemed fortune was on his side this morning. As he and the boys headed across the field to set down their picnic basket and get their kites prepared, Tyler yelled out, “Look, Father! It’s Max and Will down there by the pond!”

“Can we go say hullo?” Grayson asked.

“Of course,” Andrew replied.

He let the boys run ahead as he watched carefully to see what Miss Whittingham’s reaction would be to see them head her way. He was a few feet behind the boys when they approached their new friends enthusiastically.

“Hullo!”

“Hullo!”

“We are here flying kites. What are you chaps up to?”

Emma’s head swung around to see him. Her eyebrows rose in surprise. His eyes locked on hers, and he just knew she had to be his mystery woman. The energy between them was palpable, transporting him back to the night before. The softness of her skin, her sighs of passion, the warm heat as he sank into her body.

****

Emma’s breath hitched at the smoldering heat in the duke’s gaze. What was he doing here? She couldn’t believe her bad luck. She quickly shifted her attention to the boys.

"We are making paper boats to sail on the pond." She smiled at Andrew's sons, trying to ignore the duke's penetrating stare.

"Paper boats? Don't they sink?"

"Not if you make them correctly. I was just showing Max and Will. Would you like to make one as well? I have plenty of newsprint."

"Father, may we? Please?"

"Yes, of course. May we join you, Miss Whittingham? We have a picnic lunch we can share in return for boat-making lessons." He smiled down at her.

Emma nodded, still trying to avoid glancing at the duke. She was being silly. He didn't know it was her from last night. Still, she didn't want him to catch her staring at him with longing. He looked so handsome this morning. Freshly shaved, his black hair combed back from his brow. His coat fit him like a second skin. Which only reminded her of the strong muscled arms which had been wrapped around her last night, and the feel of his lips as they raced across her skin. Lud! She needed to get a hold on her runaway emotions.

She handed a piece of newsprint to each of the four boys and started her demonstration from the beginning to show them how to properly fold the paper into a little boat. Grayson, being the oldest, caught on quickly, but the little boys, being only five and six years old, needed a little help here and there. The duke surprised her by sitting down in the grass with the boys to help them fold their boats. Finally, everyone had a boat, and the boys raced down to the water's edge to sail their ships.

"I didn't think you would know how to make a

paper boat, Your Grace."

Andrew looked up at her from his spot on the grass, the sun on his face. "Believe it or not, I was once a small boy myself. Building paper boats is a right of passage. I thought we agreed you were going to stop calling me Your Grace."

Emma was unable to resist a small smile. "We did, but only in private. The park is a public place. You should get up off the ground before someone sees you kneeling at my feet and gets the wrong impression."

"Ah, we can't have that." Although before he got up he took her hand and pressed a quick kiss to her knuckles, giving her a wink. Emma gasped, snatching her hand away.

"Gilchrest, really!"

Andrew settled himself next to her on the bench. Leaning back, he crossed one leg across his knee. "If you are so worried about propriety, where is your maid? An unmarried young woman shouldn't be walking about London on her own."

"I am not alone. I have Fergus." At hearing his name, Fergus, who had been lying under the bench at her feet, rose and laid his large head on her knee. Emma gave him a scratch behind the ears. She turned to Andrew. "He is my protection." She raised one eyebrow, daring him to argue.

"Did you and your sister have a nice time at the Lansdowne's ball last night?"

"Yes, thanks to you and your brother, Lucy's dance card filled. She had a lovely time. And I as well, although I felt we made a scene with our laughter during that dance. Your mother seemed a bit shocked at our behavior." She grimaced.

"Don't worry, I think she was just shocked to see me laughing at all. It has been a hard year."

"Yes, of course." She looked down at her gloves. A breeze blew through, ruffling her hair and the feathers atop her hat. Andrew reached out to tuck a piece of her hair behind one ear. His fingers lingered at her throat. Could he feel her pulse race?

"You always seem to find the humor in any situation. I admire that. I need more laughter in my life."

Emma could feel a blush creep up her cheeks. He seemed so close all of a sudden. He had taken off his gloves to make the paper boats, and his bare fingers were warm as they played along her skin above her pulse. Her breath hitched in a sharp intake of air. A deep woof caused both her and the duke to startle. She glanced down at Fergus. The dog looked up at her with concern in his eyes. She scratched his head again and chuckled. "Go lie down, Fergus."

Andrew pulled his hand back and unfolded himself from the bench. "Shall we set up the food? I am certain the boys will be famished after the initial excitement of the boats wears off."

He spread out a blanket on the grass a few feet away and started unpacking the lunch. Emma settled herself on the blanket, enjoying having someone else take care of the details. Sure enough, a few minutes later, the boys came up from the pond.

"My boat sailed all the way to the middle."

"My boat sank!"

"Mine too!"

"We will just have to work on your construction. After you make a few, they will get better. Come and have some food," Emma said.

"Will you have many callers this afternoon?" Andrew asked after passing out chunks of bread and cheese to the boys.

"Callers?"

"Generally, after an event a young lady will receive callers the next day. My mother and sister will be setting themselves up in the drawing room this afternoon to receive callers, I expect."

"I had no idea! What time would callers come?"

"If I was calling on you, I would generally plan to visit around two. Didn't you ever have callers, Miss Whittingham?"

"I was never really out during the season. I was betrothed the summer I turned twenty. The year before, my mother had been expecting the twins, so my season was postponed. And then she died." She glanced away. It still ached to think of her mother. She only hoped she could do half as good a job in raising the younger children as her mother had done with her and Lucy.

"You were engaged?"

"Yes, briefly. He died in a horseback riding accident before we married." Emma shut her mouth. Why did she always end up telling him more than she meant to about her past? They must go home and check on Lucy. "What is the time?"

Andrew pulled his watch from his breast pocket. "Half one."

"Oh dear! I better head home. I shouldn't have left Lucy home unchaperoned with the possibility of callers coming. Max, Will, we must head home."

"No," the twins chorused.

"Come along. Lucy needs us."

At that the boys immediately stood. Their sense of family duty made her proud.

"Thank you for sharing your picnic." She gave the duke a quick curtsy. The boys gave sunny smiles and waved before the three of them hurried off down the path.

They did indeed have callers that afternoon. Thanks to the duke's advice, Emma made it home in time to change and have tea prepared. Lucy was over the moon because she received three bouquets of flowers that morning, all from prospective suitors. They received three gentleman callers. All seemed rather nice and rather bland to Emma. Lucy was the epitome of good manners. Emma was impressed at the amount of small talk her sister managed so beautifully.

The next day, Emma made an extra trip with Mrs. Fenway to the market for more food. Having so many visitors was going to be taxing on their grocery budget. After the market, she came home to find Lucy supervising the children in their studies. Lucy looked up with excitement in her eyes when she came into the drawing room.

"Emma, look at all the invitations that came today! Six just for this week alone." She held up a handful of envelopes. "Come help me decide which to accept."

When the duchess had offered to sponsor Lucy, she had no idea it would have such a great impact on their social standing. Thank goodness they had the foresight to order a good variety of gowns. Perhaps not so many as some debutantes, but enough so Emma had been worrying a good bit about paying for the modiste bill. It would be worth the expense now that they had parties to wear them to. Hopefully, Uncle Charles would be by soon with the proceeds from the bracelet and earrings she had given him to sell.

Emma pushed her worries to the back of her mind and gave her sister a smile. “Let’s see what we have here. How exciting.”

Chapter 11

Wednesday afternoon, Emma and Lucy were in the kitchen baking more biscuits with Mrs. Fenway when they heard the doorbell ring from the front of the house. They glanced at each other in confusion.

"Were we expecting anybody?" Lucy asked.

"Oh dear, I forgot to check the salver at the front this morning." She looked down at her hands covered in flour, at the bread dough she was kneading, and then over at Lucy whose apron was also dotted with flour. "Where are the children?"

Emma exchanged a look of horror with her sister as the creak of the rusty hinges on the front door signaled its opening. A small child's voice said, "Good day, Your Grace."

"Quickly, Mrs. Fenway, please go greet our guests and show them to the morning room. We will be right behind you once we wash up. Oh, and in a little bit, bring in some tea and some of these biscuits we made." Emma and Lucy quickly took off their aprons and went to the sink to pump water to wash their hands.

****

At the front door Andrew, his sister, and his mother were greeted by the sweet face of a young lady. Her wild blonde curls framed large curious eyes the same brandy color of her older sister's. Behind her, Andrew saw the rest of the children race by in a flurry with several dogs in their midst.

"Let's see, you must be Miss Abagail?" Andrew smiled at the girl.

She opened the door a little wider. "Yes, sir, and you are the Duke of Gilchrest. Good day, Your Grace." She gave a little curtsy, which would have been more elegant had her left stocking not been rolled down at her ankle and the ties on her dress hanging loose.

"May we come in?" he inquired.

"Surely." She opened the door wide and stepped back to let them into the foyer.

"Perhaps you could let your sister know we are here?" Caroline asked Abagail.

Just then the rest of the children came barreling again through the foyer, the boys at the front, brandishing wooden swords as they yelled out, "Die, you bloody pirates!"

Andrew let out an ear-piercing whistle. "Halt!"

The entire group skidded to a stop.

The Whittingham's housekeeper came hurrying around the corner. "Children! All of you upstairs right this minute. Pardon, my lord, ladies. We were not expecting any visitors. Please let me show you to the morning room."

"Andrew, didn't you send a note to say we were coming?" his mother asked him.

"Of course I did." He glanced over at the salver on the hall table, noting the pile of unopened envelopes.

His mother followed his glance, then looked over at the children and dogs standing nearby, and finally to the servant wearing an apron splattered in flour, looking expectantly at them. "Miss Whittingham certainly has her hands full, doesn't she?" She started forward after the housekeeper.

They were just settling into the cozy morning room when Emma and her sister came in to greet them. "It's so good to see you, Your Graces, Lady Caroline." Emma greeted them with a warm smile.

"I am so glad you are here." Miss Lucy grabbed hold of Caroline's hands. "We have received an avalanche of invitations, and we don't know which to accept. We don't want to insult the wrong people. It's all rather overwhelming."

Caroline kissed Miss Lucy's cheek. "Let's see what you have received, and we can help," she assured her.

Andrew watched Emma from across the room as she directed the housekeeper, who had brought in the tea service. She looked beautiful today. Her hair was piled loosely on top of her head, and she had a pair of amethyst earrings dangling from her ears accentuating her lovely neck. He had spent the last few nights lying in bed thinking—nay, lusting—after her. His mystery woman had not visited him again.

Andrew had become increasingly sure it had to be Emma. Or maybe it was that increasingly, he wanted it to be Emma. How was a man to get any rest remembering her warm naked body underneath him, her kisses lighting a fire in his blood? She drew him across the room to her like a moth to a flame.

****

"Thank you, Mrs. Fenway." Emma turned to find the duke stood right behind her, not two feet away. "Your Grace." She placed a hand over her heart. "I am sorry for the raucous greeting at the door. I hadn't had time to check the salver this morning, and we weren't expecting you."

Andrew gazed at her with an intensity which made her nervous.

"You always seem to arrive when we are at our craziest. I assure you the house is not always in an uproar." She let out a nervous laugh as he continued staring. "What? Is something amiss?"

Andrew slowly pulled off his glove. He extended one finger and ran it down her cheek. She saw a dab of red on the tip as he pulled it away. His tongue darted out to taste, his piercing blue gaze never left hers. "Hmmm, raspberry, my favorite."

She swallowed hard before tearing her eyes away. Warmth suffused her cheeks. The duke came to call, and there was jam on her face…brilliant. "We were baking biscuits." She wiped at the spot. "Is it all gone?"

His gaze roamed her features, then he brushed a knuckle across her forehead, gently wiping off a dusting of flour from her brow. "There, all gone."

"Emma," Lucy called out from across the room. "You must come sit with us and discuss the invitations. Do we have any more out front?"

"Perhaps. I will go check." She went over to open the door and found all four children playing jacks right in middle of the hallway. She nearly tripped over Max. "What are you all doing out here? This house is big enough for you to go find trouble elsewhere."

"But you have all the biscuits in there. We were waiting to see if there would be any leftover," Margie complained.

Emma put a hand up to cover her face as she took several deep breaths. "The biscuits are for our guests. I will make some more for you lot another time."

"Excuse me," Andrew said from her elbow. "I was thinking I could take the children outside with their dogs and teach them a few lessons in dog obedience. Would you all like that?" Andrew asked.

All of the children scrambled to their feet. "Oh, yes."

"Well then, each of you go fetch your pup and bring him to the back garden on a leash. I will meet you there in five minutes."

Emma protested, "You don't have to entertain the children."

"You could use a break to sit and have some tea and biscuits with my mother and sister. And that lot could use some lessons in dog training, don't you agree?"

"Well, yes, but still…"

"Then it's settled. Plus, I don't want to discuss the ins and outs of the social season. I just show up where I am needed. I'd much rather be outside in the fresh air." And before she could protest further, he headed through the morning room and out the french doors to the garden beyond.

Emma stalked over to where the other ladies were seated. "Does everyone always do what he says?" she muttered.

The duchess leaned over and patted her hand. "I am afraid so, dear. That's what Andrew excels at."

"Telling people what to do?" She grimaced.

"No, dear, looking after those he cares about. Have some tea, Miss Whittingham." The duchess turned back to the younger women. "No, let's go to Lady Petworth's dinner party. It always has a good mix of eligible gentlemen, although I don't know how she manages to entice them all to come."

After much deliberation, it was decided Friday evening they would be attending the opera with the Langdons. Saturday evening, they would go to Lady Petworth's dinner party. The following week there were three invitations to tea, as well as a musicale, and the duchess would host a dinner party to which they must attend. Emma leaned back against the cushions with a sigh. She desperately needed some air.

"Perhaps I should see how His Grace is faring with the children?" Rising to her feet, she headed out to the gardens. She didn't know what to expect as she approached, but it certainly wasn't her younger siblings all standing in a row, each with their dog sitting calmly next to them. They listened attentively to the duke.

"Now tell your pup to stay in a firm voice, and don't forget to use the hand signal that I showed you. Then walk toward me," Andrew said. "Will, I said use your big voice, otherwise he won't listen."

When the children had all walked about ten feet from their dogs, they turned neatly and faced the still sitting dogs. "All right, now you may call them and then don't forget to give them praise for being so good." Lord Pettigrew broke rank and bounded toward Abigail before she called him, but the pup still got praise from the little girl for sitting so long. Andrew looked up and spotted her. She gave a little wave.

"It's still a work in progress," he called out and gave a crooked smile. Emma's heart did a little somersault in her chest; this man's smile was a dangerous thing.

"I am amazed you had any of them standing at attention," she called back. In a few long strides, the duke was right in front of her; how had he moved so quickly? His proximity was unnerving.

"So when will I see you again?" Andrew asked. His gaze swept down over her from head to foot. The hunger in his eyes stole her breath away.

"When?" She tried to focus on what he was asking.

"Were you not just looking through all your invitations?"

"Ah yes, of course." Emma fumbled, trying to get her brain working. Andrew stared at her as though he could devour her. Her thoughts tumbled immediately back to his large bed, her body wrapped around him, the feel of his kisses searing her heated flesh.

You can't have him. Then she took a deliberate step back. "The opera, I believe. Friday evening, we are going to join your mother at the opera."

Andrew smiled and, taking her hand, brushed a kiss across her bare fingers, sending tingles down her arm. "Until Friday."

****

Across town, in a tiny watchmaker's shop, Mr. Dorling watched Charles Whittingham peruse the gold fobs in the glass case. He finished examining the bracelet and earrings Whittingham had brought in.

"I can do ten guinea, minus my usual fee." Dorling kept his voice firm. He never missed an opportunity to weasel out an extra few pounds from every transaction. He had dealt with Whittingham for years and years. He knew the man like to haggle; it was always best to start low with this one.

"Come now, we both know they are worth at least fifteen." Whittingham's face darkened.

"There is more onyx than diamonds, not as easy to

sell…maybe I could go as high as thirteen guinea."

"All right." Whittingham's face cleared, and his easygoing smile surfaced again. "But I need you to count it out in front of me. Every penny matters, you know. Especially now that I am merely the middleman."

"Of course." Dorling shuffled to the back room to put the jewelry away in his safe. In actuality, the onyx would sell well. He knew of a buyer who had a preference for the dark black stone.

He returned with the money, counting it out carefully under Whittingham's watchful eye. The man would be suspicious of his own shadow. Dorling didn't know who the young thief was Whittingham worked with these days, but he knew that it was steady income for him, so he tolerated Whittingham's request.

"Thank you." Whittingham tucked his money into his jacket pocket carefully. "I expect to be back soon with quite a special piece. A diamond necklace of some heft. Is that something you can handle, Mr. Dorling?"

"Certainly, easy enough to break it up and sell the diamonds loose. How many are we talking about?"

"At least thirty from what I observed from a distance."

Dorling raised his eyebrows. That was interesting indeed. "Of what size?"

"Thumbnail size and strung along three strands. Quite the prize, I'd say, worth at least fifty guinea."

Indeed. If the man told the truth, they could sell the piece to one of his rich merchant connections. Men who preferred to acquire jewelry for their mistresses discreetly. "Excellent. I will line up an auction for my very special buyers if you are sure you can obtain this necklace. That will ensure we receive the very best price."

"It is no problem for my associate. He is very talented. Go ahead and set it up."

He crossed his arms, assessing Whittingham's cocky attitude. "Whittingham, you may bring your associate with you to the auction to observe the process. It would be a good opportunity for us to meet. My door is always open to any friend of yours."

"Tut, tut. I have told you, my friend is very shy. Trust is a fragile thing, Mr. Dorling." He tipped his tall beaver. "Good day."

Dorling frowned as Whittingham walked out the door. He had a fair idea who the bastard was protecting. A good judge of character he was, and his instincts said that Whittingham would only trust family. Time to send out his investigator and see if his hunch was right. Once he knew for sure who the lad was, he would make contact personally and neatly cut out the middleman.

Chapter 12

Friday night, Emma and her sister were dressed and ready for the opera. She had finally decided to hire a lady's maid for her and Lucy. As she looked at her reflection in the glass, she decided it had been worth the expense. Her hair for once was curled and pinned into an intricate coiffure on top of her head. A few ringlets hung down to rest on her shoulders. Her dress tonight was a deep blue. The sleeves lay slightly off her shoulder and tapered down to a lacy cuff. Lucy came into the room with the new maid, Francine, trailing behind her. She looked lovely in a pale pink dress and their mother's pearls. Emma was just about to send Francine out to hail a hack for them when the doorbell rang. She and Lucy exchanged a look of surprise.

"Well, come on. Let's go see what that can be about." Sliding her feet into her satin slippers, Emma hurried down the hallway. When she arrived at the top of the stairs, Mrs. Fenway was just opening the door. The duke filled the doorway, dressed impeccably in formal black, his white cravat luminous in stark contrast; a gold stick pin topped with a fiery ruby winked at her from its elegant folds. He glanced up and smiled as he doffed his hat. Then he gave an elegant bow. Dash it all, why did he always have to look so handsome? She was trying to put her foolish attraction to him behind her, but he kept popping up looking ever so tempting. Emma took a deep breath, and with Lucy right behind her, they descended into the foyer.

"Ladies, you both look lovely this evening. Your carriage awaits."

"Pardon? We were just about to call for our own carriage," Emma protested.

"Nonsense. I am here to escort you ladies to the opera."

"But there can't be room for us all in your carriage," Emma tried again.

"Jack has my mother, Caroline, and Vivian in the other carriage." He gestured outside. Emma walked to the open door. Peering out, she found two grand carriages parked outside. The window of one was opened, and Caroline's pretty face appeared, smiling. She waved enthusiastically. Knowing it would be rude to continue to argue further, Emma waved and stepped back inside.

Lucy's excitement was evident on her face. "Thank you, Your Grace. Let's get our wraps, Lucy." Emma agreed riding in the ducal carriage would certainly be more comfortable than a hired hack. Andrew helped each of them with their wraps and escorted them out to the carriage. Emma sat with her sister on one side of the plush, well-appointed coach with Andrew across from them. On the quick trip to the theatre, Andrew gallantly filled the space between them with small talk and polite questions. The fancy carriage and the dashing man were all too much for Emma tonight. She didn't belong here. She left Lucy to respond and instead looked out the window as the streets rolled by.

She loved the night. How she wished she could be out skipping along the rooftops watching the people down below go about their business. In the night, she was free to go where she wanted. She didn't have to make conversation if she didn't feel like it. One day she would have enough money to live at her little country house, Hertford Manor, all by herself. Once her siblings were grown, that was. She would putter about the gardens or ride out in the countryside on her horse. No one would need her attention or tell her what to do.

Emma glanced surreptitiously over at Andrew. Perhaps he felt her gaze because his eyes shifted to meet hers. They were filled with good humor as he regaled Lucy with a story about his last trip to the palace. He gave Emma a wink, and her heart tripped in her chest. She turned her gaze back out the window. The only problem was, since she met the duke, her modest dream of living in the country sounded rather lonely. Curse him for making her want more than what she could have. No, she didn't need anybody. She would be perfectly happy on her own; she would have family to visit and their children to dote on.

Lucy poked her with her elbow. Glancing away from the window, she realized they had arrived. When Andrew helped her out of the carriage, he gave her a quizzical look.

"You seem melancholy tonight." He held her hand for an extra moment, giving it a squeeze. "Is everything all right?"

"Yes, of course." She put a smile on her face. "I was just enjoying riding in such a fine carriage. I love to see the streets at night. You never know what will appear out of the dark."

"Indeed." Andrew grinned. Then he walked over to help his mother alight from her carriage. Emma frowned at his back. What had he meant by that?

Caroline rushed over to stand between her and Lucy. She linked her arms with them. "Tonight shall be fun. I adore Italian opera and a good tragedy. I heard that the tenor singing tonight is fabulously handsome."

Thousands of candles lit the theatre's interior, and two grand red carpeted staircases led upstairs to the boxes. The Gilchrest box had a perfect vantage point to view the stage and of course to see and be seen by everyone below. Lucy and Emma stood at the balustrade, taking in the whole scene when Andrew came up right beside her. Emma started as he leaned toward her, her breath catching in her throat. She caught a whiff of his cologne. Closing her eyes briefly, she let the smell of sandalwood and soap fill her nostrils. Why was he standing so close? Andrew smiled as he reached into a small box mounted right by her elbow. He held out two pairs of opera glasses. She let out a shaky breath she hadn't been aware she was holding.

"Oh, how lovely!" Lucy exclaimed.

The opera glasses were delicate with a lovely filigree pattern etched into the gold-plated handles. Emma accepted her pair with a small sigh. What a ninny she was. Gathering her composure, she turned out to the theatre to look around, using her pair. Her gaze swept through the boxes. She couldn't help but notice the lovely jewelry worn by the ladies of the ton. On display were intricate necklaces, gold and gemstone earrings dancing in the light, and pearl and diamond headpieces tucked artfully into elaborate hairstyles.

A particularly large feathered headdress caught Emma's attention. Sitting next to the lady was a man she recognized immediately. Charles looked right at Emma and gave her a quick wink before turning back to his companion. Emma abruptly put down her glasses. *Oh dear*, one never knew what Uncle Charles would say or do. She hoped he would not find an excuse to come up here and try to meet the duke's family.

The gentle ting, ting, ting of a bell rang out.

"That is the signal the performance is about to start," Andrew explained. He cupped Emma's elbow and settled her into a chair nearby, taking the seat right next her. Caroline sat to his left with Lucy on the other side of her. Jack and Vivian settled behind them, and the duchess sat on a settee in the back of the box.

"Doesn't the duchess want to sit up front?" Emma asked.

Jack leaned forward. "Mother hates heights. She prefers to listen from the back."

"Truly?" Vivian asked. "How did I not know this?"

"Why doesn't she just have seats down in the orchestra then?" Emma asked Andrew quietly as the curtain went up on the stage.

"Because the boxes are the best places to see and be seen, I suppose. It's just what's done." Andrew shrugged his shoulders.

Emma gave him a sidelong look from under her lashes. "And do you always do what you are supposed to do, Your Grace?" she teased.

"Do you?" Andrew countered. His question held a challenge that made her breath hitch. Luckily, the music started, and she had an excuse to turn from his piercing gaze.

Emma had not ever been to the opera, and her first experience did not fail to impress. The music carried her away on a river of emotion. The story was tragic, but it did not dim her enjoyment. Life was often tragic. A handkerchief appeared in her lap as she tried to stifle a sniffle right before intermission. She looked over at Andrew; the corner of his mouth turned up in amusement. He probably thought she was silly to cry at the opera. Grateful for the handkerchief, she gave him a watery smile in return. When the curtain went down at intermission, everyone stood up to stretch, and a footman appeared with a tray of sparkling wine.

"Ladies, how are you enjoying the performance so far?" Andrew asked.

"Lovely!" Lucy said.

"I don't understand why the heroine is so tragic. Why doesn't she just go and track down her lover instead of pining away? I would have found him and demanded to know why he disappeared. Perhaps there is a perfectly good explanation," Vivian declared.

"Darling, you are a unique woman." Jack leaned down and kissed his wife right in full view for anyone to see. None of the family seemed fazed by the public display of affection. Emma looked around and saw dozens of pairs of opera glasses trained on their box. Her gaze automatically went toward the seats where her uncle had been sitting. His companion was talking animatedly to her neighbor, the feathers in her headdress bouncing up and down. But Charles Whittingham was missing from his seat. *Uh-oh.* Emma focused back on the conversation.

"Sometimes life's circumstances are beyond our control. She has accepted her lot. It is tragic, but that's life," Emma said. Vivian gave her a strange look but did not comment further.

Emma grabbed Lucy's elbow. "Lucy, won't you accompany me to the lady's retiring room?" She steered her toward the curtains which led out to the hallway, grabbing a glass of wine from the footman on the way out.

"Why are we out here, Emma? I'd much rather be with our friends inside the box."

"Uncle Charles is here tonight." Emma took a bracing sip from her wine. "Do you want to introduce him to the duchess?"

"Not if we can help it," Lucy agreed.

"Let's take a look around for him. He is probably making his way in this direction. I know he saw me earlier." They headed down the hall together. Sure enough, they had not gone fifty feet from the box when Charles Whittingham came strolling down the hallway toward them. Tonight he wore a suit in a peacock blue. Copious amounts of lace flounced at his throat and from his sleeves. A powdered wig, still popular with older gentlemen, graced his head, and his ever-present cane lent him a distinguished look. This evening he had added a monocle to his outfit, and Emma had to stifle a giggle as they approached him.

"My dears, how are you this evening? Imagine my surprise when I looked up and saw the two of you in the Duke of Gilchrest's box."

"Good evening, Uncle Charles." Emma and Lucy received air kisses on both cheeks continental style from their uncle.

Charles scanned the people milling about in the crowded hallway. He gestured with his cane. "Perhaps we could have a private moment of conversation?" He led them to a curtain, which partially hid an alcove with a little sofa tucked in it.

"So you are still working an angle to get to the necklace, aren't you? I thought I warned you it was too dangerous to take on such a high-profile mark."

"No, Uncle, I am not working anything. The duchess has been kind enough to sponsor Lucy this season. I would never steal from people I consider friends," Emma replied.

"Besides, she is not doing that anymore," Lucy interjected. "She has promised me she is done."

Charles gave Emma a questioning look. "Indeed?"

Lucy ignored Emma's silence, barreling on. "Yes, this season I will marry a nice gentleman of means, and he will take care of all of us. Emma no longer needs to put herself in danger. I won't have it!" Her face flushed pink.

Charles reached out and took Lucy's hand, patting it gently. "It's a lovely plan. I do truly hope you find a gentleman of means to take care of you." His eyes slid over to Emma. "And you, my dear, will you be finding a husband this season as well?"

"If I ever found a gentleman I could rely on, I suppose I would consider it. But my experience has taught me men like that are quite rare, so it is unlikely I will be marrying anytime soon."

"Hmmm, it is too bad you have given up our little side business, because I did happen to see the most divine necklace around the neck of Mr. John C. Caldwell's newest paramour this evening. Caldwell is a young man from Massachusetts. I hear he was sent to London to gain some polish. He is gambling and whoring his way through town, spending his father's money. The necklace consists of four gorgeous strands of diamonds. She must make him very happy to have received such a fine gift."

"Uncle! Really, must you be so frank in front of Lucy?" Emma admonished.

"Sorry, pet," he said to Lucy. "My dears, I can see you both are doing well, and so I have done my duty as your guardian for today."

Emma rolled her eyes at Lucy. Some guardian. He hadn't even asked after the children.

"Oh, I almost forgot. This is for you, Emma." He took her aside a few paces and passed her a small envelope.

She raised an eyebrow. How had he known he would see her tonight?

Charles shrugged. "Yes, a little birdie informed me you would be joining the duke and his family at the opera. I was all too curious to see if it was true."

Charles was keeping tabs on her social calendar? Emma peeked inside the envelope, mentally calculating. Satisfied, she tucked it into her reticule.

Charles took both of Emma's hands and said in a low voice, "Emma, I have always encouraged you to take care of yourself. Waiting for some white knight to come take care of you, that's all well and good for Lucy, but I know you can recognize a good opportunity when you see one. The necklace could help us both live well for quite a while. Even allow you to pay off that moldering manor house you love. Think about it. Contact me when you have made your decision."

Emma nodded. "Thank you, Uncle." She kissed his cheek. "Have a good evening." Emma pulled aside the curtain, and she and Lucy exited heading to the right, toward the retiring room.

****

Andrew leaned back against the wall. Emma's uncle exited after the ladies and ambled down the hallway. Stunned by the conversation he just overheard, his suspicions were laid to rest. Emma was definitely the jewel thief. But what he learned about Emma's guardian baffled him. It sounded as though her uncle encouraged her to a life of burglary. Even more troubling than the poor influence of her uncle was Lucy's comment about the danger Emma put herself in. He hadn't thought past her visits to him, but if she was sneaking into strange houses regularly, she was indeed putting herself in quite a bit of danger.

He ran a hand through his hair. What he wanted to do was confront her. Berate her for her stupidity. But at the same time, he wanted to pull her into his arms and promise to protect her forever.

Holy hell, what was it with him and rescuing damsels in distress? He'd done the same for his late wife. Lydia had cried on his shoulder, told him his brother Jack seduced her, and that Jack refused to marry her. Who would want her now that she was ruined? Andrew had felt so gallant offering marriage. He would save her from gossip and ruin. The betrothal had been encouraged by their fathers; it seemed like the right decision. Of course everything she said had been a lie. And look how that had turned out. A marriage filled with anger and betrayal, and years of estrangement from his brother.

The difference with Emma was this urge to protect was not just from a warped sense of duty; he was beginning to care a great deal for her. That had been the one thing missing from his relationship with Lydia, love and affection. Unfortunately, Emma didn't want saving. She certainly hadn't sounded like she was looking for a husband like her very practical sister.

He would just have to try to gain Emma's trust until she would allow him to help her. He knew she took great pride in caring for her siblings. But at what expense to herself? He needed to find the right time to confront her with the fact he knew her other identity. Once everything was out in the open, perhaps he could convince her to cease her nighttime escapades.

Andrew returned to the box still troubled by all he heard. A footman offered him the tray of wine, and he took a flute, quickly draining the entire thing. Looking at the empty glass in his hand, he mentally cursed. *Damn this woman.* She had him so wound up he drank the wine with only one thought, to quiet his whirling thoughts. He wanted another. Hell, he could use a glass of something stronger.

Andrew set the empty glass down with disgust. *This is not me anymore*. He wasn't opposed to having a glass of wine when the social situation called for it, but he did not want to rely on spirits to soothe his soul. What he needed was some space to breathe and think. He headed to the railing. He stared blindly, trying to calm his emotions.

She came up so quietly behind him he started when she softly said his name. "Andrew."

He turned, noting the rest of the family stood toward the back of the box, chatting with his mother.

"Look who is melancholy now." Emma gave him a small smile.

His gaze roamed her face. Was she indeed the same passionate lover who had come to his room in the night? He tried to accept the truth that the lady in front of him was a jewel thief. Her eyes grew wide and her smile wobbled. The intensity of his emotions must have shown on his face. Andrew set aside his concerns about what he'd overheard. Tonight was not the right time or place to confront her.

Thinking of jewelry, he glanced down at the unadorned creamy expanse of skin above the lace neckline of her dress. He remembered how soft the skin was there in the lovely hollow between her neck and shoulder. How she smelled delicious, like vanilla.

"I believe you could use a necklace with this gown. Something to highlight the neckline. Sapphires, I think." He almost reached out a finger and drew it along her delicate collarbone but thought better, at the last second dropping his hand back down at his side. They were in full view of half the ton, for God's sake. When he gazed at her, everyone else disappeared. She'd claimed his thoughts more than he liked to admit these past three weeks.

"I do not own any sapphires, Your Grace, else I would surely have worn them." Her fingers fluttered up to her throat, and his body heated watching them dance across her skin.

He forced a smile to put her at ease. "Are you ready for the tragic ending of this performance?" he teased her. "I fear I should have brought more handkerchiefs."

She tilted her head. Her eyes sparkled with humor again. "It's the music more than the story that brings me to tears. It is hauntingly beautiful."

Ting, ting, ting. The chimes rang out.

Andrew took her arm and escorted her back their

seats. As the lights went down, he reached for her hand. He leaned over to speak softly in her ear. "I find you hauntingly beautiful." Then he settled back, content for now to be sitting next to her with her hand clasped in his.

Chapter 13

The following week felt like a whirlwind of social events. Emma could scarcely keep her head on straight with all the different people they had met. She hadn't any time at all to do reconnaissance for the job she had decided to pursue. The diamond necklace had proven to be too tempting.

The proceeds from the necklace would pay for the expense of this social season and allow them to have a nice Christmas. She'd written to a contact of hers who, for a small fee, passed on the information that the mistress of Mr. John C. Caldwell was a woman named Esmerelda Hunt. The lady lived in a modest townhome in a fashionable area just on the edge of Mayfair. She lived alone with a small staff of three.

He had provided the address, and today Emma sat on a bench in the small park across from the row of homes. She dressed conservatively, as would a lady's companion or governess. She pretended to cross-stitch as she watched the house in an effort to learn the schedule of the lady. No one had come or gone from the house all afternoon.

In addition to finding the right time to break in, it was necessary to figure out the best way to enter and exit the house. Miss Hunt's home had an ornately carved wooden door which stood at least ten feet high. This indicated a high ceiling height for the rooms on the main level and most likely a long staircase to the second level. The upstairs windows were all open, letting the cool fall air into the bedrooms, no doubt. Sky blue curtains fluttered in the windows at the front. Next time Emma would wear her maid's outfit, and when the lady exited the house, she would take a look around the back. She could always pretend she was delivering a letter if she was caught snooping around.

Generally, she preferred to skip the trouble of picking door locks and climb from the roof through an upstairs window. Most people kept their jewelry in their bedroom or dressing room. But figuring out alternate exits was essential just in case.

She sighed and set her stitching on her lap. If she owned anything of worth, she would keep it in a safe. She found through her experience wealthy people were careless with their jewelry. Especially ladies like Miss Hunt who lived on their own. Emma shook her head. Their negligence was her gain.

The front door opened across the street, and Miss Hunt appeared with her maid. They turned left and headed toward Bond Street. *Hmm…four o'clock.* Emma noted it down in her little notebook. This first opportunity to observe the household was frustrating. She gleaned only a small amount of information. Normally, she would have time a-plenty, after she tucked the children into their rooms at bedtime, to figure out her plan of attack. Her evenings of late were filled with dinner parties and musicales. Perhaps Lucy was right; she should set this aside and concentrate on finding her sister a good husband this season. She could always revisit the job later in the year. She didn't want to attempt it ill prepared.

She glanced again at the watch pinned to her jacket. She needed to get home. Tonight they were going to dinner at Gilchrest House. She looked forward to seeing Andrew. She hadn't seen him this week at any of the gatherings they attended. It had been very hard to keep herself from visiting him at night. The highlight of her week had been when she received a beautiful bouquet of flowers from him the night after the opera.

Where had he been? She hated to admit it, but she missed him, their conversations, and their laughter. Emma stopped short in the middle of the path. It was no good to continue to moon about him. She must be practical. Pursuing a friendship with him would just lead her right back into his bed again. She couldn't risk letting him get too close. She straightened her shoulders and headed home.

Later, after she dressed for dinner, Emma walked into Lucy's room to see how her sister was getting on. Francine was just finishing curling Lucy's hair when Emma walked into the room.

"What in God's name are you wearing?" Lucy exclaimed from her seat in front of the mirror.

"I don't know what you mean." Emma looked down at her gray silk dress. It was a bit plain, but the fabric and trimmings were expensive.

"Emma, you look like you are entering a nunnery! That neckline has been out of fashion for five years at least. I know for a fact that was one of your mourning dresses from when Mother died. You absolutely cannot wear that dress to Gilchrest House."

"Whyever not? It maybe a little out of fashion, but I have worn all my other dresses already. It seemed the best choice," Emma argued.

She was not entirely being honest. She chose the unassuming dress because she didn't want to give the duke any cause to notice her tonight. She needed to keep her distance from him if she had any hope of keeping her wits about her.

"What about the mauve dress? It's the perfect shade of pink to complement your complexion. And I have the perfect ribbon to tie in your hair." Lucy stood and took Emma's arm. "Come along, Francine, and bring the dark pink velvet ribbon from my drawer."

"But we will be late." Emma tried again to protest. But Lucy was having none of it and pulled her back to her room. Her sister went straight to the wardrobe to pull out the dress she had chosen. With a shrug Emma gave up and let Francine unbutton her gray dress.

****

They were twenty minutes late. Andrew checked the clock on the mantel. He had been watching the door to the drawing room and trying to pay attention to the conversation around him at the same time.

"Don't you think so, Gilchrest?"

"Pardon? I'm sorry I missed that," Andrew apologized to his friend, Ethan Davenport.

"You are very distracted tonight," Davenport noted.

"Yes, well, truth be told, I am looking forward to seeing a certain lady this evening. But she has not arrived yet," Andrew confessed.

A slow smile spread across Davenport's face. "Really? No wonder you have been staring at the door. And who might I ask is this mystery lady?"

Just then, the door opened, and Miss Whittingham and Miss Lucy were ushered into the room by Rhodes.

She stole his breath away. Tonight, she was dressed in a gown of deep pink, her hair a shining bronze with a pink ribbon woven through her coiffeur. As usual there was no necklace marring the exquisite skin above the lace of her neckline. But she did have tiny pink earrings dangling from her ears.

Andrew gestured to the new arrivals. "Come with me, and I will introduce you to her and her lovely sister."

Lord Davenport glanced over at the two beautiful ladies. "It would be my pleasure."

"Good evening, ladies." Andrew bowed over each of their hands. "May I introduce my good friend, Lord Davenport? Davenport, this is Miss Whittingham and her sister Miss Lucy Whittingham."

Davenport smiled at Lucy. "I have had the distinct pleasure of sharing a dance with Miss Lucy at the Lansdowne ball." Taking her hand, he gave a smart bow. "It is a pleasure to see you again." He turned to Emma. "And you as well, Miss Whittingham. You both look lovely this evening," he said smoothly.

"A pleasure to meet you, Lord Davenport." Emma gave him a wide smile.

Andrew narrowed his eyes, jealousy clawing at his insides. Which of course was ridiculous. He let out a soft chuckle. "That was going to be my line, Davenport. Ladies, please come in. Dinner will be served shortly." He gestured them farther into the room.

"We apologize for being late." Emma gave her sister a pointed look.

Caroline came over to them as they crossed the room. "I am so glad you could come." She kissed each lady on the cheek. "Gilchrest, have you offered them anything to drink?"

"Not yet, Caro, they've just walked in the door."

Lord Davenport held out his elbow to Lucy. "May I get you a glass of punch, Miss Lucy?"

"Yes, thank you, Lord Davenport." Lucy laid a hand on his arm, and they walked toward the refreshment table.

"It certainly didn't take him long to claim her. I just knew they would like each other," Caroline said.

"And who do you like, Caroline?" Vivian asked as she and Jack strolled up to join them.

"Oh, none here tonight, love. You know me, I just like to flirt. Gilchrest, don't give me that look. The season has barely begun. Perhaps someone new to the scene will show up and save me from my boredom." She laid one hand dramatically on her brow, and Emma laughed behind her hand. Vivian just rolled her eyes.

Andrew wrinkled his brow as he observed his sister. Caroline was far too blasé about the season for a girl her age. Shouldn't she be all a-twitter to find some bloke to shackle? She had turned down five perfectly good offers the last two years. He had no intention of forcing her to marry someone she didn't want. He knew all too well the pain of being in a bad marriage. But he made a mental note to have a serious talk with her about choosing a husband already. How old was she now, twenty-two? Twenty-three?

Jack changed the subject. "Miss Whittingham, how goes the dog training? Andrew told me he was helping teach your siblings some simple commands."

"Fairly well, I guess. They have been practicing of sorts. But I think they did better when His Grace was there to organize them."

"Yes, well, Andrew always was good at telling people what to do," Jack teased good-naturedly.

Annoyed with his siblings, he shot them a frown. Why wouldn't they go away and leave him a moment with Emma alone? She'd barely even glanced at him since her arrival. Had she liked the flowers he'd sent? Had she thought about him? He'd missed her this week. Andrew sent his brother a glower over the ladies' heads, hoping his unspoken message to go away was expressed clearly.

Thankfully, Jack understood. "Vivian, let's go find Mother. Come along, Caro." He grabbed Caroline's elbow and ushered both women away.

Andrew let out a breath of relief. Turning to Emma, he said, "You look beautiful in pink."

"Thank you, Your Grace." She looked down at her hands instead of meeting his eyes.

Andrew tried again. "Did you receive the flowers I sent?"

This time Emma did look up at him with a smile. "Yes, they were beautiful, thank you."

Pleased, he returned her smile. "I had to attend to some business at my estate in Kent. A dispute among tenants. I was gone for most of the week." He gazed down at her. "I missed you," he confessed in a low voice.

Emma's lips parted in surprise at his soft words, but damn if he was going to hold back how he felt now that he knew her real identity. He would pursue this woman to the ends of the earth if that's what it would take to return her to his bed.

"I missed you too." Her quiet reply made him inexplicably happy.

Rhodes appeared at his elbow. “Dinner is served, Your Grace.”

“Thank you, Rhodes. Ring the gong,” he said, without taking his eyes off Emma. “If you will excuse me?”

She nodded, and Andrew reluctantly tore himself away to go escort his mother in to dinner.

Chapter 14

Emma, to her surprise, enjoyed dinner. Her nerves from earlier had been swept aside by Andrew's soft declaration he had missed her this week. He sat at the head of the table dressed in black and white formal attire. His hair was slicked back from his face and not one hair out of place. He looked every inch the Duke of Gilchrest. Caroline sat to his right, and Emma sat to his left with Lucy and Lord Davenport next to them. The duchess held court at the other end of the table with Vivian and Jack flanking her. The other guests appeared to be mixed in with no account to rank, but instead by who would get along with whom. It made for lively conversation and a relaxed atmosphere.

Lord Davenport was exceedingly charming. Between his and Caroline's many stories, they all had laughed often during dinner. Even Lucy, who normally wore her debutante persona like a shield at these events, seemed to relax. Lucy was a practical and organized soul, but like Emma, she had a wicked sense of humor. Lord Davenport elicited Lucy's laughter, and Emma approved.

She bit her lip, worried that a man like him would never offer for her sister. Lucy had no dowry. Beauty and grace could only go so far with most men. Perhaps she should speak to the duchess about her concerns and see what advice the lady could offer. Strong fingers clasped hers under the table and gave a squeeze. She glanced up to find Andrew looking at her with concern.

"Something amiss?" he asked quietly.

"No, everything is fine." She placed a smile on her face. How did he decipher what she was feeling? Damn his perceptiveness.

When dinner ended, everyone made their way into the music room where several of the young ladies took turns singing and playing the pianoforte. As Emma sipped a glass of sherry, she spied two small dark heads poking through the door across the room. She glanced around, but everyone else's attention focused on the lady singing. She stood to make her way surreptitiously over to the door. The two heads disappeared. Emma opened the door and slipped out into the hallway. Grayson and Tyler stood to the left of the door in their nightclothes, and both looked as though they were waiting to be hanged at the gallows for their crime. Emma smiled at the two little boys.

"What are you two doing out of bed?" she asked.

"We just wanted to see what was happening, I suppose." Grayson spoke for the two of them. "Will you tell on us?"

"No, I promise I won't, but you two should probably go back up to bed." A small hand slipped into hers. She looked down at Tyler's sweet, upturned face.

"I have been practicing making paper boats. Would you like to see them?"

"Oh, well…"

"Yes, come see them! Then you can make sure we went back to bed." Feeling his logic sound, Grayson took her other hand, and the two boys led her away.

****

Andrew saw Emma slip out of the music room. The perfect opportunity to catch a moment alone with her. He slowly made his way around the outskirts of the room and out the same door. Turning, he spotted a footman twenty feet down the hall standing at attention.

"Bertram, did you see a young lady in pink come out this way a few minutes ago? Which way did she head?"

"Yes, Your Grace, Masters Grayson and Tyler took her upstairs to the nursery, I believe."

"The boys? What were they doing down here?"

"Peepin' in on the party, sir. I just turned a blind eye, my lord, they weren't causing any trouble." Bertram's face turned red as he tugged at his collar.

"It's all right, Bertram. I'll go up and see they are back in bed. Thank you."

Andrew headed upstairs to the nursery. As he approached the doorway to the room, he stopped just outside to listen to the conversation going on inside.

"You've almost got it right. You see here, this flap should be folded over that way, which helps to make it float straight." Emma sat on the rug with his sons, examining several paper boats. "Now this one is just right. Good job!"

"When can we go sailing our boats again with Will and Max?" Grayson asked.

"I am not sure. Perhaps you should ask your father."

"Miss Emma, will you read us a story? We promise to get back into bed if you read us a story." Tyler put his hand in Emma's. Andrew's heart squeezed tight in his chest as he watched.

Taking a step forward, he leaned against the

doorjamb. “Is the party so boring downstairs that you needed to escape?”

All three heads swung around. His boys scrambled up to run over and give him a hug. Emma smiled up at him from her spot on the floor, her silk skirts spread around her.

“The boys had some very important business to show me. It needed my immediate attention.”

“Well, boys, I think you have monopolized enough of Miss Whittingham’s time for this evening. I believe it is far past your bedtime. Where is Ms. Fischer?”

“Downstairs having some tea with Mrs. Blume. Don’t get us in trouble with her, Father. We’ll go straight to bed now,” Grayson replied.

“Will you tuck us in?” Tyler gazed up at him.

Andrew reached down and gathered his son into his arms. “Of course.” He carried Tyler over to his bed on the other side of the room. He kissed each boy goodnight before returning to Emma, who still sat on the rug in front of the fire. He offered his hands to help her off the floor. And he didn’t let go of them as he led her out of the room and shut the door behind them.

“I’m sorry to keep them up, but I saw them peeping into the music room, and then they dragged me upstairs…”

Andrew cut her off with a kiss. For a moment she stood stock-still. But he moved his lips gently across hers, waiting for her to respond. *Kiss me back, Emma. Remember how perfectly our lips fit together.* Then she sighed and melted against him, and he sank into the kiss. A low growl of satisfaction rose unheeded from a deep primal place inside him. He wrapped an arm around her waist. *Mine.*

Emma's hands moved up around his neck, and she kissed him back, heating his blood. He moved to kiss her neck, breathing in the scent of vanilla as his lips caressed her soft skin. The rapid beat of her pulse fueled his hunger for her. He felt like a starving man. It had been two weeks since he last had her in his arms.

Then Emma pushed her hands against his shoulders in an effort to push him away. "Andrew, we cannot be doing this in the middle of the hallway outside your sons' room. Andrew!"

He pulled back enough to gaze down into her face. Her skin was flushed, her lips swollen pink. She looked delectable. "You're right. We can't do this here." He held on to one of her hands tightly and led her down the stairs. Instead of going back to the music room, he walked three doors down to his study. Pulling her in, he firmly shut the door, turning the key in the lock.

Andrew captured her mouth once more. She fit perfectly against him. His body hummed in response as it remembered her curves. He maneuvered them slowly over to the couch by the fire. Placing kisses along her jaw and across her cheek, he tumbled them down onto the chaise. Emma landed in his lap. She giggled as she fell against his chest.

"What are we doing, Andrew? This isn't proper at all." She kissed him and then pulled away enough to put her forehead against his, laying a hand on his chest. His heartbeat thundered under her palm. That wasn't the only body part responding to her soft curves. She sent his thoughts into disarray as she wiggled, trying to slide off his lap. He tightened an arm around her waist.

"I can't help it. I have been dreaming about holding you again ever since you disappeared from my bedroom two weeks ago." He kissed the tip of her nose.

She froze. "What did you say?"

"Did you think I wouldn't recognize your kisses? The feel of your body?" He ran a hand up to brazenly cup one of her breasts. Emma scrambled off him, backing away, her face draining of color. Perhaps this hadn't been the best moment to bring up he knew she was the thief. Nevertheless, now they could have a real discussion about her future, about their future.

"I don't know what you are talking about." She continued to back away.

Andrew stood up and approached her slowly. "Don't be afraid. I won't tell anyone. Emma, you can trust me." She had backed herself right up against his desk, the wooden edge hitting her in the backside.

"W-When did you know?" she stammered. "H-How did you know?"

Andrew came up close, putting his hands on the desk, one on each side of her, trapping her neatly. "I recognized your laugh."

Her eyes went wide, darting left then to the right as if looking for an escape route. It tore at him that she looked so frightened. Andrew reached out a hand to cup her chin, forcing her gaze to him.

"Emma, your laugh brought me back to life. I thought I was doing better. I'd stopped drinking. I was spending more time with my family. The truth is, I was just going through the motions each day. Until you made me laugh." He gently rubbed his thumb across her cheek. "Let me take care of you. Stop this thievery. It's too dangerous. I can take care of you if you let me." It surprised him how fervently he believed each word. He would do anything to keep her safe.

Emma shook her head vehemently. “No. I can take care of myself and what is mine.” Her voice hitched. “This has been a dream that I cannot have. Let me go, Andrew.”

But he could not. She had to feel how much he needed her. How they needed each other. “This isn’t a dream. What’s between us, this is real.” He kissed her. His arms trapping her against him. His mouth demanded she understand. But she held herself stiff and unresponsive against him. When he broke the kiss, Emma turned her head away from him, unshed tears glimmering in her eyes.

“Let me go, Andrew.”

He dropped his arms and took a step back. He barely held himself in check as she slid from the desk. He was no beast, but he wanted to howl in frustration at her retreat.

She pushed past him as she fled toward the glass-paned door, which led out to the gardens. “I must go. Please make sure Lucy gets home safely.” She dared to meet his gaze from across the room.

“This isn’t over, Emma,” he said with quiet conviction.

“This never should have started.” She wiped an errant tear from her cheek. Turning, she opened the door and disappeared into the night.

Chapter 15

Emma hurried down the block, her heart pounding. He had known it was her for two weeks! Why hadn't he turned her in? Why hadn't he turned away from her in shock and dismay? Her instincts screamed for her to run far away, but Emma forced herself to walk straight home. It would be dangerous to wander around London at night in an evening gown, no money, no plan. She slowed her pace, taking deep bracing gulps of the cold night air.

Her mind scrambled to understand why he had kept her secret. Perhaps he was hoping to continue their amorous activities; it had certainly seemed like that tonight. If she said yes and became his mistress, she knew he would take care of her…for now. But what then? When he grew tired of her or found another? No, she was better off on her own. Her heels clicked an angry rhythm against the cobblestones.

What must he think of her? A common harlot, no doubt. It had been the height of folly to be with him. She wiped at the wetness on her cheek. *You fool! It's too late to be crying over your poor decisions*. Now she had to trust he would not turn her in to the authorities. Fear clawed in her gut. Perhaps she should just disappear.

The idea took root. If she left the city, Lucy could still carry on her connection with the Langdons, and

Emma wouldn't have to see Andrew. If she were honest, she didn't believe he would turn her in to the authorities. But she was certain he planned to press her to become his mistress. She needed to get away, or else she didn't know if she had the strength to say no to him.

She would do this job for the diamond necklace. It would bring in a sizable sum, enough to keep the family provided for a while. She would steal the necklace and leave the proceeds for Lucy to manage. Then she would disappear. Charles could damn well step in and take his guardian duties seriously. She could go to Hertford Manor. It wasn't entirely livable yet, but it would be a roof over her head. No one knew her there. Emma took a deep breath through her nose. She felt calmer now that she had made a plan. She would allow herself a week to prepare. She could avoid the duke for one week.

She arrived home, hollow from the emotional upheaval of the evening. She made her way up to her room. When she entered, Fergus woke and walked over to greet her from his bed in the corner. Emma took one look into his sympathetic face and burst into tears. Kneeling down, she flung her arms around his great shaggy neck and wept.

****

Much later in the evening, after all the guests had gone home, Andrew sat at his desk, staring into a glass of brandy. He swirled the amber liquid around in the glass but didn't drink. It called to him, promising oblivion from his churning emotions if only he were to consume enough. A knock sounded, jerking him from his trance.

His brother entered the room. "May I join you?"

Andrew looked up. "Be my guest." He gestured to the bottle on the corner of his desk.

"So why are you in here staring into that glass instead of heading to bed?" Jack asked as he poured himself two fingers.

Andrew got up from his seat, leaving his drink behind. He came around and slumped down on the sofa. The same sofa where he had, just a few hours earlier, held in his arms the most confounding, the most desirable woman he had ever met.

"Does this have anything to do with Miss Whittingham leaving early?"

Andrew nodded. "She is a woman with secrets, Jack. They are not mine to tell. I want to help, but she doesn't trust me, or rather she won't let herself trust me. It's damned frustrating!"

"Do you love her?" Jack asked.

Andrew jerked his head up, surprised at his brother's blunt question. The answer crystallized with a clarity he could not deny. "Yes, I think I do."

"Then you must exercise patience. Just be there for her when she needs you. That's all you can do for now."

"What if her secret puts her in danger?"

Jack's face registered astonishment. "Well, not knowing the particulars of the situation, I cannot advise you." He took a sip of brandy. "But if she could possibly be in danger, then I would do whatever it takes to help her whether she wants you to or not."

Andrew nodded in agreement. He would figure out some way to help. He just couldn't let her know it was him. Perhaps the uncle could be just the ticket he needed.

"Jack, do you know someone who can dig up information for me about a Mr. Charles Whittingham?"

****

Several nights later, Emma sat crouched on the roof of a row house across from Miss Esmeralda Hunt's residence. The cold night air cut through her light jacket, causing her to shiver. It was two o'clock in the morning, and Miss Hunt was still not home. She had been watching the house each evening for the past three days, hoping to figure out if Miss Hunt had any type of regular schedule Emma could use to her advantage.

So far it seemed Miss Hunt spent hardly any time at home. She came home to change clothing, and then she was out again. Unfortunately, her erratic comings and goings didn't leave Emma with any sort of plan for when she could slip inside. The only pattern she had surmised was that Miss Hunt did go out regularly in the evenings, at least for dinner.

Emma yawned. She'd better get home and get some rest or else she really would get sick, just as she had been feigning all week. She felt guilty about lying to Lucy. But feeling guilty was nothing new.

She shimmied down the drainpipe, landing silently in the garden. She exited through the garden gate, which led to the street, when a carriage pulled up in front of Miss Hunt's house. Emma flattened herself against the brick wall in the shadows of the alley. Mr. Caldwell jumped down from the carriage, and he held out a hand to help Miss Hunt alight. They embraced passionately.

Then Miss Hunt pulled away, laughing. "Now Mr. Caldwell, you've had your fun tonight. Go home and sleep."

"But I'd much rather come inside and sleep with you." He wrapped an arm around her waist, pulling her close.

Miss Hunt smiled and placed a hand on his chest. "Now, now, I need my rest too. I will see you on Friday evening. You're taking me to the theatre, aren't you? I do so love going to the theatre. Off you go, be a good boy, and I promise you a special surprise Friday after the show." She gave him a languid kiss and, turning, went up the front steps.

The young man gave a jaunty wave. Then he stepped up into his carriage. Elated at what she heard, Emma watched the carriage roll away down the street. She couldn't believe her good luck. Now she knew exactly when the lady would be out of the house for a good chunk of time. She would return Friday night and hope Miss Hunt wasn't planning on wearing her diamond necklace to the theatre.

Chapter 16

The next morning Emma was up early for once. She hummed as she prepared bread dough. She was making sweet rolls for her siblings for breakfast as a special treat. Her conscience poked at her for making plans to abandon her brothers and sisters. She frowned as she punched down the dough. She wouldn't be gone forever, just until Lucy could make a good match. Once her sister was settled, she would happily return to care for the whole lot again.

She would leave them a note to explain her absence, although what this alleged note would say she had not figured out yet. Emma paused her kneading. Biting her lip, she wiped away a tear with the back of one floury hand. Looking over at her loyal companion lying on the hooked rug by the fire, she sighed. "Fergus, what am going to do?"

"What are you going to do about what?" Lucy's voice came from the doorway.

Emma didn't turn around. "Oh nothing, just this bread dough isn't rising properly."

"Well, don't beat it to death, let it rest on the counter for a bit." Lucy went over and got two mugs from the cupboard. "Come and have a cup of tea with me. Are you feeling better, then?" She asked Emma as she poured the tea.

"Yes, thanks." Emma cleaned her hands and then

sat down across the table from her sister. "How was the dinner at Lord Greenville's last night?"

"Oh, dull. I sat between the distinguished Colonel Fairlight and the newly home from university, Sir Lawrence. Both were dull as dust." She sighed and took a sip of her tea.

"What of your Lord Davenport? Was he not there?"

"No, he is out at one of his estates, attending something or other. He did write me this lovely note." Lucy pulled it out of her pocket and, opening it, read it out loud.

"Dear Miss Whittingham, I am away again to my estate in Kent. I shall miss the opportunity to call on you this week. I hope your affections will not be swayed by some other swain trying to win you with pretty words and flowers while I am away. I look forward to seeing you again this Saturday at Lady Heathrow's ball. Yours truly, Davenport."

She then clutched the note against her heart for a moment before folding it carefully and placing it back into the pocket of her apron.

"He sounds interested. What do you think about him, Lucy? I don't want you to just choose the first man to show interest in you. Is he kind? Does he gamble? Drink?"

"Oh, Emma, you are too cynical by far! Davenport is a true gentleman," Lucy huffed.

"All right, but I had a very close call with my engagement to Longwood. If he hadn't fallen off his horse and died, I would be married to that horrible philanderer. I want you to know I would never have you marry unless you were absolutely sure of the man's good character." Emma reached out to give Lucy's hand a squeeze.

"You are a good sister, Emma. The best." Lucy returned the squeeze. "Now tell me, what do you think of Lord Gilchrest's character? He is always present at functions when you will be there. He sent three notes this week and stopped by to see how you were faring. He seemed very concerned for your health, Sister," she teased Emma.

Pain flashed like a hot knife through Emma's heart. She stood quickly, turning to put her cup in the sink lest Lucy see it in her eyes. She'd not returned any of his notes, which all insisted he needed to speak with her. He was so domineering! She simply needed to ignore him for a few more days, and then she could disappear.

"He has a very fine character. But he is a duke and therefore is far out of my league. Besides he has no need to remarry, he has his heir and spare. He has done his duty."

Lucy came up behind Emma, wrapping her arms around her waist, and settled her chin on Emma's shoulder. "Perhaps next time he will choose to marry for love," she said quietly. She gave Emma a quick hug and left the room.

****

Charles Whittingham smiled as he set down his niece's missive on his mahogany desk. He picked up his glass of wine, raising it in a toast to himself. Emma was making preparations to steal the diamond necklace. Her note had been brief, saying she was doing reconnaissance this week, and she would get back to him when the job was done.

The only troubling thing was her mention of taking

a break from London. Some blather about needing to disappear for the benefit of Lucy's season. He certainly would steer her away from that idea. Emma was the most talented thief he had worked with in years, nimble, unafraid, with a natural penchant for the art.

His lips curved up. He would always remember the first time he had seen her pinch something. It had been about six months or so after his brother Henry had died. They had received endless invitations to teas and dinners so everyone could coo about what a tragedy the viscount's death had been. He and Emma had both been under scrutiny for different reasons. His return after fifteen years abroad had caused much interest. The reason for his banishment had been mostly forgotten, and he enjoyed the opportunity to move in society again. Emma had been the recipient of pity. Poor girl, they said, lost her fiancé and lost her father within weeks of each other. Tsk-tsk, what bad luck.

At one event, he had noticed Emma was missing. He found her in the library meandering along the shelves, looking at the titles while the other ladies chatted by the fire. While he watched from across the room, her hand had darted out and snatched a golden paperweight in the shape of a small angel from a table nearby. It had disappeared into her small silk purse in the blink of an eye.

"So is the angel still in your purse?" he casually asked, as they made their way home in the coach. Her hands had jerked in her lap, and she blinked rapidly as she stared across at him. He simply waited for an answer.

Then she had squeezed her eyes shut and shook her head slowly side to side. "No, I put it back. I always do." When she opened her eyes, she pressed her hands against her cheeks. "It's…just that when I am upset, I can't seem to help it. Mama used to call it my sticky fingers problem. She always made me return whatever it was. I do, I always return the items." She shrugged her shoulders.

He had reached over and patted her hand. "You have given me a brilliant idea, my dear. We'll talk about tomorrow, I promise."

Charles took another sip of his drink and set the glass down next to his ink pot on the desk. He'd worry about talking some sense into her later. He turned his attention to writing a quick note to Dorling.

Mr. Dorling,

Please note that I will be able to obtain the item we discussed for auction within the next few weeks. You may set up prospective buyers. I will be in touch soon.

W

Charles folded the note carefully. He melted a bit of wax over the flame of the taper next to him and dripped it over the seam to seal the letter. He was about to ring for a footman to deliver the note when there was a knock at the door. His butler, Greer, came into the room looking quite flustered. This was some cause for alarm as the man never showed an ounce of emotion.

"What is it?" Charles narrowed his eyes.

"Sir, there is a gentleman here to see you." Greer glanced down at the card in his hand as though he was double checking the name. "The Duke of Gilchrest, sir."

"Well, don't keep him waiting! Show him in." *The Duke of Gilchrest calling here? That was a first. Didn't the aristocracy usually summon those they wish to speak with?* Charles stood and put on his jacket. He had just enough time to straighten his cuffs before the man strode in, his presence filling the room. He wore a hard expression, which made Charles want to take a step back. Instead, he made himself step forward, placing a friendly smile on his face.

"Mr. Charles Whittingham? Are you the guardian for the children of the late Viscount Newton?"

"Technically, just for the four younger siblings. Miss Whittingham and her sister Lucy are of age. Do you know them, Your Grace? Oh yes, of course, my niece did tell me your family was sponsoring Lucy this season. Please, come in, and have a seat." He gestured to a chair by the fire. "Would you care for a brandy, Your Grace?"

"No, thank you."

The duke sat down, one leg crossed across his knee. His expression did not soften. His eyes were hard as ice chips.

Charles settled himself in the chair opposite. He catalogued the possibilities to why the Duke of Gilchrest was sitting in his study. Was he here to ask permission to marry one of the girls? He didn't exactly wear the expression of a man with the intention of betrothal. Maybe one of the children had insulted him? Stolen something from his house? They were a bit of a handful.

"Your Grace, with what may I help you?" he prompted.

"To start, I would like you to stop encouraging your niece to a life of crime."

Well, that had not been on his list. Luckily, years of cons had taught him to control his reactions. "I beg your pardon?" He raised an eyebrow as if he were confused.

The duke didn't mince words. "I think you know exactly what I am speaking of. You are putting her at great risk."

Charles steepled his fingers and put an expression of concern on his face. "I am sure my niece would not be involved in anything remotely criminal."

The duke sighed. "So we are sticking with denial." He pulled out an envelope from his breast pocket. "And you? Are you not remotely involved in anything criminal? Because I have evidence here which would contradict that assertion."

Charles narrowed his eyes. *What was this man's angle? What could he possibly know?* In the next moment, his heart sank.

"It seems to me you left England quite in haste in '93, Mr. Jones, Mr. Barnabus Jones, is it?" The duke thumbed through the papers. "Or perhaps it is Monsieur Blanchett, or…oh yes, I rather like this one, Adriano Escalanta. It has so much flair." As he looked up, the smile vanished. "You see, I believe the Home Office would be very interested in all this information about your various reincarnations. It seems they were very frustrated they could not pin down the Ghost before he disappeared fifteen years ago."

Charles resisted the urge to pull at his cravat which was suddenly too tight as he swallowed. How had this man dug up all his old identities?

"What do you want?" he choked out.

"What I want is for you to step away from Miss Whittingham and her siblings. What I want is for you to stop setting up opportunities for her to steal. Stop encouraging her." With each syllable, the duke's anger singed the air between them.

Charles composed his features. "I am their guardian. I have done the best I could to take care of them during a very difficult time." He looked off into the fire. "I am rather fond of them."

"You know, I almost believe you. But now I am going to take care of them. And I won't need her to steal for me to accomplish the task." His features were fierce and his voice possessive. "Now, what is your decision? A nice long trip to the continent, or a nice long chat with the Home Office?"

Charles glanced at the letter sitting on his desk. It didn't appear the duke had discussed his plans with Emma yet. High-handed bastard. The sale of the diamond necklace would set them up with quite the nest egg, enough to take the whole family out of England. There were rich nobs all over the continent ripe for the plucking. With his contacts and Emma's nimble fingers, they could make a fortune. He would not leave without the proceeds from the auction. Nor would he give up Emma.

"Yes, well, perhaps I am tiring of London. It could be a good time for trip abroad." He sighed, trying to look defeated.

The duke nodded and then stood, slipping the papers back into his pocket. "Then our business is finished." He patted his pocket. "Just make your exit quickly. This deal has a time limit. You don't want to be around when I turn this information over to the investigators. Good day, Mr. Whittingham."

Chapter 17

Friday evening, Emma entered the nursery. The boys were tucked into their beds asleep. She gave each small cheek a kiss goodnight. She walked along the hallway. The flame of her candle danced in the dark. Next, she peeked in to say goodnight to Margie and Abby. The girls were tucked in together, heads bent over what was no doubt the latest gothic novel. They looked up at her with owlish eyes.

"You two should go to sleep. You'll hurt your eyes reading with only that taper for light." Abby set the candle down on the nightstand, and her sister tucked the book under the pillow. "Blow it out," Emma commanded. With a roll of her eyes, Abby blew out the candle and settled back against the pillows.

Emma closed the door. She headed to the wing she and Lucy shared. Her last stop was to see that her sister was dressed and ready to go to Almack's tonight with the duchess and Lady Caroline. She was required to wear all white for this rite of passage. Emma, thankfully, had been able to bow out of the event. She had said she was not up to crowded ballrooms just yet after having been sick most of the week.

She leaned against the doorjamb. "You look lovely, Lucy. I am sure you will get through tonight without issue."

"I hope so." Lucy turned to face her, running her

hands down the front of her gown. "I have heard it's an awful crush. I guess I understand why you wouldn't be feeling up to it yet."

"I promise to be rested for tomorrow night. We will go to Lady Heathrow's ball and see your Lord Davenport." Emma gave her sister a kiss on the cheek. "Have fun tonight."

Emma walked swiftly to her room. When she was sure her sister had left the house, she changed into her men's clothing, donning the shirt, pants, and loose jacket. She braided her hair, winding it high on her head. Using soot from the fireplace and her dingy oversized cap, she transformed herself into a dirty street urchin.

The theatre performance always ran at least three hours with the intermission. It should leave her plenty of time to pinch the necklace and make her way home. Her blood thrummed though her veins. Giving Fergus a scratch on the head, she said, "Wish me luck."

Then she hopped onto the windowsill and jumped with ease over to her tree. Climbing down to the grass, she made her way across the darkened garden and into the alley beyond.

The evening air chilled her even through her jacket. Clouds blew across the sky, covering the moon. *The darker the better*. She strode through the park, enjoying the freedom of movement her boy's clothing allowed. Spotting a low-hanging branch, Emma jumped up to swipe a leaf from its branches. She could never do that in layers of skirts. Grinning, she sprinted the last fifty yards to the street corner.

As she reached the street Miss Hunt resided in, she strolled by to assess the house. It was past ten, so Miss

Hunt should be gone for the evening. No lights shone from the front of the house. Based on earlier surveillance, Emma knew the lady's bedroom faced the street on the second floor. Which meant she would have to enter through a back bedroom and cross the hallway.

Doubling back, she made her way down the alley between the houses. The back garden gate lay closed right in front of her. Praying it wasn't rusted, she carefully pushed the gate open and walked into the garden. The kitchen door swung open. Light spilled onto the grass. Emma ducked behind a tree, flattening herself against its trunk.

A husky feminine chuckle came through the open doorway. "Come on, Betsy. Let's go have some fun. You know the missus doesn't like anyone in the house when she is entertaining her gentleman friends. Let's go to Vauxhall Gardens. I hear they have a tightrope walker!"

Two women emerged from the house together. She didn't hear the scrape of a lock. "Well, it will be right nice to have some entertainment, maybe get a pint of mead." The servants passed right by where Emma hid, chatting animatedly, then out the gate to the alley. Emma remained still in her spot until she heard the women's voices fade. Smiling to herself, she emerged. *What luck! Not a soul home.*

She entered the house through the unlocked kitchen and made her way up the back stairs. The second floor comprised of only three rooms, two bedrooms in the back and one large one in the front. Emma slipped soundlessly into the front bedroom. She crept across the room, deciding to start her search at the lady's vanity. She rifled through all the drawers. Finding nothing but perfume bottles and hairbrushes, she moved to the wardrobe. She found no jewelry there either.

Emma let out a frustrated breath. All right, Miss Hunt was not careless with her valuables. She stood in the middle of the room, hands on her hips, considering the possibilities. If she wanted to keep her jewelry in a safe place, where would she hide it? Her gaze scanned the room in a slow sweep. Then she spotted the shadowed form of a lock box tucked in a corner under the desk.

This lift might not be as easy as she anticipated. Picking the lock on a safe box required more time and patience than the average door lock. Getting down onto her knees, she peered at the small iron box, evaluating what kind of lock it had. She pulled out her leather roll of picks and chose the tools she needed for this delicate lock.

After a little finessing, the lock turned, and the lid popped up. She rolled her picks back up and tucked them away in her jacket pocket. Inside the box lay a large stack of money and several velvet boxes. Choosing the largest, she brought it over to the window so she might have more light to see its contents. As she opened it, a small sigh of pleasure escaped her lips as dozens of diamonds twinkled in the moonlight.

Then from downstairs a male voice boomed. "Next time, remind me that I find the theatre boring, before dragging me to another play. I couldn't sit through another minute of that blather."

Emma froze, then her survival instincts kicked in. She stuffed the necklace into her jacket pocket, and quickly crossing the room, she returned the velvet box and closed the lid to the lock box. She moved to the open doorway to listen.

"Darling, I know just what will make you forget all about that idiotic play." Female giggling drifted up the stairs.

They were headed up the front stairs. Emma slipped out of the room. As she pulled the door closed behind her, it let out a loud creaking sound. She halted, one hand on the doorknob. Had it creaked when she opened it before? She silently moved across the hallway, hoping her dark clothing would help her blend in with shadows.

"Hey! Stop! What are you doing in here?" Damn! Mr. Caldwell and Miss Hunt were already at the top of the main stairs.

Emma raced down the short hallway to the back stairs that led to the kitchen and her exit. Panic, thick and bitter, rose in the back of her throat. The loud report of a pistol rang out right before her arm erupted in pain. The force of the shot bounced her against the wall of the stairwell, then she stumbled, falling down the rest of the stairs.

At the bottom she pushed herself up and shook her head to clear it. A dark figure loomed at the top of the stairs. She scrambled to her feet, adrenaline propelling her through the kitchen and out into the night. Another shot blasted into the brick wall next to her as she raced out the back gate. Lungs burning, she ran for the park as fast as her legs would carry her. The dark hulking shapes of the houses lining the street blended together in a blur as she ran for her life.

Was he following her? She couldn't hear any footsteps from behind her over the thunderous beating of her heart. Emma didn't dare look back until she reached a familiar grove of trees. She stepped into the bushes behind one giant oak and tried to catch her breath. She doubled over, the pain in her shoulder and arm sending her to her knees.

She ran her fingers gingerly along her right arm. Wetness seeped through her jacket. Pulling her hand away, she could see it was covered in blood. Her hand shook violently. She'd been shot. She knelt in the bushes, terrified she would hear the sound of footfalls running in pursuit. But when several minutes went by in silence, she took in an unsteady breath.

Emma slowly stood, keeping to the deep shadows provided by the tree. She'd lost her hat somewhere. The long braid of her hair had come loose and was hanging down her back. She pushed at wisps of loose hair stuck to the side of her sweaty face.

She could not go home bleeding and battered; she would scare Lucy and the children to death. Closing her eyes, she swayed on her feet. God, the scandal it would cause if she was found in the middle of the park unconscious with a gunshot wound. Lucy would never be able to marry decently, and the boys would inherit a bankrupt title smeared in scandal.

Her vision blurred, the edges darkening. Panic coursed through her once again. Emma leaned against the rough bark of the tree, trying to breathe through the pain. She refused to die out here in the middle of Hyde Park. Then with sudden clarity she knew what to do. Stumbling forward, she headed to the only person she knew who was powerful enough to help her.

Chapter 18

Andrew and his brother sat in companionable silence by the fire in Andrew's study, he with a glass of cider and Jack with his usual whiskey. Tonight, the ladies had hied off to Almacks, and both men, along with Jack's wife, Vivian, had made their excuses and stayed behind. He was grateful for the easy friendship he and his brother now enjoyed.

The two of them had come far from their previously strained relationship. In his youth, Jack had been in love with Andrew's late wife, Lydia. She led Jack to think she returned his affections, and then had cruelly laughed off his proposal of marriage. Devastated and angry, Jack ran off to join the Royal Navy. Because of Lydia's scheming, for the last decade Jack and he had rarely seen each other and had only been on the most formal of terms.

During those early adult years, Jack's life had unraveled. His reckless behavior landed him a court martial, he nearly died in an ambush, went to work for pirates, and was coerced into working as a spy for the crown in return for forgiving his desertion. Eventually though, he was able to buy his first ship. He had since built up an impressive export business.

Jack returned home this past summer bent on repairing his connections with the family. As they spent time together again, they had forged a new friendship which had healed old wounds. Andrew leaned back in his chair, content to spend a quiet evening in the company of family. He couldn't be happier to have his brother back in his life.

His head whipped around as a thud sounded against the french doors which led out to the garden. The door burst open, and a man stumbled into the room. Andrew and Jack shot to their feet. The man braced himself against the desk, and a pair of large brandy-colored eyes peered out from a soot-stained face. No…it couldn't be.

"Andrew…" the figure moaned. Then slowly sank to the floor.

"Dear God, Emma!" He raced over and scooped her up off the floor. She let out a cry of pain. He immediately set her back on her feet but left one arm around her waist to prop her up. Andrew looked down and saw a dark red stain on her jacket that could only be blood. "Oh, Emma, what's happened?" He pulled her gently against his chest.

"I believe…I've been shot." Then her eyes fluttered shut, and with a sigh she slid into unconsciousness.

"This is Emma Whittingham?" Jack said, his mouth agape.

"Yes. She's been hurt badly from the looks of all this blood. Help me get her upstairs to my suite without anyone seeing us."

Jack, to his credit, quickly shook off his initial shock. He went through the door and out into the hallway. Andrew could hear him send the footman on an errand to the kitchens. Then he motioned for Andrew to follow him. They went directly up the front stairs, with Jack turning the corners first, checking that the hall was clear before motioning for Andrew to continue. Just as they reached the doorway to his suite, Vivian came out of a sitting room four doors down.

Her eyes travelled over both men and then to the bleeding figure in his arms. "What in bloody hell is going on here?" she demanded.

There was no time for questions. Andrew motioned with his head for Jack to get the door. He strode in, placing Emma gently on his bed. She lay motionless, and he was appalled at the blood which spread across the sleeve of her jacket.

"Winston!" Andrew yelled. "Winston!"

"Will someone please tell me what the hell is happening? Who is that?" Vivian repeated her question from the doorway.

Jack pulled her into the room and shut the door. "That is Miss Emma Whittingham. She's been shot. That's all I know."

"What!" Vivian peered more carefully at the unconscious form on the bed.

From the dressing room Winston came bustling out. "You bellowed, my lord?"

"I need some towels and some help getting her out of this jacket. She is bleeding profusely. We must stop the bleeding." Andrew could hear the panic leaking into his voice.

Winston's eyes bugged out of his head. But he immediately ran back to the dressing room and emerged a moment later with a stack of towels. Andrew turned to his brother.

"Jack, can you send for Davis? He can be trusted to have discretion, yes?" George Davis had been Jack's ship's surgeon for many years before resigning last year to settle in London and get married.

"Yes, of course. I will ride out and fetch him immediately." Jack swiftly left the room.

Vivian seemed to take stock of the situation, for she hefted her skirts up and climbed onto the bed next to Emma. "Andrew, you lift her up gently, and I will try to get her arms out this jacket."

Andrew slid an arm under Emma's shoulders, and together the two of them managed to slide the oversized jacket off one arm. As they tried to slide it off the injured one, Emma came to with a scream of pain, her eyes wild. She groaned as Andrew laid her gently back against the pillows. Winston handed over a towel, and Andrew pressed it against the wound on her upper arm, hoping to stanch the bleeding.

"Andrew…," she croaked, "my arm is on fire."

"You said you'd been shot, my love." He brushed his fingers across her cheek. Looking up, he saw Vivian gaping at them, mouth hanging open. He didn't know what had shocked her more, Emma being shot or the endearment that had slipped out of his mouth. At the moment, he didn't have any inclination to explain his relationship with Miss Whittingham.

"Vivian, can you go wait for Jack and George Davis and escort them up here without the staff seeing the surgeon arrive?"

Vivian nodded her head and shimmied off the bed.

Andrew turned to Winston. "Nobody comes into this room except the surgeon, or Jack and his wife. No one knows she is here. Can I trust you to make sure of that?"

"Yes, Your Grace. Shall I bring up some spirits?

The surgeon may need them to clean the wound."

"Not until Davis arrives. Right now, I need you to stand sentry at the door."

"Yes, sir."

When Andrew was alone with Emma, he took a towel to the wash basin to dampen it; he wiped her face clean of the soot she used to disguise her features, revealing a deathly white pallor. He again put pressure on her wound, trying to stop the blood which was quickly soaking the towel. Emma still had her eyes closed, so Andrew jolted when she spoke.

"I'm sorry. I didn't know where else to go. Didn't want to frighten the children. You said you wanted to take care of me. I wager you didn't imagine a scenario like this." She opened her eyes, and her mouth turned up in a wry smile. How could she smile at him when she was quite possibly bleeding to death?

"I will take care of everything. You just hang on until the surgeon gets here. If I can just get this damned bleeding to stop!"

Emma eyes fluttered closed again. Andrew leaned his forehead against hers. "Emma, hang on." His voice rasped. "Please don't die. I won't have it, you hear me! You are absolutely not allowed to die."

Time passed impossibly slow as he watched Emma's pale face and kept pressure on her wound.

"Andrew, I've brought Davis." Jack's voice came from across the room.

Andrew stood to greet the surgeon. "Thank you for coming so quickly."

"It's no problem. I'm glad I was at home and not at the hospital. What is the situation?" Davis strode over to where Emma lay on the bed.

"She was shot in her right arm. I've been trying to put pressure on the wound to stanch the bleeding, but I have no idea if it's working." He scrubbed a hand over his face. "She has been in and out of consciousness."

"May I assess the wound?"

Andrew nodded. Jack laid a comforting hand on his shoulder, giving it a firm squeeze as Davis tore the sleeve of Emma's shirt to look at the wound.

Davis called out, "Could you come here and help me roll her gently onto her side so I can see if there is an exit wound? If we are lucky, the ball isn't lodged inside her shoulder."

Andrew climbed on the bed and gently rolled Emma toward him. She moaned, her face taut with pain. His stomach clenched in response.

"It looks as though the ball just grazed her arm and took with it a chunk of flesh. Flesh wounds often bleed profusely, but the bleeding is slowing and starting to clot nicely. I'll need to clean the wound, then I will sew it up as neatly as possible." The doctor rolled Emma onto her back. "But I see her shoulder is dislocated. We must push it back into the socket before I can do anything else."

Andrew exchanged a grim look with his brother. A dislocated shoulder was thankfully not life-threatening, but this was going to be painful. Davis looked down at Emma. "I need you to stand up, my dear. I'm going to have to fix your shoulder if you want to use this arm in the future. I won't lie. It will hurt to pop it back into place."

Emma lost any color she had left, but she nodded her head. Andrew helped her to get off the bed.

"How can I help?" he asked.

"Let's help her over here, back against the wall, and hold her steady."

Andrew pressed Emma against the wall, using his body to prop her up and a steady hand against her good shoulder. He whispered in her ear. "Be brave, my sweet. I will take care of you."

Then he nodded to Davis, who with one swift push and a sickening pop, thrust Emma's shoulder back into place. Emma screamed, her eyes rolled back, and she collapsed into Andrew's waiting arms.

Davis gestured for him to bring Emma back to the bed. Then he reached into his bag and took out needle, thread, and a bottle of laudanum. Turning back to Andrew, he said, "Do you think you can get her to drink a small amount?"

Andrew laid Emma carefully on the dark blue counterpane. He leaned in close. "Emma, darling, wake up just for a few moments." He brushed gentle fingers across her pale cheek. "Emma."

Her eyes fluttered open. They were glazed with pain. "Andrew? Everything hurts."

Davis handed Andrew the bottle of laudanum and then went to gather up the rest of what he would need to stitch up her arm.

"I know, love, here drink a little of this. It will dull the pain. The surgeon will have to stitch you up. Drink," he commanded.

She obliged him. She swallowed two sips of the bitter liquid. Then she leaned her head back against the pillow and closed her eyes as if it was too much effort to keep them open.

"Lucy is going to be so angry with me," she mumbled. "I promised her I'd quit."

Comprehension rushed through him. “Emma, what were you doing tonight?”

“The necklace.” She raised her hand weakly, gesturing to her throat. “I was going to give the proceeds to Lucy and the children when I left. They are better off without me. I am just a scandal waiting to happen.” She let out a small sigh. Her head rolled to one side as she succumbed to the effects of the poppy.

He closed his eyes. She had been planning to run away. Just as he feared. A necklace? He looked over at the bloodstained jacket lying next to her on the bed. Picking it up, he checked the pockets. Sure enough, in the left interior pocket, Andrew pulled out a gleaming diamond necklace. He shoved the necklace back into the jacket pocket before anyone else could see.

“You fool,” he quietly berated her unconscious form.

Chapter 19

"I will need to remove her shirt. Perhaps Vivian should come over and help me?" Mr. Davis asked.

Vivian stepped forward, but Andrew just held up one hand. "No, I will help you."

"But Andrew," Vivian murmured. "It is unseemly for her to be unclothed by a man who is not her husband. Think about her reputation."

Andrew snorted. "Her reputation? She stumbled into my house with a gunshot wound. Her reputation is the last thing I am worried about tonight." His instinct to take care of her was bone deep. "No, I will help take care of her. She is going to be my wife."

Everyone in the room froze at his pronouncement. Vivian glanced at her husband. Jack just shrugged his shoulders in response.

But Andrew didn't care he had shocked them with his statement. The words that had tumbled unguarded out of his mouth were the utter truth. Emma belonged with him.

"All right, Andrew. We will go get her some fresh clothing, a nightshirt," Vivian soothed.

"No one knows she is here, understood? Winston, you stand sentry at the door again."

The three of them vacated the room. "What's next, Davis?"

"Let's get this shirt off, and then if you can hold

her steady. With her head in your lap, I will start to get this closed up. After the wound is stitched, I will check her for any other injuries."

Andrew sat cross-legged on the bed, cradling Emma's head in his lap and brushing her hair back gently, while speaking soothing words. How everything was going to be all right, how he would take care of her. Davis cleaned and sewed up the gash with efficiency.

Ten minutes later, Davis looked up. "That's the best I can do. I tried to make the stitches as small as possible." He wiped his brow with a handkerchief.

Andrew looked over and saw twenty neat stitches in black thread marching up her smooth pale skin. The stitches were small and the line of them about four inches in length.

"You did an amazing job, Davis. Thank you."

"The ball missed hitting her bone by perhaps an inch. She is a very lucky girl. Let's see where else she is hurt." He methodically examined Emma's legs, arms, and even her scalp. "She is bruised in several places as though she took a fall, which would also explain the dislocated shoulder. But most concerning is that she has lost a lot of blood. She needs to rest and to keep the arm immobile for a least two weeks." He applied a bandage over the stitches and wrapped a length of linen around her arm to keep it in place. "Keep watch over her tonight, and come and get me if her breathing changes or if the wound begins to seep blood. If she doesn't catch a fever in the next twenty-four to forty-eight hours, she should recover. I will come back in the morning to check her."

Davis got up and washed the blood off his hands in

the basin. There was a knock on the door, and Vivian appeared with fresh linens and a nightgown for Emma. They gently pulled it over Emma's head. Her eyes were glazed with pain and unfocused. She didn't make even the smallest sound as he guided her uninjured arm through the sleeve. Vivian pulled off Emma's boots and pants. Then she pulled the flannel nightgown down over her legs. Andrew ever so gently gathered Emma up in his arms, holding her close against his chest while Vivian made quick work of changing the blood-spattered sheets. Laying her back down, Andrew pulled the blankets up around her and stared down at her pale face.

His anger with her boiled over. He wished he could roar like a wild animal. How could she put herself in such danger? How could she think to run away from him, from her family? He said he would take care of her. Why would she choose to reject his offer without even giving them a chance? Fool! Stupid, precious fool. A hand tugged on his arm. Turning, he looked over to find Vivian next to him.

"Andrew, we need to talk to you. Now. Come with me. Let's go sit down."

Andrew shook his head. "No, I don't want to leave her alone."

Winston came up beside him on the other side. "I will watch her for a few minutes, Your Grace. Go change your clothes. You are covered in blood."

Andrew glanced down at himself. His jacket and shirt were indeed smeared with Emma's blood. "Winston, thank you for standing guard. I will be back shortly."

"We will meet you in the sitting room." Vivian

gave him a look that brooked no argument and disappeared through the connecting door. Andrew changed clothes and splashed cold water onto his face. Then he picked up Emma's jacket, which lay discarded on the floor. He headed into his private sitting room which sat between his bedchamber and the bedchamber for his duchess. Each bedroom had its own dressing room, and the suite was complete with a private bath.

He sat down on the couch, a bone deep weariness weighing him down. His brother handed him a glass with two fingers of brandy, which he promptly threw back. The liquid burned his throat and warmed his belly, a familiar feeling he had missed the past few months. Jack offered him another pour, but Andrew shook his head. As much as part of his mind screamed for him to dull the shock of the evening, another more sane voice reminded him this was not the time to lose his wits.

"Andrew, do you know what in the hell is going on tonight?" Vivian, always the direct one, jumped right in with her questions. "How did Emma Whittingham come to arrive at our doorstep shot and dressed as a street urchin? What was she doing tonight that would put her in the path of a revolver?"

Andrew reached down into the jacket on his lap and pulled out the sparkling diamond necklace. "This is what she was doing tonight." Holding it up for them to see. "She has been supporting her family by stealing jewelry from those who won't miss a bauble or two."

An audible gasp came from both Jack and Vivian. "This is the secret you alluded to the other night?" Jack asked.

"Yes, her father left them without a single penny

which was not owed for some gambling debt. I don't know all the details, but her guardian, the errant younger brother, knows about it and encourages the thieving. I overheard them talking at the opera." Andrew set down the necklace on the table in front of him, its many strands of diamonds winking in the candlelight. "I can only assume she got caught in the act tonight, and she was shot fleeing from the scene."

He studied their shocked expressions. "Are you very shocked my future duchess is a jewel thief?"

Vivian answered first. "Shocked, yes, but I admire her." Jack's head swiveled to face his wife. His mouth gaped. Nonplussed, Vivian continued. "There are not many opportunities for a gentlewoman to support herself and a family without resorting to selling her body. She did what she needed to keep her family afloat."

"But I proposed to her just the other night, and she ran away. She chose to put herself in danger instead of accepting my protection," Andrew protested.

"You proposed? When?" Jack asked.

"The night of the dinner party." Andrew ran a hand through his hair in frustration. His mind ran over the last conversation he had with Emma. "Well, maybe not proposed, but I told her I would take care of her."

"That's hardly the same thing," Vivian replied tartly. "For a woman who has spent the past several years trying to not end up as someone's mistress, your offer probably did not sound gallant, Andrew."

Andrew sat back to reflect on Vivian's observation. He thought about the pain and indignation he had seen in Emma's eyes. She had been frightened. But why? He had meant it sincerely even if he had bungled the wording.

"I need to send a note to her sister Lucy. She will be worried if Emma is not home tonight." Andrew stood up, every muscle protesting, to go over to his desk by the window. "Are Mother and Caroline home yet?"

"No, not yet. They shouldn't suspect anything is amiss. Their suites are down in the east wing," Jack replied. "I think the fewer people who know about what's happened to Emma the better. Especially if you are determined to make her your duchess. Are you sure about that, Andrew? You could choose any number of nice girls who would make you a suitable duchess. This lady is trouble with a capital T."

Andrew glowered at his brother. "I have already had a suitable wife, as you well know. No, this time I marry for love."

Jack exchanged a look with his wife. She gave a slight shake of her head. Then Vivian took his hand and guided him out of the room.

****

Emma woke up the next morning, her mouth dry, and her shoulder and arm throbbing. She forced herself to open her eyes. She found with some relief instead of lying in the park she rested in Andrew's bed. He lay next to her fully clothed on top of the counterpane, his sharp features softened in sleep. Instinctively, she reached out her hand to brush the hair from his face, and pain shot through her so sharp that she whimpered.

Andrew's eyes popped open. "Emma? What happened? Are you in pain?"

Emma just nodded her head, trying to keep her right arm perfectly still as she let the pain ebb. Then she blew out a breath. “That was stupid of me. I lifted my arm without even thinking.”

Andrew propped his head up on one hand and looked down at her. “Try to be still. Do you want some laudanum?”

“No, I’d rather not. I think I’ll be all right if I’m careful.” She bit her lip as she searched his face for signs of his ire. “Are you very angry with me?”

“Extremely,” he said. But he gently traced a finger along one eyebrow and down her cheek with a gentleness which belied his fierce frown.

She closed her eyes. “I’m sorry. I didn’t know where else to go.”

Andrew sat up abruptly. “You think I’m angry you came to me for help? Emma, open your eyes,” he demanded. She did as he asked. “I am angry because you deliberately put yourself in danger last night. Because you were going to run away rather than accept my help. I am angry because you scared ten years off my life stumbling into my house, bloody and barely conscious.” As he ranted, he came up onto his knees, his hands slicing through the air at each offense.

When he took a breath, Emma extended her good hand to grab hold of his. “I’m sorry I scared you. Can you help me sit up a little? If we are going to argue, I would like to be able to look you in the eye.”

She smiled up at him, and with some relief, she saw his anger sputter out. He sighed as he leaned down to gently lift her forward. He propped up several pillows behind her back before letting her lean back again. Emma gritted her teeth against the pain, but as she settled, she found she was more comfortable than before. Andrew got off the bed and went over to pour her a glass of water.

"I thought I was doing what was best for everyone," she said.

He handed her the glass. "You were sorely mistaken. In fact, your decisions almost got you killed last night. But you are here with me now, and I will be making the decisions moving forward."

Emma bristled at his tirade. But Andrew took no notice as he continued to pace back and forth across the thick blue oriental carpet. "We will be retiring to Stoneleigh where I will take care of you while you recuperate. And you will let me. Is that clear?"

"You cannot just whisk me away. I will go home and recuperate in my own bed, thank you," Emma countered. She could not believe his arrogance. She would never say yes to a proposal like that. She was trying to save her family's reputation, not ruin it by joining the duke at his estate. Even if what he described did sound like heaven. A chance to get away from town, from her responsibilities, and time to recover.

"And you will no longer by any means steal another bauble. You are officially retired."

Emma's eyes widened at his audacity. Then it struck her. "My necklace! Where is my necklace?"

"It is somewhere safe until it can be returned. From whom did you steal it?" Andrew crossed his arms in front of his chest.

Emma glowered at him. But she didn't get the chance to respond because the door opened, and Lucy rushed into the room. Her long blonde hair was pinned back carelessly and tumbled about her shoulders. She wore a plain green cotton dress. A wool shawl lay askew across her shoulders as though hastily donned.

Her face was a study in worry. Winston pulled the door shut behind her.

Lucy addressed Andrew. "What's happened? Your note said she had been hurt."

"Your sister was shot last night. She stumbled into my study bleeding, her shoulder dislocated," Andrew replied succinctly.

Emma gasped. "Andrew!" He needn't make it sound so dire. He would scare Lucy. She looked over at Lucy, expecting to see her distraught, but instead Lucy's eyes blazed with anger. Her sister stalked over to the bed.

"I cannot believe you would go behind my back and do another job! You promised me you were done." Then her eyes filled with tears. "This is exactly the kind of scenario I picture every time you go out into the night. How could you be so careless with yourself when you know how much we love you?" Tears spilled down her face.

The sharp bite of guilt stole her breath. She reached out her good hand. "Oh, Lucy, I'm sorry. I wasn't being careless, I swear. It was just bad luck. They came home early from the theatre and saw me before I could get down the back stairs. When he shot me, I was thrown back, and I tumbled all the way down the stairs..." Both Lucy and Andrew stared at her, slack-jawed.

Andrew turned to Lucy. "She really doesn't understand, does she?"

"No." Lucy shook her head. "She thinks she can do whatever she wants with no consequences."

Andrew walked over and gently wiped a tear from Lucy's face with his thumb. "Don't worry, this will never happen again. Emma is officially retired. I am going to take her to my estate in Kent to recuperate."

"Will you two stop talking about me like I am not in the room?" Emma snapped. A hot bolt of jealousy had sliced through her when Andrew touched Lucy. Heat flushed her cheeks. She knew it was ridiculous and peevish. She despised that Lucy and Andrew were both angry with her. The pain in her arm and shoulder throbbed like a heartbeat. She bit her lower lip as tears pricked at the backs of her eyes. She had really made a mess of things.

Andrew looked over at her, concern radiating from him. "Are you in pain?"

Emma nodded, though it was not the type he meant.

"Do you want some laudanum now?" he asked.

"Yes, I think I would. My arm is burning."

Andrew fetched the bottle and gently tipped it to Emma's lips. "Just a little and you should be able to rest more comfortably." His eyes were so kind. He would take care of things if she let him. Exhausted, she almost wanted to let him.

Andrew spoke to Lucy. "Do you think you could get together some clothes and things she will need? I will have someone pick them up tomorrow. I think you should write a note to my mother. Act as if you are Emma; explain she must go out of town for a few weeks to take care of an ailing elderly aunt or something along those lines. And would she watch out for you, Lucy. I know Mother would gladly help you. She is not familiar with either of your handwriting yet, and Emma won't be able to write anything with her arm. Are you comfortable with a little deceit?"

"Yes, I think so," Lucy replied.

"Humpf!" Emma snorted from the bed.

This time it was Lucy who glared. "This is hardly the same thing, Emma. Our little white lie will not be putting anyone in harm's way."

"What about the children? What are you going to tell them?" Emma asked.

Lucy bit her lip. "I think I will just keep the stories consistent and tell them the same thing. That you are visiting a sick friend of Mother's. I can handle them." Straightening her shoulders, she turned to Andrew. "I will get her things ready."

"And Fergus," Emma said, her head starting to feel fuzzy. A pleasant feeling of calm replaced the pain.

"What? No." Andrew shook his head.

"But he has never been without me for so long. He will be beside himself with worry." She hoped her argument wasn't tempered by the fact she couldn't seem to keep her eyes open. She snuggled back against the pillows. "If you insist on being so high-handed, I must have an ally."

Andrew let out a long sigh. "Fine, we will bring the damn dog."

Chapter 20

It was almost eleven when Andrew dressed and headed downstairs to have some breakfast. He was not looking forward to having to face his family and lie about what was happening. His mother and sister were both still eating.

"Good morning, Mother, Caroline. Late night last night?" He went to the sideboard, happy to find breakfast hot despite the late hour of the morning.

"Yes, Almack's is unbearably tedious. But Miss Whittingham's presentation went off beautifully, so it was well worth it," Caroline replied.

"Indeed, I know of several gentleman interested in her despite her lack of dowry. She is making quite a splash," his mother agreed.

Andrew ate like a starving man. Then it occurred to him Emma hadn't eaten either. Even though he left her sleeping, she would most likely be hungry when she woke. She still looked deathly pale this morning. He would have the kitchen send up something hearty, maybe eggs and ham. He wondered what she liked for breakfast.

"Andrew, hello in there." Caroline playfully poked him with her fork.

"What? Oh, sorry, I wasn't paying attention."

"Yes, I gathered that. My question was will you be escorting me to the ball tomorrow evening?" Caroline asked.

"Oh, I cannot. Unfortunately, I have been called to Stoneleigh. I will be leaving first thing in the morning."

"Does this sudden departure have anything to do with the letter I received not an hour ago?" his mother inquired. "Miss Emma Whittingham has been called away to help nurse an ailing family friend, a friend of her mother's in Kent." She arched an eyebrow in question.

"In Kent? I did not know." Andrew shoveled more eggs into his mouth, trying to look blasé.

"Yes, she has asked if I would keep an eye on Lucy for her for the next couple of weeks."

"And will you?" Andrew asked.

"Of course. She can accompany Caroline and me out to events." She caught her son's eye. "I am very fond of both the Whittingham ladies."

Andrew returned her smile and then got up and bussed his mother's cheek. "Thank you. I will see you both in a fortnight." He gave a small bow and left to go find Winston.

When Andrew entered the upstairs hallway, he ran into Jack and Vivian. "Good, we were just coming to find you, Andrew," Vivian said.

"What do you need?" He glanced at the door to his suite. Would Emma be awake?

"We wanted to tell you we discussed the matter, and we are coming with you to Stoneleigh," Jack replied.

"What? That's not necessary."

"Yes, it is, Andrew," Vivian replied. "Even I know you cannot abscond with an unmarried young lady without causing damage to her reputation. We will accompany you as chaperones. She can be my guest, that way the staff at Stoneleigh will have no need for gossip."

Andrew crossed his arms across his chest. "I don't care what the staff thinks. I am taking her out of London so I can take care of her without prying eyes."

"And if you convince her to marry you? Don't you think she will care what her staff thinks of her? And what if you get visitors coming by while you are there? No, we are coming with you." Vivian looked over her shoulder at her husband for confirmation. Jack nodded his head. But when Vivian turned back to face Andrew, Jack gave him a shrug and a look which said, "Sorry, this was her idea."

"Very well. You two will have to take your own carriage. I promised Emma she could bring her behemoth of a dog. There will not be enough room for four of us and the dog. Vivian, have your maid ride with Winston and the luggage. I am sending him ahead this afternoon to make preparations."

Vivian clapped her hands together. "Excellent, I will let Molly know and write a note to Gabrielle and talk with Caroline." Vivian wandered down the hallway muttering to herself.

"How is she feeling this morning?" Jack asked, his expression grim.

"Not great, I think. I left her sleeping." Andrew took a key out of his pocket to unlock the door to his suite, his mind already on Emma.

"All right, we will meet up tomorrow morning and see about getting your girl safely whisked out to the carriage without anyone noticing." Jack gave him a pat on the shoulder and headed down the hallway.

****

Emma spent most of the day asleep. She'd woken twice, but the pain burning in her arm quickly made her decide sleep was the better option. She smelled Andrew's spicy scent and knew he was nearby. Comforted by his presence, she slid back into slumber.

When she truly awakened, the late afternoon sun streamed through the windows. Emma blinked against its glare as she glanced around the room. She was alone. Feeling well rested, she stretched her legs and used her good arm to prop herself up. Yes, despite the pain in her arm, she definitely felt better. She would get up and dressed. Then she could go home and get away from one very overbearing duke.

Emma swung her legs around and paused a moment at the edge of the bed. Her head was a bit fuzzy, but that was probably due to the aftereffects of the laudanum. Her right arm ached, so she used her left arm to push off the bed to stand. She made it only two steps before she felt faint. Her legs gave out, and she crumpled to the floor, landing with a thump on her backside. Pain radiated into her arm and shoulder. She pulled in a long breath through her nose, waiting for pain to subside.

Perhaps she'd overestimated the extent of her recovery. Leaning back against the side of the bed, she closed her eyes, and a giggle escaped her lips. What a ridiculous sight she must make sitting on the floor, her nightshirt a white puddle around her, wearing a pair of fuzzy gray socks. She wiggled her toes in the oversized socks and giggled again. She must have hit her head last night as well, because really there was nothing remotely funny about socks.

"Emma!" Andrew entered the room. He hurried over to her. She looked up at him, and her laughter abruptly fled. His face revealed a mixture of worry and anger, his eyes a stormy deep blue.

She tilted her head to one side. "I thought I felt better, but when I stood up, I realized I am weak as a kitten."

Andrew scooped her up, careful of her right arm. She turned to bury her face in the crook of his neck, drinking in his scent and his warmth. He sighed, and his lips brushed against her brow.

"Stubborn fool. You lost a lot of blood. Of course you're weak." He set her on the bed, propping some pillows behind her carefully.

"What time is it?" Emma asked.

"Half four. Are you hungry? I have a tray for you out in the sitting room. You've been asleep all day."

At the mention of food, Emma realized she was starving. "Yes, very hungry in fact."

Andrew left the room for a moment to retrieve the tray. Emma used her good hand to run her fingers through her hair. She made it only a few inches before getting caught in a tangle. What a fright she must look.

He returned, setting the tray to her left on the bed. He picked up a bowl of what smelled like beef stew and a spoon. Emma took the spoon from him, and he held the bowl up for her to scoop a bite. Using her left hand felt awkward, and most of the stew slipped off her spoon.

Andrew didn't say anything. He took the spoon, and scooping a small measure of stew, he offered it to her. Emma pursed her lips in displeasure at the idea of being fed. He raised one eyebrow. She rolled her eyes and obediently opened her mouth to take the spoonful. It tasted even better than it smelled. She stopped feeling foolish and let him feed her.

"Mr. Davis was here earlier to check your arm but didn't want to wake you. He said to make sure to feed you lots of red meat to help your body recover from the blood loss, and you need lots of rest. Your shoulder will probably be inflamed for four or five days. He said you should keep it immobile. The stitches can be removed in two weeks as long as the area does not get infected," he told her while feeding her mouthfuls of warm stew.

After she'd eaten the entire bowl, Andrew set it down and handed her a piece of bread he had slathered with butter. "We will leave for Stoneleigh at first light. My brother and his wife will accompany us to help keep your reputation intact. You will be Vivian's guest, recovering from an illness in the fresh country air."

Emma took a bite of the bread, feeling a little better about being kidnapped. At least she wouldn't be totally at the duke's mercy.

Andrew caught and held her gaze. "Are you ready to tell me to whom the necklace belongs? I will need to arrange to have it returned, discreetly of course, before this evening." His expression stern, he waited patiently for her to answer. Emma knew it would be foolish to withhold the information. He offered an opportunity to put last night's debacle behind her. If the necklace was returned, there would be no reason for anyone to continue to search for the thief. It still stung, though.

"Miss Esmeralda Hunt. Stanhope Place. Number 7." She bit viciously into her piece of bread. Then looking up through her lashes at Andrew, she asked, "Could I see it one more time?"

Andrew frowned, but he walked over to a tall wooden bureau, opened a drawer, and pulled out the necklace. He handed it to Emma. She held it up to admire the many strands of diamonds. Five in all, each a neat row of small sparkles. The first row would wind around the lady's throat like a gleaming cuff, the rest cascading down the throat and collarbone. Emma sighed in feminine appreciation.

"It is beautiful and extravagant," Andrew noted.

"Not as lovely as your mother's ruby necklace," Emma said without thinking. She quickly looked down at her lap. *Fool!* Andrew sat down on the edge of the bed. After taking a deep breath, she dared to look up at him.

"That's what I was after the first night, when I came to your room. My information said this was the duchess' suite. I also thought the family was out of town," she confessed.

"Well, I can't say I am sorry you ended up in here with me." A grin tipped up the corners of his mouth. "Although I thought you were a figment of my imagination the next morning. What I can't fathom is how a viscount's daughter became a jewel thief. Will you enlighten me?" He took her free hand in his.

Emma tried to pull her hand back, but Andrew held it fast. She looked down at his hands with their long fingers and tanned skin. They should be soft and pale, as befitting a man of leisure, but instead callouses ran along the palms. She was comforted by the quiet strength of his hands.

She shook her head. "What I told you before was true. My father drank too much and gambled away his fortune, our dowries, everything. His last hope was marrying me off in exchange for what I assume was a sizable loan from his new soon-to-be son-in-law. No one bothered to tell me the details. When Longwood got himself killed, my father went into his study and shot himself in the head. The coward," Emma spit out. The bitterness she still held on to churned in her chest. She was appalled at the tears running down her face. She took a deep breath and continued.

"The doctor was paid by Father's solicitor to say it was an accident. That the pistol had misfired while being cleaned. When my father's Last Will and Testament was read, the solicitor broke the news as kindly as possible that there was nothing left. The debts and the mortgages were huge. I had very few options available to earn enough to pay the bills. To keep the family together and in the only home we've ever known."

She straightened her shoulders. She didn't regret her choice. Better than to sell her body to some aging lecher. "I steal from the rich, a few baubles here and there, and no one is really hurt. Most probably think they have simply lost the item, easily replaced. It just takes careful planning and some luck."

Andrew reached out and wiped a tear from her cheek. "Who found your father's body?" he asked quietly.

Emma locked eyes with him. "I did." She loathed the pity reflected there. Turning her head away, she closed her eyes. "I'm tired. Perhaps I should rest awhile."

Andrew pulled his hand away and stood. He tucked the covers around her. She could feel the weight of his gaze, so she kept her eyes tightly shut. He sighed, the soft clinking of the necklace being lifted followed, and then he left.

In the morning, Lady Vivian bustled in with a bundle of clothes. Emma hadn't slept well the night before. Her injured arm prevented her from finding a comfortable position. She lay staring up at the canopy, contemplating her life. Her shoulder and arm ached, a constant reminder of her poor choices. She needed a new plan for taking care of her family moving forward. What that would be she wasn't sure yet.

"I have brought some clothes I thought might work for you to wear for the ride. You certainly can't go around in a nightshirt. They are Caroline's clothes. Mine would be far too short on you. She won't miss them. She has so many things." Vivian winked at her.

Emma struggled to sit up straight. "Um…thank you. Could I ask you to help me over to the privacy screen? I am still too weak to walk over there myself."

"Absolutely." Vivian helped her to the chamber pot behind the screen. She turned her back to give Emma some privacy before helping her back to the edge of the bed.

"I also brought a brush and some ribbon to put your hair to rights." She pulled out a blouse and separate skirt. "I didn't think your shoulder would be able to maneuver the sleeve of a dress. This shirt has buttons all down the front and loose blousy sleeves. Let's see if it will work."

Vivian helped Emma out of her shirt and into the fresh change of clothes. The blouse was roomy enough to slide on easily and hide her bandaged arm. After tucking it into the skirt, Vivian retied the sling around her injured arm. She stood back and assessed Emma.

Nodding her head, she climbed onto the bed behind her and tackled the task of brushing out Emma's tangled locks.

"You are too kind to help me. I couldn't possibly brush out the tangles with just my left hand." Emma bit her lower lip. She met the lady's eyes in the tall mirror across from them. "You are not too scandalized about me being here under these circumstances…in Andrew's bedroom?"

"Are you joking? I have never met someone more scandalous than me. I am thoroughly enjoying myself."

"I hardly believe that," Emma replied.

"Did you know my father was a pirate? I grew up in the Caribbean aboard my father's ship running around barefoot and free." A smile played across her lips. "Trust me, when I arrived in England, I was scandalous."

"A pirate? Truly?" Emma was impressed. "I thought all the pirates were long gone."

"Well, the government would like the public to think so. My father hasn't been looting ships since right after I was born. These days he runs an aboveboard shipping business…mostly."

She braided Emma's long hair and tied off the end with a lilac ribbon. Just as she was finishing, Andrew came into the room.

"You look much improved," he said briskly. "Ready to go?"

Much improved? Emma grimaced. Carrying a cloak, Andrew came over and wrapped it around Emma. He tied the strings, pulling the hood up to cover her head. "Up we go." He lifted her into his arms. "Jack is making sure we have an empty path to the carriage."

They were soon settled into a plain black carriage. It was well-appointed with velvet-covered seats and fuzzy, knit blankets stacked neatly in one corner. Andrew tucked one around her. "Warm enough? This carriage is rented. I didn't want to make a fuss in front of your house with the ducal crest. Let's go get your Fergus, shall we?"

Emma grinned. Fergus must be beside himself with worry. When they arrived at the house, Lucy came out with Fergus. Andrew sent the footman and the driver into the house to retrieve her trunk.

Fergus looked warily up at the carriage, but his ears perked up when she called to him from inside. He jumped in and found her, licking her face, his tail wagging furiously. Andrew gave the dog's hindquarters a shove to keep Fergus' long tail from beating on his leg.

"Fergus, sit," Emma ordered. She scratched his ears. "Now, Fergus, my right arm is hurt, so you must be careful not to jostle me, all right?"

"He can't possibly understand you. This might be a mistake to have him in here with such tight quarters."

"Nonsense. There is plenty of room. Of course he understands me." Fergus laid his large head down on her lap and gave a whimper. "See?" She gave him a kiss on the head. "Now, Fergus, you lie down on the floor like a good boy. We are going to the country." Fergus obediently lay down at her feet and gave a great doggie sigh of contentment.

****

Andrew just shook his head and moved over so he could stretch his own long legs out behind the dog. They travelled in silence. Andrew assumed Emma had nodded off. But when they got out of the city, the roads became considerably bumpier, and after the third large jolt of the carriage, a muffled whimper of pain came from Emma.

"Why do you insist on refusing to ask for help?" he muttered. "Come here at once." He reached for her hand, and as she scooted closer, he lifted her into his lap. He braced his feet and wrapped his arms carefully around her waist, settling her against him. At first, she was stiff in his arms, but after a few minutes she relaxed into him. She laid her head in the crook of his shoulder.

He had missed her this past week. He had definitely missed having her in his arms. The soft curve of her derriere rubbed against his groin as she shifted to get comfortable, and he sucked in air sharply at the flare of lust which shot through him. She was hurt and vulnerable; this was no time to be thinking about the contours of her body. Andrew turned his mind to mundane thoughts like crop rotations and financial statements, ordering his manhood to stand down.

Emma's breathing soon slowed as she fell asleep in his arms. Andrew turned to kiss her forehead. He thought about the turmoil of the last twenty-four hours. His brother was right; this woman was trouble with a capital T. But it was no use telling his heart. Her laughter and her sensuality had captivated him from the beginning. True, her feeling of responsibility to her family had led her down a dangerous path. But he admired the way she lived life on her own terms. When he had seen her sitting on the nursery floor with his two sons, examining the seaworthiness of their paper boats, his fate had been sealed. Emma belonged with him. He planned to spoil her rotten these next two weeks. Then he would propose properly and make her his duchess.

Chapter 21

The following four days flew by. Never in her life had Emma been so pampered. This morning the sun streamed in to her pretty guestroom at Stoneleigh. She spied a tray by her bed which she knew would contain a steaming mug of hot chocolate and several biscuits. Heaven indeed. She stretched in her comfortable bed, testing her shoulder. It was much improved, if still a bit sore. Her arm still hurt around where she had been shot. The muscle had been ripped to shreds, and it still burned when she tried to use the arm.

Andrew had been attentive to her every need. The morning after her first full day at Stoneleigh, Andrew swept into her room bearing a small tray of hot chocolate, toast, and raspberry jam. She tried to shoo him out of her room. "Andrew, you are not supposed to be in here! I am not presentable in the least!"

"This is my house. I can be anywhere I choose." His boyish grin had been irresistible. "Besides, I come bearing breakfast."

Setting the tray down, Andrew presented her with the cup of hot chocolate.

"How are you feeling this morning?" he asked.

"Disheveled." She shouldn't be surly with him, but she was never her best first thing in the morning. She felt uncomfortable and raw this morning.

Andrew walked over to the dressing table and

picked up a brush. He moved to come sit on the bed. "Turn please," he ordered gently.

Emma scooted to present her back to him, and he started to brush her hair. With each stroke of the brush, the tension slid from her body. With his warm body behind her and his deft hands running over her hair, she relaxed inch by inch. She closed her eyes, and taking a sip of her hot chocolate, she let herself be taken care of by someone else. It was a new and strange feeling.

He had the hot chocolate sent up every morning since. Then Andrew would show up later with a tray laden with eggs, sausage, toast, and jam. She suspected he was coddling her, making sure she ate, but she felt so well rested she couldn't muster any annoyance. She couldn't remember the last time she had had no one to take care of, no tasks to complete.

She smiled as she scooted herself up to a sitting position. It really was sinful. She took a sip of her drink.

Andrew had not just been making sure she ate but also had been a pleasant companion. He came by later in the afternoon again to have tea with her. He didn't stay too long, not usually more than an hour, but they talked of all manner of things. He hadn't pressed her for any more information about her past. He talked about family, the boys, and about his childhood here at the estate.

Darn him for being so charming. She needed to remember this was a temporary situation. Once she recovered fully, she would return to London and her real life. She swung her legs over the edge of the bed. Perhaps she would call for a bath this morning; it had been more than a week since she last had one.

An hour later, Emma lay neck deep in warm water with her hair piled high on her head. She examined the row of black stitches running down her upper arm. The skin around the stitches looked angry and red, but the water lapped at the wound, soothing her skin. The wound was an ugly reminder of her encounter with Mr. Caldwell.

She closed her eyes. The memory of her panic as she raced down that hallway clogged her throat. The pain of the ball searing through her flesh and the fall down the stairs all stood out cold and clear in her mind. She'd never been as scared as when she forced herself to run through the garden and away from that house. It wasn't the first close call. She had always felt so clever when she escaped unnoticed from a house where the owners came home unexpectedly. Emma scrubbed a wet hand over her face, and the bath water splashed against the sides of the tub. Not this time. This time had been horrible and frightening beyond belief.

The sound of the door opening and shutting pierced her thoughts.

"Emma?" Andrew's voice rang out. "Are you all right?"

He came around the screen, his eyes widening in surprise to find her in the bath. His gaze swept over her, and Emma's first reaction was to cover herself with her arms. Her eyes collided with his. The heat that flared between them stole her breath.

He pivoted away abruptly. "I'm sorry. I didn't realize you were in the bath."

"Wait," she called out to his retreating back. He paused but didn't turn around. Why did she feel so shy around a man whose hands had roamed over every inch of her body? Granted, it had been in total darkness; he had never seen her naked before. Screwing up her courage, she said, "Andrew, don't go. Will you help me out of the bath? My arm is still sore when I try to use it for leverage."

"Of course."

Andrew reached out a hand and, using her good arm, pulled her to her feet. Then he lifted her over the side of tub. They stood there, inches from each other, his fingers still entwined with hers. Emma's heart raced. She shivered as the cool air hit her wet skin.

Her shiver broke the spell. Andrew grabbed a towel from the chair next to them, and he wrapped it around her. She flinched as the towel rubbed against her injury. He immediately pulled the towel away from her arm. Then he began to pat her skin dry.

The soft terry cloth caressed her skin as he made his way down the length of her body. He knelt to dry her legs, and she gasped at the whisper soft brush of his lips on one hip. He leaned over to place a kiss on the other hip. Then one right above her navel.

Andrew looked up at her, a silent question in his eyes. Emma ran her fingers through his thick dark hair and nodded. In return, Andrew gave her a wicked smile. His hands ran up her legs, caressing each calf, trailing up the outside of her thighs, then settled on her hips. He nuzzled one breast, giving the underside a leisurely kiss. At her sigh of pleasure, he captured her nipple, and he gave it a slow suck. His tongue slid around its peak, and her fingers tightened in his hair lest he think of pulling away. A moan of pleasure escaped her lips. Her eyes fluttered closed as she savored the hot feel of his mouth on her breast.

He pulled away to switch his attentions to the other breast, taking the puckered nipple into his mouth. Emma opened her eyes to look down at him as he licked her nipple and ran kisses along the curve of her breast. It was incredibly erotic to watch him, and her womanhood throbbed in response.

He rose from his knees, never taking his eyes from hers. Then he captured her mouth in a searing kiss. Dear God, the heat of this man could scorch her soul. Andrew's hands cupped her bottom as he picked her up, and she wrapped her legs around his waist.

Emma could feel the hard evidence of his desire for her pressed up against her core. He carried her over to the side of bed, laying her down gently. She felt bereft without the warmth of his body pressed up against hers, but soon forgot as he started to undress. Andrew's gaze captured hers, his eyes more gray than blue and stormy with desire.

He removed his cravat, untying it slowly and tossing it aside. His waistcoat joined the cravat on the floor. He unbuttoned his shirt one button at a time, exposing the taut golden skin of his well-muscled chest. A light dusting of dark hair led down from his chest to his navel and then disappeared into his waistband. He made quick work taking off his shoes and stockings. When he unbuttoned his falls, Emma's mouth went dry, and she grew wet between her legs in anticipation. Then he stood there totally naked for a long moment, his eyes locked on hers. She unconsciously licked her lips in anticipation.

****

Andrew groaned, "Emma you're driving me mad with lust."

"Then come here and let me see if I can help you with that." She beckoned to him with one hand. All the blood had drained from his head the moment he saw her naked for the first time, the bath water lapping at those pink nipples. Now, he drank in every curve. Curves he'd known with his hands and his lips but had never seen in the light of day. Her naked body was like a beacon leading him to crash onto the shore. But what a glorious way to go.

He knelt down beside the bed. He wanted to bury his tongue into the sweet center of her womanhood. With a swift tug on her ankles, he slid her right to the edge of the bed.

"Andrew, what are you doing?" Emma propped herself up with her one good arm. Her brow furrowed in confusion.

For all her bravado, he had a feeling her past lovers hadn't a clue what pleasured a woman. He placed a kiss on the sensitive flesh on her inner thigh. He left a trail of kisses up the soft skin there until he got to her core. He gave a slow lick up the seam of her sex. Emma gasped out his name and fell back against the covers. He continued to lick and nibble at her, taking his time to enjoy each sigh of pleasure he elicited. When she bucked her hips up to meet his mouth and cried out his name, he knew she was close to her crisis. He slipped two fingers into her wet warmth, pushing her over the edge. Her fingernails bit into his scalp as she cried out in ecstasy.

Andrew placed one more kiss on Emma's quivering center. He lifted his head to look at her as she lay panting, her face flushed pink. She was breathtaking.

His cock throbbed with the need to bury itself in her warm wet sex. He stood and climbed over her, careful to keep himself propped up on his arms above her so he wouldn't harm her shoulder or arm. He dipped his head to kiss her, his tongue diving into her mouth, urging her to taste herself on his lips. She ran her left hand up into his hair. Emma's hips lifted, and she rubbed herself along his cock. Groaning against her mouth, he lowered himself into her heat with one swift thrust. This was where he wanted to be for the rest of his life, tangled up with this woman.

She called out his name in a hoarse shout, and his control snapped. He thrust into her over and over, losing himself in her body. She met each of his thrusts with her hips in a rhythm which was uniquely theirs. His balls tightened, and his orgasm built at the frantic pace of their coupling. Emma called out his name as her orgasm rolled through her, her sex convulsing around his cock. He pulled out, twisting to let his seed spill out onto the bedsheets.

Andrew buried his face for a moment in the crook of her neck. He had almost lost control and let himself come inside her, his desire to mark her as his so strong. His chest heaved in an effort to catch his breath. Then he kissed his way across her cheek to her mouth, nibbling at that full lower lip of hers. Looking down into her satisfied smiling face, he couldn't hold back how he felt any longer.

"Marry me, Emma."

Chapter 22

"What?" Emma's eyes popped open.

"Marry me, Emma. Be my duchess." Andrew's lips curved in a smile, but his eyes were serious.

Her heartbeat skipped in her chest. She shook her head. "No."

Andrew rolled to her good side. He wrapped one long leg across both of hers, his head propped by one elbow. "I'm sorry, did you say no?"

"Yes, I mean no…I mean yes, I said no." She tried to pull her scattered thoughts together. "Andrew, you can't marry someone like me." Why would he ask such a ridiculous question? She turned her head away to stare up at the canopy.

"Someone like you?" Andrew hooked one long finger under her chin, and she reluctantly turned her face back toward him. "A woman who brought laughter back into my life. A woman who my children clearly adore. A woman whose strength and sense of responsibility I admire. That someone?"

His sweet words were like honey seeping into Emma's well-guarded heart. She raised an eyebrow. "A thief."

"Ex-thief, remember."

"A ruined spinster," she countered. "Andrew, I am twenty-five, and not a virgin as I'm sure you figured out. I was compromised a long time ago. Which is why when my father was eager to sell me off to Longwood, I agreed without argument. I was lucky anyone would marry me at all."

Andrew frowned, his expression thunderous. Emma knew that would be his reaction to her confession, but she needed to make him see. She was not worthy of him. "See, it has you upset. You are the Duke of Gilchrest. You need an unblemished proper young lady to be your duchess."

Andrew rolled his eyes. "I'm not upset that you are not a virgin. Neither am I. However, I am upset you were taken advantage of by some scoundrel." His frown deepened. "And I'm incensed your father would match you with that reprobate Longwood simply for coin.

"Also, why is it everyone keeps telling me to marry some proper young miss who would likely bore me to tears, and be afraid of me in the marriage bed?" Andrew rolled onto his back to stare at the canopy as well. After a moment he asked, "Emma, what do you want?"

Emma's head whipped back to stare at his profile. It was the first time in her whole life anyone had asked her that question. It was her turn to roll on her side toward him. She draped her injured arm over Andrew's stomach, resting her chin on his chest. His eyes shone with confusion and hurt.

She couldn't deny that she did want to be with him. But marriage? Her hand roamed across his stomach, teasing the hair there. "Maybe I should be your mistress? We could have lots of fun." Her hand trailed lower to stroke his softening cock.

The next moment Andrew had her flipped onto her back. He loomed over her. "So you simply want my body? But you'll not take my heart, my name?" His eyes snapped with indignation.

"N-no. That's not what I meant," Emma stuttered, taken aback by his fierce countenance.

His expression softened. "I am beginning to understand why you don't trust me yet. The men in your life have been less than admirable. But I will not dishonor you by having you as my mistress. Either you marry me or it's nothing at all. I'll give you some time to decide what you want." He bent to place a scorching kiss against her lips. "But not forever," he warned.

Then he got up, donned his shirt and pants, gathered his things, and left without another word.

Later that afternoon, Winston brought up her afternoon tea tray.

"His Grace will not be able to join you for tea this afternoon," he said with the utmost formality.

What did she expect? She had spurned his proposal of marriage and made a mess of explaining why. "Thank you, Winston," she murmured.

Winston poured tea into a china cup adorned with blue roses. "My lady, you don't remember me, do you?"

"From the night I was shot? Yes, of course I do. You were very kind and sat at my bedside for a while." Emma smiled at him tentatively. "You must be terribly scandalized."

Winston's lips twisted into an ironic half smile. "This is not nearly the most scandalous thing I've ever seen on the job. I used to serve the Marquis Longwood."

Emma recoiled. Longwood?

"Yes, we've met at Longwood's residence once

before." He handed her the teacup.

She tried to place him, but she could not. The one and only time she had set foot in the Marquis Longwood's residence had been a blur of shock and horror. Her father set up the match. He had been so pleased with himself for landing such a rich, titled son-in-law. Emma only met her intended twice, once at a ball where they danced, and once at her house when her father announced their betrothal. The three of them had dinner together to celebrate.

Two weeks later, she sat brooding that her betrothed hadn't bothered to call on her since their engagement was announced. Emma decided she could not marry a virtual stranger. She resolved to remedy the situation. She needed to pay Longwood a call and get to know him better whilst having tea perhaps. She hadn't sent a note ahead, a grave mistake which ended up serendipitous. She and her maid Bridget simply walked over and knocked on his door.

They were shown into a well-appointed drawing room where they waited for almost thirty minutes without seeing hide or hair of anyone. Outraged at being ignored, Emma stepped out into the hallway in search of a servant. The marquis' home was quite large, and she wandered down a long hallway with marble flooring and dark green silk wall coverings. She emerged into the main foyer. Dark mahogany railings wound up a grand staircase.

At the top of the stairs hung a large painting depicting a dying man lying prostrate. Around him half-naked women lay on couches and divans, staring entranced at a dancing devil. The devil's grotesque face laughed, and a large pitchfork pointed down at the man as the devil taunted and poked him. Reflecting on it now, she should have seen the painting as a warning of trouble ahead. What sort of man hung such disturbing artwork prominently in his home?

Emma headed down another hallway. She paused, hearing muffled voices from behind a nearby door. She knocked but received no answer. Annoyed, she tried the knob, and opening the door, she said, "Excuse me please, but…" She froze at the scene she stumbled upon. She had entered into the dining room. Bent over the dining room table was a maid, her skirts bunched up around her waist, her bare bottom exposed. In between her legs was the marquis, pants lowered, enthusiastically rutting the maid.

At Emma's loud gasp, Longwood had paused to look over to where she stood in the doorway. He smiled slowly, his gaze ran the length of her, then he gave the maid's bottom a slap.

"Ahh, my dear Miss Whittingham. Would you like to be next?"

Emma whirled around and fled. His laughter followed her down the hallway. She'd raced back to the drawing room and, grabbing Bridget's hand, pulled her from the room. They escaped quickly out the front door. In her haste she stumbled and nearly fell down the front steps. A strong hand caught her arm and steadied her.

"Careful, milady, are you all right?"

She had nodded her head, mumbled thank you, and quickly moved past the man with only one thought in her mind, to get back to the safety of her home.

Emma's eyes focused back on Winston's face. She stood abruptly from her chair. "Wait, you were the man on the stairs. The one who caught me before I fell."

"Yes, you were in an awful rush to leave that day."

She clasped her hands together tightly. "He had…I had walked in…he was taking advantage of one of the maids. He just laughed at me and said, would I like to be next?" Her face grew hot at the horrible memory.

Winston picked up her teacup and pressed it into her hands. "He did that often, abuse the servants." His face was a mask of fury. "You are very lucky he died before you were married. We are all lucky that bastard is gone from this earth." His gaze flew up to meet hers. "Beg your pardon, miss."

Emma shook her head. "You don't even know the half of it. I went home and told my father what I saw. I asked him to call off the engagement." She sat back down. "He was appalled, not at what I had seen, but that I would dream of calling it off. He told me men were lusty creatures. Soon I would be married and be able to care for my husband's needs myself. That under no circumstances would he call off the wedding. He said how lucky we were to have such a wealthy gentleman willing to marry me.

"I felt trapped. I had no choices. A fortnight later, Longwood was dead. It's likely a terrible sin, but I was overjoyed by the news of his death. My father did not feel the same way."

Sunshine streamed in through the window, and she turned toward it, wishing its warmth could somehow burn away her memories of the past.

****

Miss Whittingham stared out the window with a look of anguish on her face, which broke his heart. Winston knew she must be reliving the events in her head. He had many such memories of the odious Marquis Longwood. When the Marquis had been thrown from his horse and died, Winston poured himself a celebratory drink from his master's best brandy. Then he promptly left the house in search of better employment. He carefully chose the Duke of Gilchrest based on his excellent reputation among the staff employed at Gilchrest House. Winston never had a reason to regret his choice. He would do absolutely anything for the duke.

"He's not like them," he said after a moment.

Miss Whittingham turned toward him. "Who?"

"His Grace. He is not like those other two. He is not after using you. He is after saving you."

"I don't need saving. I am doing fine on my own. I make my own decisions. I take care of what's mine."

Her defiant expression won him over entirely. He allowed himself a small smile as he gathered up the tea tray. Everyone needed saving, His Grace included. This strong, resilient lady would make a fine match for the duke…if she would ever let down her guard and let him take care of her.

Chapter 23

"Miss Whittingham, if I may say so, you are quite distracted this afternoon. Is something troubling you?" Ethan Davenport took one of Lucy's hands and gave it a squeeze. It was a bright sunny afternoon, and the two of them were seated outside on the veranda.

"Oh dear, I'm sorry. My mind is tumbling over all the tasks I must handle while my sister is out of town. I do apologize."

"Your sister is out of town? I hadn't realized. Perhaps I should not be here when you are unchaperoned." He stood up to take his leave, but Lucy tugged on the sleeve of his jacket.

"Lord Davenport, I doubt you have any nefarious intentions here in the garden with a house full of children behind us. Stay. I could use some pleasant adult conversation this afternoon."

Davenport looked down at her beautiful face. She had no idea how easily he could picture himself ravishing her right here in the garden. He would lay her down in the grass and kiss every soft inch of her graceful neck. Nibble on those delectable earlobes while he unfastened each of the buttons on her dress one at a time. He would unwrap her carefully, like a special gift at Christmas. Lucy didn't know how alluring she was; it was one of the things he liked best about her. She was entirely unaware of her beauty. He was not, though. Which was exactly why he should leave.

But when she gave another tug, he let himself be pulled back down next to her on the bench. She bestowed another sunny smile upon him. He reached out a hand and ran a finger down her cheek. "Do you not know how tempting you are?"

Her eyes went wide, the blue depths pulling him in. He leaned in to touch his lips to hers. Just a taste…but he found one taste was not enough. Her lips, like a sweet wine, were intoxicating. He dipped closer for another kiss. She sighed, and her hand came up to rest against his heart. Everything around them blurred as the warmth of her lips drew him in. He cupped the other side of her face, changing the angle and deepening the kiss. Finally, he broke away, leaning his forehead against hers, he smiled. "I should go."

Lucy's smile disappeared, and she stood abruptly. Walking a few steps away, she looked out at the roses that climbed the wrought iron bars of the fence.

"Don't you ever get tired of being proper and good? Of always doing the right thing?" Her voice was clipped and angry.

Davenport frowned. "I am not sure what you mean. Would you like me to be wicked, to be hiding some deep dark sin?"

Lucy whirled around, eyes wide. "No! I guess I was speaking more about myself." She sighed and wrapped her arms around her waist. "My sister is the bold one. She is head of our household, and she does whatever she wants without worrying about breaking the rules. I'm quite angry with her right now. Once again, here I am, making my lists, supervising the staff, and taking care of the details while she is…she is missing." Lucy caught her bottom lip between her teeth.

He reached out, and she put her hand in his once again. This time it was he who tugged her down onto the bench. He chose his words carefully.

"I admire your ability to run the household in her absence. And I don't think there is anything wrong in being responsible, in taking care of the details. In fact, I have often been accused of those things myself." He gave a self-deprecating smile which Lucy returned.

"Miss Lucy."

They both looked up to find Mrs. Fenway a few yards away. "Your uncle is here. I have put him in the library."

"That's odd. I was not expecting him. Do you mind waiting here for a few moments? I will just see what he wants, and then perhaps we can all have some tea together." He nodded his agreement. Lucy disappeared through a set of french doors at the other end of the patio.

****

Lucy shut the glass doors behind her, and squaring her shoulders, she walked across the room. Her uncle stood near the fireplace, examining the ornaments hung with red ribbon from the mantel. There was one enamel ornament for each of the six siblings. Her mother had painted them herself. She held her breath as her uncle flicked at one carelessly, and it swung wildly back and forth for a moment.

Lucy was just as angry with Charles as she was with her sister. "Uncle Charles, I was not expecting you today."

"Lucy." He walked over to give her a kiss on the

cheek. “I am looking for Emma. The housekeeper said she is not home.”

“No, she is not here. She was injured last weekend while attempting to steal a diamond necklace.” She gained some satisfaction at his shocked expression. “Sound familiar? The necklace you told her about at the opera.”

“What happened? How badly was she injured?” Charles, to his credit, looked concerned.

“She was shot in the arm while escaping the house. Shot!” Taking a breath in through her nose, she lowered her voice. “I told you she promised me she was going to quit, but you still encouraged her to do another job. I am furious with you both.”

His eyebrows drew down, and his eyes narrowed. “Where is she now? Where is the necklace?”

“Where is the necklace? Is that all you can say? Emma could have been killed!”

“But she was not. Burglary is inherently dangerous. Emma understands this. Where is your sister?” Charles’ expression darkened.

Lucy couldn’t believe his cavalier attitude about Emma’s well-being. She realized if her sister would ever have a chance at a fresh start, their uncle needed to exit their lives. She crossed her arms across her chest. “She is recuperating somewhere safe. The necklace has been returned anonymously to the owner.”

“Returned.” His voice rose, and he took a menacing step toward Lucy. “Where is Emma?” he shouted.

“Emma now has someone looking out for her best interests, someone who wants to take care of her, not just use her.” Lucy stood her ground, although she had never seen her uncle look quite so furious.

"The duke," Charles spit out derisively. He took hold of her upper arms, squeezing them painfully. "Listen carefully. Emma works for me. How do you think you can still live in this house, still have all your pretty frocks for your husband-hunting? I am the reason you all are not paupers on the street." He gave her a shake, and the first tendrils of true fear grew in her belly. "Where is she?" he demanded.

"I suggest you unhand the lady immediately." A welcome voice boomed from the doorway. Charles dropped his hands in surprise, and she stumbled backward a little. Davenport strode across the room toward Charles, his face a stone mask of fury. She grabbed at Ethan's arm as he stepped in between her and Charles.

Turning to her, he asked, "Lucy, are you all right?"

She nodded, their eyes met, and the anger reflected in his boosted her own. She faced her uncle. "I would introduce you, but my uncle was just leaving." She injected as much ice as possible into her tone. "He is not welcome in this house any longer."

A strong hand slipped into hers and gave a squeeze. She welcomed the warmth and knew she was not alone.

****

Charles strode down the street. His cane clicked against the bricks. He couldn't believe the necklace was out of his reach. How could she agree to return such a valuable piece? What would he tell the buyers? Dorling and his associates did not take bad news lightly. His neck was on the line with this auction.

Thinking about Emma ensconced somewhere with

her precious duke made him ill. She was his. He had trained her, groomed her to be an exceptional thief.

This was not over. What he needed was something of equal value to replace the diamond necklace. A plan began to form. What did the aristocracy fear more than anything? Scandal, of course. He smiled to himself as he headed home. He had a letter to write. Emma would be his again soon.

Chapter 24

When Andrew did not arrive for afternoon tea, Emma was thrown off balance. Had she hurt him? Why couldn't he see it was foolish to care for her? She set her teacup down with a rattle. She needed some fresh air to clear her head. She found a pair of half boots and a wool shawl. Calling for Fergus, she left to take a walk in the gardens. She hadn't been outside in days. It was a crisp clear day with the sun shining down. It warmed her as she and Fergus strolled through the manicured gardens. Fergus had been very patient with her, but she could tell he needed a good run outside.

Eventually, she meandered over to the paddock where several beautiful horses were grazing. One mare noticed her and came over to say hello. Emma petted her nose. "Sorry I don't have a treat for you," she said to the horse as he nuzzled her hand. "Next time I will come better prepared. I promise."

The clatter of hooves had her turning to find Jack and Vivian arriving on horseback. Both were flushed and windblown from their ride. Jack dismounted first and then helped his wife off her horse. Emma lifted her eyebrows when she saw Vivian wore breeches and boots as opposed to a riding habit.

Vivian laughed out loud. "I never did like to ride sidesaddle. And when we are here at Stoneleigh, I have the freedom to be myself." She reached out a hand to her husband who grasped it, giving her a kiss across her knuckles.

"How are you feeling, Miss Whittingham?" Jack asked.

"Please, call me Emma. After all you have seen and all of your help, Miss Whittingham seems too formal." She smiled at them. "I'm feeling much better thanks to Andrew's coddling."

"Where is my brother? I am surprised to see you out here without him."

Emma turned away to pet the horse. "I don't think Andrew is very happy with me right now."

"I find that hard to believe. Why?"

Squaring her shoulders, she pivoted back to face Jack and Vivian. "Because he asked me to marry him this morning, and I said no."

"What!" Vivian gaped. "Why did you say no?"

Emma lowered her eyes. She didn't need to see the censure in their eyes. She tried to explain succinctly. "He deserves someone much better than me. It wouldn't be right."

When she summoned the courage to look up, she found instead of condemnation, Jack wore a thoughtful expression.

"Actually, I know exactly how you feel." He looked over at his wife and then returned his gaze to Emma. "I was once given a very good piece of advice by a wise lady. She said that there is always opportunity to change the direction of our lives. I chose to be a better version of myself, but I had to let go of my past. It wasn't easy, but with the right partner it's definitely possible." He leaned down and surprised Emma by brushing a kiss on her cheek. "I'll just go take care of the horses." He grabbed up the reins and led the horses over to the barn.

Emma stood there, stunned. She looked over at Vivian. "I don't know what to say. It's not that I don't care for him. It's just that he is so very kind and wonderful, and a duke for goodness' sake." She waved her hands about, clearly doing a poor job of convincing Vivian of her unsuitability to be matched with Andrew.

Vivian came over and gave her hand a squeeze. "Well, you have had a very rough week. You have a lot of thinking to do about your life. Come on, let's go do something diverting. Do you like to play cards?"

****

In the ballroom the sound of metal on metal rang through the room as Andrew and his brother fenced. Andrew attacked, his foil whipping through the air. It felt damn good to take his frustration with Emma out on Jack, a willing partner. When they were younger, Andrew had always beaten Jack at fencing, being much lighter on his feet than his brother. But in the years since, Jack had improved. Instead of playing like a hothead, as he had in his youth, he handled his foil with lethal calm. Jack was currently trouncing him.

"You are much better than you used to be, little brother."

"I have had a lot of practice. You can't survive in the Caribbean without knowing how to defend yourself with a sword. Pirates fight dirty."

The large round tip of his foil struck Andrew in the shoulder. That one would probably leave a bruise. They never wore protective padding when they fenced. It was too cumbersome, and Andrew trusted his brother not to harm him…too badly.

Andrew shuffled back and reset his stance. Two servants hurried over to offer water and towels as the men paused. He wiped sweat out of his eyes. Then he focused on Jack, foil at the ready. "Again."

"All right." Jack shrugged. "You are a glutton for punishment." Foils clashed as Andrew went on the offensive. Jack nimbly backed away, turning lightning quick to one side. "So does all this aggression have anything to with the fact that your recent marriage proposal to Miss Whittingham was politely declined?"

"How did you hear about that?" Andrew asked. He blocked a jab of the foil.

"She told us. She seemed very upset you would be angry with her indefinitely."

"I am angry, but because she still doesn't trust me. I am going to back away and let her think on it awhile. I don't know what else to do." Clank, clank went the metal as the men sparred.

"I think you have the wrong idea, Andrew. I recognized the misery on her face. She does not think she deserves happiness, that she is unworthy. I know because I felt the same way when I met Vivian. If you leave her to her own devices, she will just continue to justify her own ideas that you are too good for her." Jack paused, lowering his foil. "Which we both know is bullocks." He grinned devilishly. "My advice would be to seduce her into your bed and keep her there until she says yes."

"Are you actually suggesting I take the young lady hostage in bed until she agrees to marry me?"

"Like I said, sometimes you have to fight dirty." While Andrew was distracted by thoughts of Emma naked in his bed, Jack neatly pushed him up against the wall, the long edge of his foil an inch from his throat. "See?" Jack smiled, then stepped back. "Besides, if you have to take her hostage, big brother, then you're definitely not doing it right."

Andrew just shook his head and laughed. He moved back to the middle of the room and resumed his ready stance. "Again," he said.

****

Emma walked through the downstairs hallway on her way to the library to find a book to read. She hadn't seen Andrew since yesterday morning. Disappointment warred with boredom, so she decided a good book was exactly what she needed to distract her. As she passed by the ballroom, clanking sounds and male grunting drifted out. Curious, she approached the door which was halfway ajar. She peeked in.

Oh my. She drank in the sight of Andrew and his brother fencing. Neither man wore a shirt. Sweat glistened across broad shoulders. Emma could not take her eyes off Andrew. The muscles in his back stretched and bunched as he pushed forward with his soft-tipped foil. He was quick on his feet. The concentration on his handsome face made him look like a fierce warrior of old. She sighed a little to think what it would be like to have a strong knight fighting in her defense. Emma shook her head; what a silly schoolgirl fantasy.

The men paused, and servants ran up to offer them water. Andrew took a deep swig. Emma got a perfect view of his well-muscled chest and the planes of his hard stomach. She took in a sharp breath as she remembered running her hands down through the hair there. How he groaned her name as she leaned over him to lick his flat nipples. How he had tangled his fingers in her hair. She knew she should walk away before they noticed her. But her feet were rooted to the spot.

Andrew lowered his drink; he spotted her in the doorway. Their gazes locked. Andrew's eyes darkened with desire, as if he knew exactly what she was thinking. Embarrassed to have been caught ogling him, Emma turned and fled down the hallway to the library.

****

A half hour later, Andrew entered the library properly dressed, his hair clean and slicked back from his face. He found Emma sitting on the rug in front of the fireplace reading a book. She regarded him warily over her shoulder when he entered. After seeing her in the ballroom doorway with such raw desire in her eyes, he'd come looking for her. His intention was to take his brother's advice, spend some time scrambling her wits with passion. But now, he could see the apprehension written across her face. He decided on a different tack with this woman.

Andrew crossed the room to sit behind her on the rug. He stretched his legs on either side of her and bent to nuzzle her neck. "What are you reading?"

He could feel her release a breath. "*Macbeth*," she replied.

"Isn't that a rather dark tale for an afternoon read?" Andrew was surprised at her choice.

"Perhaps. Macbeth thought he would be king, and life would be grand. But no matter who you are, life is hard. It does me good to remember that." Emma leaned back against his chest. He wrapped one arm around her waist.

"Of this tenet I am well aware. The trial of being stuck in an unhappy marriage is something I would have gladly endured to spare my sons the unfairness of losing their mother so young. The guilt nearly consumed me." He paused. It wasn't so hard to talk about it anymore.

"This past summer I came to the conclusion I need to leave things from my past behind in order to look toward something better. I want to show my boys how to move forward after tragedy. I want to show them what hope looks like." Andrew stared into the fire, remembering the anger and bitterness he had been mired in after his wife died. How he had tried to drown those feelings in liquor.

"Your brother said something to that effect to me earlier. About leaving the past behind," Emma murmured.

"Will you tell me more about what happened after your father's death? How did you become a thief?" Andrew prodded gently.

Emma stiffened in his arms. He brushed another kiss to her neck.

"I suppose it's best if you know all of it. Then you will believe me when I say you can't marry me." She turned in his arms so she leaned up against one of his knees and could look at his face while she spoke. "After the will was read, I just sat there in my father's library, tears streaming down my face. My uncle got up to leave, but I caught his arm and asked him to stay. I don't know if it was my tears or the desperation in my voice which pricked his conscience that day, but he did stay, for a little over a year. He was the only adult willing to be totally honest with me about the dire financial situation we were in. He himself was in no financial position to care for all of us. He is what you would call a lothario. He moves from one lonely lady to the next, his 'amours,' he calls them.

"In the end, he taught me the only thing he knew how to do well, to be a thief. You see, he was once a notorious thief, never once caught. But as he explained to me, it's a young man's game. So he trained me as his protégé. He sells the jewelry to his fence, a man he has worked with for many years. I have been stealing from the rich ladies in Mayfair for almost four years now."

She frowned up at him. Perhaps she could sense his pity for the young girl whose world had crumbled in one short day.

"Stop." She held up a hand. "Don't romanticize the tale. You're feeling sorry for poor, desperate Emma. But the truth is I enjoy the hunt, the freedom of being out at night, of taking what I want. Listen and see clearly who I really am." She lifted her chin, defying him to argue.

She was right; he did think how fearless she must be to brave the night and earn a living for her family in such a difficult way. Her declaration of her enjoyment in her misdeeds struck him as a well-placed strike to scare him off. Not that it was going to work.

"Your uncle, does he take a cut from the sales?" Andrew asked.

"Of course, as does the fence."

"And do you know what the size of his portion is when you hand him a piece of jewelry?"

Her brow wrinkled. "Well, no, it depends on what the fence says he can sell it for…are you implying Charles is cheating me? He dotes on us! He gave me a way to pay the bills, to care for myself. I will always be indebted to him," Emma protested, but the furrow between her eyebrows showed she was considering his words and did not like the implications.

"What I am suggesting is, like you said, Charles is not a young man anymore. He is using you to make a living for himself. He needs you just as much as you need him," Andrew stated.

Had there been any man in her life who had not tried to use Emma to their own advantage? Anyone who had put her needs ahead of their own? After all that had happened to her, how did she still so easily find the humor and joy in the small things around her? He admired so much her ability to bounce back from adversity. Andrew knew better than to let her see how much her struggles affected him. She would recoil from any sympathy. So he schooled his face into a bland smile.

"Why don't you read to me? The part with the witches is a particular favorite of mine."

Emma's pensive expression cleared, and she smiled. "That is my favorite part as well. I do an excellent witch's cackle." Turning, she again rested her back against his chest. She began to read aloud.

Chapter 25

Mother Nature could be fickle in December, teasing them with a few mild sunny days before turning cold and blustery again. Emma didn't mind the cold weather one bit. She had decided to enjoy every moment of her forced vacation. Andrew continued to coddle her with hot chocolate in the mornings and raspberry tarts at teatime. She didn't have the heart to tell him she preferred gooseberry. They passed the time playing cards with Jack and Vivian or reading in the library with the fire roaring to stave off the chill.

One morning at breakfast Andrew said, "Today I must attend to a few things in the village. Would you like to come along? It's a short carriage ride, and we could have lunch at the inn if you like."

"That sounds diverting. I must admit I do have a bit of cabin fever."

"Dress warmly. I don't want you to catch a chill when your arm is still recovering."

"Yes, Mother." Emma smirked at him. He was the most managing man alive! Jack tried to muffle his laughter from behind his newspaper, and it made her smile to realize she had an ally.

Andrew just ignored her comment. He turned to the others. "Do you two want to join us?"

"No, you have fun. We can entertain ourselves," Vivian replied. Her husband lowered the paper, and he gave her a smoldering look.

"Indeed." Jack took Vivian's hand and kissed her fingers.

Emma blushed, and sent Andrew a sidelong glance. He rolled his eyes, returning his focus to his eggs.

"If you will excuse me. I will just go change." She set down her napkin. Andrew and his brother stood as she rose from her chair. "I can be ready in thirty minutes." She hurried from the room.

****

An hour later they were ensconced in the carriage. Andrew tucked a warm throw around Emma's legs and a hot brick at her feet. He settled himself next to her, then tapped on the roof twice to let the driver know they were ready to go.

Andrew enjoyed the view from the carriage as they rode to the village. Around Stoneleigh, the grassy fields stretched as far as the eye could see. White fluffy sheep dotted the landscape, their bleating the only sound for miles. Andrew let Emma drink in the scenery quietly for a while, content with his view of her lovely face. They passed across a bridge by the new mill not far from the village.

"The village is not very large, but it has been growing steadily since I opened the mill two years ago. It has most all the basics which are needed for shopping and a few stores for frivolities. A bookshop, a dressmaker, stationer, even a sweetshop if you care for a treat."

"What do you make at the mill?" Emma asked.

Surprised at her interest, he replied, "We make tweed cloth from the sheep's wool. Lengths for tablecloths and napkins, also blankets and saddle cloths.

When I inherited the duchy, much of the land around here was sitting unused. The mill provides jobs. I have more than enough land to graze sheep, and still have plenty for farming. My father and his land steward were too stuck in their ways to make any positive changes. It took me several years to pay off the mortgages, and to invest in the improvements which were sorely needed."

Emma turned her brandy-colored gaze to him. "You and I are not so different, you know. Of course, you have far larger responsibilities than I, but we have both been working to right our inheritance. To leave our families a better legacy than we received."

Andrew sat back as the truth of her statement hit him. He had accused her of being selfish, but really, she had only been thinking about her family. Doing what was necessary to protect them. He considered her profile as she gazed out the window of the carriage. It was past time someone protect her, thought of her future. If only he could convince her to let him.

****

When they reached the village, Emma let Andrew tuck her hand into the crook of his arm as they meandered through the main street. The sun peeked out from behind the clouds, and its rays warmed her face. The tiny town had neat little shops with brightly colored doors and shutters. The cobblestone sidewalks in front of the buildings were swept clean. People in the village square stopped to doff their hats at the duke or call out a friendly hello. Their curious looks made Emma self-conscious. She tried to put some space between her and Andrew, but he held fast to her hand, giving it a reassuring squeeze.

They stopped in at the general store. Andrew

pointed out the lengths of wool fabric which were made at the mill. As Emma wandered about the store, she observed him from under her lashes. He spoke easily with the shop owner, asking after the business and how the man's family fared. It was the same all through town. Andrew knew everyone; he introduced Emma to local gentry and shopkeepers alike.

"Ahh…the sweetshop! Let's go inside."

"Andrew, sweetshops are for children."

"True enough, I come here all the time with Grayson and Tyler. Mrs. Trenwick will be mad if I don't stop in and say hello."

He escorted her into a small store filled with heavenly scents. The walls were whitewashed, the moldings painted a bright pink. Three small round tables were covered in pastel-colored tablecloths. A long marble countertop along one side held trays of delicious-looking sweets. It was the most cheerful establishment she had ever entered. An older lady stood behind the counter. Her equally cheerful expression told Emma she must be the owner.

Mrs. Trenwick smiled widely as she rushed around the counter to wrap Andrew in a hug. Andrew laughed out loud at Emma's surprise. She closed her gaping mouth and smiled at the proprietress.

"Mrs. Trenwick, may I introduce you to Miss Emma Whittingham? She is a guest of ours at Stoneleigh."

"It is a pleasure to meet you, Mrs. Trenwick. Your store is lovely."

"Thank you, Miss Whittingham. It is nice to meet you. You must excuse my exuberant welcome. I've known His Grace since he was a boy. I worked as a cook up at the manor once upon a time. I reserve the right to hug him whenever he visits me. Where are young Master Grayson and Master Tyler?"

"They are still in London. We are here briefly, just a fortnight. Miss Whittingham is recovering from an illness. Lady Vivian thought it would be a good idea to whisk her out here for some fresh country air to aid her progress."

"I never did take to the city myself, a country girl I am." Then she frowned. "Jack and his wife are here, and they haven't come to visit me? You tell that boy I missed seeing his face these many years. He better come over for a visit. Come along, pick out something yummy to eat while I put together a box for you to take back to London for the boys." She bustled through a door behind the counter and disappeared into the back.

"So what is your fancy?" Andrew put a hand on her lower back to guide her down the counter, causing a warm tingle of awareness to spread at the base of her spine. Emma wanted to snuggle back against him and feel his arms wrap around her. She wished they weren't in public.

She focused her attention on the delights in front of her. "Ooh, orange jellies. I love those, and look—chocolate-covered cherries." Emma clapped her hands in delight. "What is your favorite, Your Grace?"

"Mine is the gingerbread, or anything with frosting." Andrew reached out and, swiping some frosting off a small cake, dabbed it on Emma's nose. She attempted to throw him a stern look but couldn't hold back a giggle. The fool. She retaliated with a finger full of the same frosting, running a smear across his cheek.

"Now that's a decided improvement. You looked far too handsome this morning."

Andrew got a wicked look in his eye. He grabbed up a tart covered in powdered sugar, holding it aloft in his palm. "This means war, my lady."

"You wouldn't dare!" Emma backed away from him. He took a menacing step toward her, and she let out an embarrassing squeak. She darted around one of the tables, putting it between them. Emma couldn't help but laugh out loud at how ridiculous he looked in his impeccable jacket and cravat while holding the tart high, powdered sugar drifting down onto his sleeve.

She looked over his shoulder and spotted Mrs. Trenwick emerging from the back. The woman's eyes widened.

"Help, Mrs. Trenwick! The duke has gone quite mad!"

Andrew froze. She burst into fresh laughter at the horrified expression on his face at being caught by Mrs. Trenwick mid-strike. She put a hand over her mouth and collapsed into a nearby chair.

Andrew briefly closed his eyes. Then he straightened his shoulders, pivoting toward the counter. "Pardon me, Mrs. Trenwick, we were just discussing how much I adore your frosted cakes." He bit into the tart and gave her a winning smile. The lady just shook her head and returned his grin.

She handed him a towel. "Well, if this doesn't remind me of you as a boy, always causing trouble, he was. Better wipe that off before you head out onto the street."

"Thank you." Andrew wiped at his cheek.

Finally managing to catch her breath, Emma came

over, and Andrew wiped the frosting off her nose as well. He looked so handsome when he laughed. She wanted to trace a finger along the dimple that formed when he smiled down at her.

She might like to make him smile like that every day. Perhaps she should take a chance and trust him. It seemed to come naturally to him to care for all that was his. His family, the land, and those who live on it. What would it be like to be his, not just for now, but for a lifetime?

Andrew raised one questioning eyebrow, but she was not ready to share her thoughts just yet. She turned to the proprietress. "Mrs. Trenwick, may I have one of those chocolate-covered cherries, please?"

Later that afternoon, Emma sat in her comfy chair by the fire and opened a letter from her sister. She feared her sister would still be rather angry with her, so she sighed in relief when the letter was chatty and full of news about the children and how they missed her. Lucy wrote about Lord Davenport. He had not yet formally asked her to marry him, but they had been talking about their future. Then in the last paragraph Lucy wrote about an unsettling visit she'd had with Uncle Charles. Apparently, he had been very angry about the necklace having been returned. Lucy said he grabbed her roughly, demanding to know where Emma was. Lucy told him he was no longer welcome at the house.

Emma set the letter down. Lucy had to banish Charles from the house? She had put her sister in a bad position with Charles. And she had let Charles down and not been able to explain to him what happened. She bit her lower lip and contemplated what she could write to Charles.

Folding the pages, she set them back on the desk. Then she noticed the second letter. She recognized the writing and grimaced, Charles. With no little trepidation she opened the missive.

My dearest girl,

I was very upset to hear of your bungled attempt to acquire the item we discussed and your subsequent injury. Your sister told me where to reach you. The truth of the matter is you have left me with buyers looking to bid on a diamond necklace and no necklace to present. You and I have had a successful partnership for several years, but now you have put me in a very difficult position.

So here is how we will proceed. I will allow you to continue your relationship with your duke, and you will in return set up an opportunity for you to wear the dowager's ruby necklace out to an event. The necklace that you once coveted. Then we will coordinate a time for you to hand off the necklace to me and pretend you were robbed. I will have a suitable replacement for the auction, and you may keep your duke. A good deal for both of us.

Now I don't need to tell you how damaging a scandal would be for you if the magistrate was to be tipped off about a certain thief. Not to mention what an investigation would do for Lucy's chances with her earl. You need to return to the city immediately. Contact me to set up the time and place for our ruse.

Charles

Emma leaned forward in her chair, rocking back and forth. She tried to pull air into her lungs. The threats Charles made were no jest. All pretense of the loving uncle had been stripped away by the words on the page. He had her neatly trapped. She couldn't run away; his well-placed insinuations could ruin Lucy's chances for a respectable marriage. But how could she stay and use her relationship with Andrew to steal from him? No, she could not!

She stood up to pace across the carpet in front of the fire, trembling. The paper in her hand shook. *Think!* Andrew's comment from the other day came back to her. Charles needed her as much as she needed him. She stopped pacing as the truth of what she must do came to her.

When they returned to London, she would have to sever her friendship with Andrew. If they were not in contact, she couldn't put Charles' plan into action. She would just steal something else for Charles. There were other pieces which could be stolen for his precious auction.

Did she have it in her to do another job? Emma crumpled to her knees. Stealing into a darkened house to search for the perfect item to acquire would once have excited her; now it made her stomach turn. She rubbed her arm, feeling the stiches through the thin material of her blouse. The phantom report of a gun echoed, and she remembered the burn of the bullet as it entered her flesh. A lump formed in her throat. Her eyes burned with tears she refused to let fall. What was she going to do?

Chapter 26

The next morning, Andrew knocked on Emma's bedroom door. The only response he received was a low woof. Shrugging, he opened the door and let himself in to the darkened room. Fergus jumped off the bed to come over to sniff his boots. He patted the dog's large head before heading across the room to the four-poster bed. He set a mug of steaming hot chocolate on the bedside table.

"Emma, rise and shine. There is a surprise to be found outside your window."

He went to the window and pulled aside the curtains, letting the bright morning sun spill in to the room. Andrew smiled when the lump on the bed groaned and pulled the covers over her head. Emma was not a morning person.

Rounding the bed, he climbed on, settling himself on his side facing Emma's blanket-covered self. He poked her with one finger.

"Andrew, get out of my bed! You know you're not supposed to be in my room," Emma admonished him from under the covers.

"If you would wake up, sleepy head, you would see it snowed overnight. It is a white wonderland outside."

The covers flipped down, and Emma's head popped out. "Truly?"

"Yes, truly." He leaned in and gave her a swift kiss

on the mouth. "Go see for yourself."

Emma tumbled out of bed to rush over to the window, giving Andrew an excellent view of her long bare legs and one tantalizing bare shoulder as she crossed the room in her nightgown. He had not made love to her since she had turned down his offer of marriage. He hoped by giving her some space from the intimacy, she would come to him when she was ready to trust in their relationship. But it was damn hard to keep his hands off her.

She stood in front of the window, her nose pressed against the cold glass. The sunlight filtered through her thin cotton nightgown, giving him an outline of her luscious curves. He shifted off the bed. Perhaps it was a mistake to be in her bedroom. His pants felt uncomfortably tight across his growing erection.

Despite his better judgement, he was pulled toward her. "Care to go for a walk?" Coming up behind Emma, he wrapped his arms around her waist and nuzzled her neck.

"That sounds lovely, Andrew, but I have to tell you something." She turned out of his arms and walked over to pick up the mug of hot chocolate. She blew across the top before taking a cautious sip. "Yesterday, I received a letter from Lucy. It sounds as though she is quite overwhelmed with taking care of the children and the household. I think it's time I go home."

Andrew frowned. He had hoped for a little more time before they were thrown back into the craziness of everyday life. She looked up at him, eyes wide and plaintive.

"I suppose I cannot keep you prisoner here forever."

"Thank you, Andrew. When do you think we can leave?"

"Well, it snowed a good four or five inches. It may take a few days for the roads to be passable. Will that be all right?"

"Yes, that's fine." She smiled. "Now let me be alone with my hot chocolate, and I'll get dressed so we can go on our walk after breakfast."

Andrew tugged her toward him for one more kiss. Her lips were warm, inviting, and tasted sweet. Kissing this woman was beginning to be as important to him as breathing. Reluctantly, he broke away and left her to her hot chocolate.

****

Outside, everything sparkled. Emma marveled at how fresh and new the whole world looked as she and Andrew ambled down the path which led around the lake. Tree branches were coated in a layer of ice. The snow on the ground reflected the bright winter sunshine. As she walked, Emma kicked her booted feet up, watching the powdery snow spray.

Fergus ran ahead, loping through the snow, leaving giant paw prints for them to follow. He caught scent of something, and snuffling his nose into a large bush, he let out a deep woof. A rabbit streaked out the other side of the bush, and the race was on.

"Fergus! Forget about it," she called out. He disappeared through the trees. "Oh dear, do you think he will get lost?" She bit her lower lip.

"No, he has been walking around the property for two weeks now. I think he should be able to find his way home," Andrew replied. Always able to discern what she was feeling, he took her hand, and he hooked it into the crook of his arm, pulling her close. "Let's follow him. Through those trees, it opens up to the sheep pasture. Perhaps the herd will distract him from his prey."

They needn't have worried. As they emerged into the field behind the stables, they saw Jack and Vivian on the other side of the stable yard. Her puppy frolicked in the snow. Fergus was with them, keeping an eye on the beagle puppy as it tumbled around, trying to maneuver in the snow. Jack gave them a wave. Andrew waved, then steered Emma back to the path to continue their walk.

"Don't you want to go say hello?" Emma asked, glancing back over her shoulder.

"No, I just want to have you to myself for now, especially as I will soon have to share you with your brood back in London."

Emma sighed. "True. I never thought I would say this, but I miss them. The whole crazy lot. I think I miss all the snuggles the most. The boys always race into my room in the mornings and jump into bed with me."

"The time when they are small is so short. That's one reason I couldn't send Grayson off to school just yet. I know it's unfashionable, but my father didn't send me to school until I was eleven. I much prefer to have Grayson home for a little while longer."

"Their schooling is the one thing I worry about the most. My mother always insisted on a good education. Even we girls got to learn more than just how to run a household. I had to let our governess go last year. I am afraid I am not doing a very good job of continuing the children's studies. I am simply not cut out for teaching," Emma replied.

Andrew squeezed her hand. “I know I wouldn’t have the patience for teaching either.”

Emma stopped in her tracks. “Oh, look at the lake. It looks like a fairy wonderland.”

They paused to take in the view. The lake was so still it looked like a mirror reflecting the blue sky above. All around, snow glistened on the banks and along the trees. A bird whistled, and Andrew pointed, silently calling Emma’s attention to a deer as it emerged from the trees. It nibbled on the leaves of a large bush near the water.

“I wish I had any talent at all for drawing. What a perfect winter scene,” she whispered. The deer must have smelled them because his head snapped up. In a flash, leaving a last glimpse of his white tail, he disappeared.

Andrew took her hand in his, and they walked back slowly to the house. Their stride matched perfectly as they strolled, his hand warm around hers. Despite the lovely surroundings, Emma couldn’t relax. How was she going to break off her relationship with Andrew? She knew no matter how hard it would be to say goodbye, she could not consider stealing the ruby necklace from him, or from the duchess for that matter. She had a bad feeling her uncle wouldn’t stop at that one piece. Her throat constricted. She recognized he was never going to let her be free of the life.

Perhaps the best way would be to start an argument of some sort on the way back to London. She would be her surliest most-awful self and hope something might come up naturally that she could use as a springboard for a fight. But until then, she had every intention of enjoying her last days of being his captive in this beautiful place.

Fergus bounded up the path toward them, his happiness at finding her evident in his exuberant greeting. Emma bent down to give him a hug around his wet shaggy neck. The soft wet slap of a snowball hit her backside. She straightened and turned toward Andrew, outraged, hands on her hips. "Oh, you brute!"

A boyish grin spread wide across his face. "It was such a lovely target."

Reaching down, Emma quickly made a snowball and launched it at Andrew's head. He was too quick, though, ducking behind a tree, and her snowball missed its mark. From behind his cover he threw another at her, hitting her in the stomach this time. Emma darted to the left and, crouching behind a tree, made her own arsenal of snowballs. Her pride stung. Her aim would be better if she could use her right arm properly. This was not her first snowball fight. She would just have to improvise. Peeking around, she lobbed one underhand that grazed Andrew's shoulder.

"Ha!" she called out.

A snowball hit the tree right above her head.

Andrew came out to launch another at her, but she popped out from the other side of her tree and nailed him in the chest as he raised his arm to throw. It left behind a satisfying white splotch on his black coat. Emma giggled at the look of shock on his face.

"Oh, you're going to get it now." He advanced toward her hiding spot. She squealed and turned to run away. Andrew was faster, and he grabbed her around the waist from behind.

"You're at my mercy," he whispered in her ear. Then he lost his footing on a patch of ice, and they both tumbled to the ground, falling into a drift of snow, which cushioned their landing.

Andrew sat up. “Did I hurt your shoulder?”

“No, I’m fine.” She glanced up at him through her lashes. “Come here.”

As Andrew leaned down, she wrapped an arm up and smashed the snowball she held in her glove into the back of his neck. She cackled in glee at his expression as the cold snow rolled down his collar.

“If you think a little snow could deter me from your lips, you are sadly mistaken.” He leaned in and kissed her. His lips were warm against hers despite the cold. She delighted at the instant heat that lit between them. Then a cold wet nose broke in, and Fergus’ rough tongue licked her cheek.

“Fergus! Get away, you fool, this isn’t a group activity.” Andrew pulled away. He gave Fergus a shove. “Sit, you behemoth.”

He glanced back to Emma, and they both started to laugh at the dog’s innocent expression. Fergus sat on his haunches, his tongue lolling out to one side. Andrew fell back into the snow next to Emma, and they lay there breathless. Emma stared up at the tree branches glistening with ice as they stretched into a blue sky.

“This place, Stoneleigh I mean, is wonderful. The children would love it here. Most of them have never been out to the country. My parents preferred the distractions of the city.”

Andrew turned on his side, his head propped up on one hand. He ran one gloved finger down her cheek. “Marry me, and we will bring the whole lot out here where they can roam free and explore. The dogs too.” He smiled before kissing her cold lips.

She broke the kiss. Rolling away, she sat up. "It sounds wonderful. But don't you see, I can't."

Andrew's expression shuttered. He stood up and reached down his hands to help Emma to her feet. He pulled her into his arms and stared down at her silently.

"Don't you see?" Emma was desperate to explain, desperate to get away from his kind eyes and his warm embrace. Both of which threatened to crumble her carefully constructed walls of self-preservation. The truth tumbled out of her mouth, heedless of the warning from her brain. "I can't risk it. If I marry you, I will most certainly not be able to keep myself from loving you. And I will be devastated when the other shoe drops. I don't think my heart can take another betrayal…it is too fragile. It has been pieced back together too many times."

"The other shoe? I don't understand. I would never hurt you intentionally."

Emma stepped away from him. "You are a man, aren't you?" A well-aimed barb meant to slice at him, make him pull away. His eyes went hard. He advanced toward her, and she took a couple of steps back.

"Do not compare me to other men you have known. I recognize I have faults. We all do. Thief." He took another step forward, his face coming within inches of hers. "Your fear is blocking you from reaching for happiness, nothing else. And you know what? I think you already love me."

"No! No, I don't." Emma shook her head back and forth in denial. But inside she knew he was right. When had her foolish heart betrayed her? She was so careful. She took her pleasure but knew not to risk her heart.

Images flashed one after another in her mind. The

two of them laughing while they danced around the ballroom. His handsome face smiling down at her as he handed her hot chocolate. Andrew in the garden organizing the children and dogs into neat rows. His kind words and genuine concern for the people he talked to in the village. His eyes stormy with desire as he made love to her. She did love him! Panic coursed through her, and she did what any animal does when cornered. She ran.

****

Andrew cursed as Emma turned and flew away from him down the snowy path.

"I love you too," he murmured. Nobody but the dog was around to hear the words. He spun to face out toward the water and let out a frustrated breath in a puff of white air. That confounded woman was so stubborn.

He would be damned before he proposed to her again. Any woman in Briton would be happy to be his duchess, but no, he wanted the one woman who wouldn't have him. He could force her hand easily enough. She had just spent two weeks with him. Chaperones or not, he could threaten her reputation…but then he would be just as manipulative as all the other men in her life had been.

He took another deep breath of frigid air. No, with this skittish lady he would just have to be patient. But he could damn well make it difficult for her to keep her distance. He smiled to himself. It was time he took his brother's advice. Andrew whistled as he made his way back to the house and looked forward to executing his next move.

Chapter 27

It was late that night when Andrew finally walked down the hall to Emma's room, holding one long-stemmed rose in his hand. All afternoon he had mulled over his conversation with Emma. How she had run away when he accused her of being in love with him. It finally dawned on him he had not once told her how he felt. How could she trust her own feelings if she was unsure of his? What was a good marriage proposal without the declaration of love? How could he have forgotten that essential part?

He turned the handle and found the door locked. He tried again. Definitely locked. The little minx had locked him out on purpose. So much for the element of surprise.

Andrew stalked back down to his room. Setting the rose down carefully, he pulled on a pair of boots and his jacket. She thought she could hide from him? Well, she's not the only one who could sneak into other people's rooms. He headed downstairs, rose in hand, swung to the right, strode past the ballroom, and stalked into the kitchen, startling two scullery maids. Ignoring their wide eyes, he quickly exited into the frigid night air. Pulling his jacket closed against the chill, Andrew tromped through the snow until he stood under her bedroom window. Assessing his options, he decided to use the drainpipe to climb up to the stone balcony. He put the rose stem between his teeth, thankful Mrs. Tuttle had already removed the thorns.

The drainpipe was quite cold and slick with ice after last night's snowfall. Andrew paused, one foot in the air. He shook his head; if Emma could sneak into his room, certainly he could manage to climb to hers. He had climbed almost to the bottom of the balcony when his left foot slipped. Reaching blindly for something less slippery to grab hold of for balance, his hand found a dried wisteria vine growing up around the balcony's stone balustrade. He grasped it for dear life.

Regaining his equilibrium, Andrew took a deep breath. How did she do this night after night? He shimmied up another foot. If he stretched an arm out, he could perhaps grasp the top of the balustrade. He had one chance to get the momentum he needed. He closed his eyes briefly. In for a penny, in for a pound. He let go of the drainpipe with one hand, and with one great push of his foot, his fingers grabbed hold of the stone edge. He found a foot hold, just managing to roll up and over onto the floor of the balcony. Not a graceful entrance. He lay flat on his back in the snow, but at least he hadn't fallen and broken his damn neck.

"Ahem."

Andrew turned his head and found Emma glaring at him from the doorway. Her hair fell soft as silk around her, her hands fisted on her hips, and Fergus stood at attention by her side. He took the rose miraculously still clenched in his teeth and held it out.

"For you, milady."

"You'd make a terrible burglar. I could hear you grunting all the way up." But she reached out and took the flower. Holding it to her nose, she took a sniff, and her expression softened.

"You locked me out." Andrew rolled to his knees.

The dog growled low in warning.

"Fergus, it's all right. Go lie down." She gestured for the dog to go back inside. Emma pursed her lips. "What are you doing here, Andrew? I thought I made myself clear today why I can't marry you." Her arms were wrapped tightly around her waist. Her eyes stared at a point over his right shoulder.

"I realized that maybe I hadn't made myself entirely clear." He sucked in a breath of frigid air. "Damn it, Emma, look at me." Her gaze swung back to meet his, her eyes wide. He scooted closer on his frozen knees.

"I love you, Emma. I know it was not your intent, but you have stolen my heart."

She shook her head in denial. One single tear slipped down her cheek. That tear felt like an arrow to his heart. He quickly got to his feet and closed the gap between them.

"I know you're afraid. But will you let me love you tonight?" Her eyes fluttered shut. He placed a kiss at the corner of one eyelid, and another on the opposite one. Slowly, still afraid to spook her, he brought his hands up to cup her face. She jerked back, and his stomach dropped.

"Andrew, your hands are freezing!"

He let out a short bark of laughter. "Not just my hands. May I come inside, my love?"

She held out one hand and nodded.

Andrew wound one arm around her waist, pulling her against him. He leaned in to kiss her lips. With one taste, the tight leash he had kept on his desire for her broke. He crushed her to him. His other hand skimmed down her body. Pivoting them, he pulled her into the bedroom. With one hand he slammed the french door, shutting out the cold. Emma seemed equally frantic for him, her hands trying to push his jacket off his shoulders.

"First thing we must do is get you out of these wet clothes," she murmured against his mouth. His jacket slid to the floor. He really was quite wet from his drop onto the snow-covered balcony. He turned them away from the bed and toward the warmth of the fireplace, never breaking their kiss. Her lips were both soft and demanding. He tugged off her dressing gown impatiently. They bumped into a wingback chair, and rotating again, Andrew sat down, pulling Emma into his lap.

Her hands slowly burned a path up the cold skin of his torso, raising his shirt inch by inch. He lifted his arms over his head and let her rid him of the garment. She released a hum of satisfaction. Emma ran her nails down over his chest, lightly scraping down along its planes and ridges.

"I was fascinated watching you fence with your brother. You were so fierce, you moved with such grace. I found it very arousing." She leaned in to kiss his neck and then bit him in the same spot. The sharp pain heightened his arousal. Her hands were everywhere, one impatiently undoing the buttons on his pants. He slid his hands along her calves, trailing his fingers up to the soft skin of her thighs. Why was this nightgown so voluminous? He ripped her nightrail over her head. Emma let out a small cry of pain, and Andrew froze.

"What's happened? It's your arm, isn't it?" He studied her face. She bit her bottom lip and nodded her head. "Damn it, I should have been gentler. I'm sorry."

"Andrew, it's all right. My arm is fine now. It just hurt to have it up over my head like that. I'm all right, I promise." She grabbed his face and kissed him. But he chastised himself. His plan had been to cherish this woman tonight, to show her how much he loved her. He needed to slow things down.

He stood up, taking Emma with him, and then he gently laid her on the soft rug in front of the fireplace. The firelight played across her skin, making it almost luminescent. Her long hair spread out around her. Her eyes glowed with desire for him, and dare he hope, love? What an amazing gift she was.

He shed the rest of his clothes, not once taking his eyes from hers. Then he joined her on the rug. He cupped her face and kissed her with all the love he could give. She sighed softly against his mouth. Thank God for small victories. He trailed his fingers slowly down her throat, then down along the curve of one breast.

His lips followed, placing hot kisses along the same path. His tongue made lazy circles around her breast until it reached the peak, and taking the rosy tip into his mouth, he sucked hard just as she liked. She rewarded him with a gasp of pleasure, her hands tangled in his hair. He lavished attention on the other breast, and Emma bucked her hips up against him, straining for more intimate contact between their bodies.

"Ah, not so fast, darling." Andrew placed one kiss in the valley between her breasts. Looking up, he caught her gaze. "I love you, Emma." Her eyes widened, then she turned her head away. But Andrew would not be deterred. He trailed kisses down to her navel. "I love you," he said again. He feasted on her soft skin lower still, until he reached the curls of her womanhood. Then he lost himself in the warm folds of her sex, tasting and teasing until he had her writhing and calling out his name.

Until he could not hold back anymore. He rose up, and positioning himself between her thighs, he leaned in to capture her mouth. Then he sank into her. She felt hot, tight, and glorious. "Emma, I love you," he murmured against her lips. Then her hips rolled against his, and he could go slowly no longer. Andrew pulled out almost all the way and thrust back into the glory that was her body.

****

Emma could not take his tenderness any longer. His words of love were an assault battering at the wall protecting her heart. She hooked a leg over his thigh and with a shove rolled him onto his back. Sitting astride him, she exulted in his look of surprise. Then she started to move up and down, her hips rolling in counterpart to his thrusts. His hands splayed across her hips. He sat up to kiss her neck, but she pushed him back down onto his back. Now it was her turn to ravish him. Emma rode him fast and hard, furiously racing toward that edge of pleasure. When her orgasm hit her, she arched back and let it wash over her. Andrew called out her name. His fingers dug into her hips, and he threw his head back in a silent roar. It was magic, and she gloried in her ability to give him such pleasure.

Later, they lay on the bed, Emma curled around

Andrew, her head on his chest. Andrew had moved them at some point, and Emma was glad for the soft mattress and the warmth of his body under the covers. She blinked sleepily at him, trying to judge if he was awake. She found him staring at her with his deep blue eyes. A smile played across his lips. “Emma, I…” She placed a finger on his lips to shush him.

“Please don’t ruin this lovely night with another proposal of marriage.”

“Oh, I won’t.” Andrew casually reached out and brushed a piece of hair from her shoulder.

“You won’t?” Emma sat up. Instead of relief, a sharp pang of disappointment ran through her. Was he really giving up? She bit her lower lip. Isn’t that exactly what she wanted?

“I am done asking. If you want to marry me, you will have to ask me. And it better be a proper proposal, romantic, perhaps down on one knee,” he mused.

Emma’s mouth dropped open. Andrew just chuckled. He leaned up to kiss her lips softly. “Best if you think on it, yes? Let’s get some sleep.” He tugged her back into his arms.

For a while, Emma lay awake, thinking about Andrew and his marriage proposals. He’d shifted in his sleep, and now he lay curled behind her, his arm a welcome heavy weight, circled around her waist. Dare she trust in his love, that it could last? She sighed. Here in the dark, it was not so hard to admit to herself her heart already belonged to him. “I love you, Andrew,” she whispered. Then she finally closed her eyes and slept.

Chapter 28

Three days later, Emma woke to bright morning sunlight streaming through the open curtains and found herself alone in bed. She felt strangely bereft. Even Fergus was missing from his pile of blankets in the corner. The past few days had been idyllic. She had decided to enjoy her remaining time with the duke.

Andrew had, true to his word, not mentioned marriage again. Emma was relieved but a little suspicious. Since he was not the kind of man to give up on something he set his sights on, she sensed a strategic retreat.

The delicious aroma of chocolate had her sitting up. A cup of the hot beverage sat on the bedside table along with the slightly worse for wear long-stemmed rose from three nights ago. She smiled as she took a sip from the warm mug. These past two weeks had been beautiful, a memory she would cherish for the rest of her life.

Today, however, was the day she must go home and face her future. A future which could not include the duke, for his own good. She rose and moved across the room to the desk. Opening the drawer, she pulled out the letter from Uncle Charles. Reading through it again strengthened her resolve. Charles was never going to let her quit. If she tried, the scandal of her secret life would ruin the lives of all the people she loved.

Emma folded the letter. She glanced around and spotted a small stack of books she had selected from the library to bring along in the carriage. She slid the letter into the pages of one of the books for safekeeping, then turned to get ready for her day.

An hour later, Emma emerged from her room, dressed for travelling. Her small trunk was packed thanks to help from one of the maids. She went in search of Fergus and Andrew. She found both the dog and the man outside in the garden playing with a ball. Andrew smiled when he spotted her, his hair windblown and his cheeks pink from the cold.

"Look how high he can jump." He threw the ball high and long. Fergus ran at full speed and launched himself into the air with a great leap, neatly catching the ball in his mouth. "See? Fantastic, Fergus! Good boy." Andrew ruffled the hair on the dog's head when Fergus deposited the ball at his feet.

"I see you have been making friends at last." Fergus, the traitor, stared adoringly up at Andrew.

"I thought he could use some exercise before being stuck in the carriage. He's not so bad when he is not knocking me down or drooling on me." Andrew shrugged his shoulders. "Are you ready to travel? I hope the carriage ride won't be too bumpy for your shoulder and arm."

"Yes, I am ready. I even have reading material for the trip." Emma lifted the stack of books she carried. Fergus finally noticed she was there, and he came bounding over to greet her. He jumped up and put his front paws up on her chest, giving her a lick on her face and jarring her enough so she stumbled backward, dropping all her books. Andrew came over to help her gather everything from the ground. Her heart rose into throat as she recognized Charles' letter lying on the ground.

"I hope they didn't get too wet," Emma said. "Fergus, bad dog. How many times must I say you are too big to be jumping up?"

"What's this? A letter from your uncle?"

Emma's head shot up. "Uh yes, he was concerned about me after Lucy told him what happened," Emma lied. The letter hadn't expressed concern about her health at all, only concerns about how she had botched the job.

Andrew frowned as he looked at the letter in his hand. "He wasn't supposed to contact you anymore," he muttered.

"Excuse me?" Emma snatched the letter back. "What do you mean?"

Andrew shifted his eyes left, watching the dog bound across the snow-covered lawn. He exhaled loudly, his breath a stream of white in the cold air. Then he met her gaze again.

"I met with him. I asked him to exit your life." Andrew crossed his arms in front of his chest. "He has been a poor influence."

Emma couldn't believe her ears. The audacity. "Ordered him, more likely. When exactly did you speak with him?"

"After you ran from me that night at Gilchrest House. You were so sad, so resigned. I did some digging into his past. He is not a good person. I don't think you should be corresponding with him in the future."

"He is my uncle, and he helped me and the children when we needed someone most. I cannot just cut him out of my life."

"Emma, if you want to make a fresh start, you will have to stop listening to him. Can't you see he has been using you?"

"Stop telling me what to do, you overbearing, infuriating man!"

"Don't be so obstinate. I am not telling you what to do. I am just trying to offer my advice."

"You do not get to tell me whom I can and cannot associate with, Your Grace. We return to London today, and I will be making the decisions in my life once again. I take care of what's mine. I make my own choices." Emma's voice rose higher with each statement.

"I can't keep having this same argument with you." Andrew tugged a hand through his hair. His eyes snapped with barely controlled temper. He paced away from her, his movements jerky.

Finish it, this is your opportunity. Her chest tightened in response.

"I have tried to earn your trust." He swung back to face her. "How many times are you going to push me away? To refuse my help?"

"I don't know. How many times is this time?" Emma narrowed her eyes to glare at him.

Andrew froze. His jaw clenched, and then he gave a mocking nod of his head. Turning on his heel, he strode away. Emma swallowed a large gulp of cold air. She had accomplished what she wanted. She'd made him angry enough to walk away. But she was unprepared for how much it would hurt to be the cause of the pain she had seen flash across his face. She closed her eyes and took another steadying breath. Then she called for Fergus and slowly walked back into the house.

The ride back to London was a lonely one. Andrew decided to ride back on his horse, leaving the carriage to Emma and Fergus. It was for the best, Emma kept telling herself as she tried to concentrate on the book she had brought. She must use her head, not her heart, to make decisions. This was for the best.

When she arrived home, her family greeted her with enthusiasm and cheerful chatter about all she had missed. Lucy gave her a warm hug, but then she took hold of her hands, giving Emma a stern look.

"We need to talk. There are things to say."

"I know, but not tonight. I am truly worn out from travelling. Can we speak in the morning?" Emma could not face any more recriminations today. She was still too raw from her argument with Andrew.

Lucy squeezed her hands. "Certainly. We can talk tomorrow."

After having supper together, she tucked all the children into bed with extra kisses before finally slipping between the sheets of her own bed. Exhausted from the day, she fell asleep immediately after her head hit the pillow.

The next morning, she spent time with the children, discussing their studies and listening to stories about all that happened while she had been gone. She was stalling, but she wasn't sure how much she should tell Lucy about Charles' letter. The thought of lying to Lucy was killing her, though. Lucy was not only her sister but her closest confidant. How could she bear to place a wedge of deceit between them?

Lucy waited for her in the library, patiently working on her embroidery. Emma came into the room with a tentative, “Hello.”

Lucy put her stitching away in its basket. She patted the couch next to her. “How are you feeling? How is your arm healing?”

Emma sat down and distractedly rubbed her arm. “It is doing fine. It hardly pains me at all.”

“Emma, I’ve some news. Lord Davenport has asked me to marry him, and I have accepted.” Her whole face lit up, happiness shining in her eyes.

“That’s wonderful news, Lucy! When did he ask you?”

“Two days ago, he asked if there was anyone he should get permission from before announcing our engagement. I told him no, but that I wanted to tell you first. Oh, Emma, he is wonderful.”

Emma leaned over and gave her sister a hard hug. This is exactly what she had hoped for Lucy. It confirmed that she was making the right decision to follow Charles’ orders.

Lucy pulled back but took hold of Emma’s hands. “We need to talk about Charles. I wrote you he came to see me, and he was quite angry when I said you were not in town. He grabbed me roughly by the arms. His face was red with rage. I had never seen him like that.” A small furrow appeared between her eyebrows. “He physically shook me. He demanded to know where you were. Lord Davenport was out in the garden, heard us through the door, and came in to intervene. I told Charles he was not welcome in this house any longer. I’m sorry to not have consulted you first, but I don’t regret my decision."

Emma slumped back against the cushions. Charles had actually tried to hurt Lucy? Lucy banned him from the house? Her whole world spun upside down. This was all her fault. Sitting up, she reached into her pocket to pull out the letter.

"Charles sent me this letter a week ago." She took a deep breath in and handed it to Lucy. As she waited for Lucy to read the letter, she stared out the window at the bare trees and the muddy street. The gloomy weather outside matched her mood.

"He's trying to blackmail you! And using me as well—despicable. What are you going to do? What did the duke say about the letter?"

"I didn't show him. I can't steal from him or the duchess."

"Of course, you can't. But I know His Grace would help if he knew. Why didn't you show him?"

"He did offer his support, but I pushed him away." She swallowed hard; it still upset her to think about how she had hurt him. "Don't you see? His reputation could be threatened, all because of me. It's best if I am not in his life, then Charles can't use him as leverage. I will just steal something else for Charles' auction. Everything will be fine."

"Emma, you're being a fool. Stop trying to fix everything yourself. I love you, and I wager the duke loves you as well." Emma looked down at her hands clasped together in her lap. She didn't want to talk about Andrew's feelings for her right now. Lucy grabbed hold of her hands again. "We can figure out a way to stop Charles together. Starting with this blackmail letter."

"No, don't you see he will start a scandal? He can disappear at any time. But the rumors he leaves behind will ruin us. What about your engagement? What if Lord Davenport finds out about my secret life?"

"He knows already."

"What!"

"I've already told him everything, well mostly. After I kicked Charles out, I felt it was best to explain. I don't want any secrets between us."

"And he wasn't appalled? He still wants to marry you?"

"He was shocked at first, but he loves me. He wants to take care of me. It doesn't matter to him about the past. Of course, I assured him you were retired." She arched one eyebrow. "Right?"

Eyes wide, Emma stared at her sister. Lord Davenport knew she was a thief? Knew Lucy had no dowry, and he still wanted to marry her? Was that love? Being with the person you love no matter what the challenges? As the truth dawned on her, Emma squeezed her eyes shut. "Lucy, I've made a terrible mistake."

"Go to him. Fix it," Lucy urged her.

She shook her head. "I've hurt him. He proposed, twice. But I refused."

"Tell him how you feel. He will forgive you." She gave her an encouraging smile. But Emma wasn't so sure.

Chapter 29

Andrew sat down heavily into his favorite leather chair. He set down a bottle of brandy on the round side table next to him. Then he took a long swallow from his glass. He let the burn roll pleasantly down the back of his throat and into his gut. He was finally alone.

Since he returned home, he tried to keep himself busy and his thoughts off Emma. The boys had missed him. He'd taken them to the park the past two mornings to fly kites or to sail their paper boats. He spent the afternoon reading through new bills put forth in the House of Lords which required his review. After dinner with the family last night, he sat up late reviewing estate accounts until he became so tired he could safely tumble exhausted into bed.

Unfortunately, he was out of tactics to avoid thinking about his thief. So tonight, he would spend time with an old friend. One who always helped him to escape his thoughts, at least for a little while. He poured a generous finger of brandy into his empty glass. Then another.

Caroline and his mother were attending a dinner party this evening, but Andrew had bowed out. He had no desire to accidently run into the Whittingham sisters. He'd firmly ignored Caroline's questioning looks across the table at breakfast. He did not need his little sister meddling in his romantic affairs. It wasn't anything she could help with anyway.

Emma made it clear she did not need him in her life. He'd been a fool to think just by loving someone you could make them love you back. He couldn't control her feelings any more than he could control her actions. The walls she built to protect herself proved indestructible. He took another swallow, staring miserably out through the french doors into the darkness. He'd really thought during those last few days at Stoneleigh she had begun to trust in him. Stupid.

Suddenly, she was there beyond the window. A fuzzy apparition through the leaded glass, Fergus sitting at her side. He glanced down at his brandy. He hadn't had enough yet to drink to be hallucinating. Fergus let out a loud bark, and Andrew knew he wasn't dreaming.

****

Emma stood with Fergus outside the french doors of Andrew's study. She hadn't wanted to come to the front door unannounced, so far outside of proper calling hours. Andrew sat slumped in a wingback chair. His dark hair fell across his forehead, his cravat untied, hung loosely around his neck. He looked as miserable as she felt. A bottle of spirits sat at his elbow. Oh dear, that didn't bode well for her apology. She had enough experience with her father to recognize the face of a man determined to get drunk.

She shook her head. She would not compare Andrew to her father. Andrew was a far better man. She studied him as he drank. All this time, she fought against the notion she needed anyone's help, but maybe Andrew needed her in his life just as much as she began to realize she needed him.

Should she knock? Slip inside? Fergus put an end to her indecision as he spotted Andrew through the glass. He let out a loud woof of excitement. Andrew's head snapped up, his eyes squinting as he peered through the glass. He glanced down at his glass and then back up before straightening.

"Fergus, stay." She bent down and gave him a kiss on his nose. She whispered, "Wish me luck."

Emma opened the french door and stepped inside. The warmth of the room enveloped her. Andrew stood as she entered, his posture stiff, his face schooled in a formal mask.

"What are you doing here, Emma?"

She launched into the speech she had prepared on the walk over. "I wanted to apologize…for the things I said the morning we left Stoneleigh."

"Why?"

His question threw her off guard. His expression was so cold and remote. She wanted to say she couldn't bear that she had hurt him. That she loved him despite her best efforts not to. But the words got stuck in her throat. She couldn't find the courage to voice them.

"Because…our friendship means so much to me. I wanted to explain…"

"Oh, you made it very clear you don't want my help, that you don't need anyone." He turned to pace over to the desk, his drink still in his hand.

Emma didn't know how to respond. Everything he said was true. Her heart plummeted. He wasn't even going to listen to her apology. She crossed the room and put a hand on his forearm. "Andrew, I—"

"Emma, why are you here?" He glanced down dispassionately at her hand on his arm. "If you've come to find your way back into my bed, I'm afraid, no matter how tempting, I cannot service you any longer."

Emma's temper snapped to life. Her gaze fell onto the glass of brandy he held. Damn the liquor that made men act like utter beasts. She snatched it out of his hand. "I am going to ignore your last comment because you are clearly not yourself tonight."

Then she walked over to the fireplace and flung the drink into the marble hearth. The shattering of glass was exceedingly satisfying. Equally so, the look of utter shock on Andrew's face.

"I came to apologize for what I said the other morning. I hope you can believe I never wanted to hurt you." She met his eyes, pleading for him to listen. "I was letting my fears speak for me." That much at least was the truth.

Her answer surprised him, she knew. His expression softened, but his eyes still held hurt. He ran a hand through his hair, further disheveling the raven locks.

"Emma, our relationship cannot survive without at least a modicum of trust."

"I know. I do trust you."

He let out a snort, crossing his arms in front of his chest.

She pulled Charles' letter from the pocket of her cloak. Stepping closer, she handed it to him. "I do. Please try to understand, it's hard to trust when you have never had anyone to rely on but yourself."

"What's this?" Andrew asked as he unfolded the letter.

"The other shoe dropping. You may not want to have anything to do with me after you read this letter.

But I want you to know I would never take advantage of your affection for me. It's too precious."

Andrew read the letter. "That two-faced son of a bitch! When did you receive this letter?"

"Five days ago, the day before it snowed." Emma bit her lower lip.

Andrew frowned down at the letter in his hand. "And you thought if you pushed me away, if you made me angry enough, it would protect me from being pulled into his scheme. Is that it?"

Emma nodded, keeping her eyes downcast. Now he knew the full ramifications of her secret life. Lightning quick, Andrew reached for her. His arm snaked around her waist. "You foolish girl, you could never make me angry enough to give up on us."

Her eyebrows rose in surprise at his abrupt change of mood. One side of his mouth turned up.

"Not permanently, anyway." He pulled her body flush against his, and she placed her hands against his chest.

"I'm sorry, Andrew. I didn't want your reputation to suffer because of my mistakes."

"You belong with me. It's now my job to protect you. Get that through your stubborn head." He leaned his forehead against hers. "I love you, do you at least trust in that?"

Tears filled her eyes. The sincerity of his words slid into her heart. She believed him. This amazing man loved her and wanted to protect her. Overwhelmed by emotion, all she could do was nod. Then he kissed her with such tenderness, such care. Emma poured all of her love into the kiss. Willing him to feel what she was too much of a coward to say aloud. When they broke apart, Emma captured his face with one of her hands.

"What I am about to say is really hard for me." She paused at his sharp intake of breath. Closing her eyes, she said, "Andrew, I need your help."

Andrew threw back his head and laughed. The sound eased some of the anxiety she had been carrying around with her since receiving her uncle's letter.

"Well, let's get started then." He took her hand and led her out of the room. "What we need is Jack. We need to find out what your uncle's plan is for the necklace. Who are his associates? Maybe there is something we can use against him. Did you know Jack used to be a spy?" He laughed as her jaw dropped, then gave her a swift kiss. "You see, my dear, you are not the only one who has secrets."

They found Jack and Vivian in the library sitting together on the couch. Jack reviewed a stack of documents while Vivian sketched, her feet tucked under her skirts. Jack looked up as they walked into the room. Neither of them seemed particularly surprised to find her in the house at such a late hour.

Andrew put his arm around Emma's waist and looked down at her. "Go on, each time it will get a little easier." He grinned at her obvious discomfort.

She frowned at his teasing. "This is serious, Andrew!"

"What's serious?" Jack set his correspondence down on the table.

Andrew gave Emma's waist an encouraging squeeze, and she took a deep breath. "I need your help."

Chapter 30

Emma arrived at 101 St. George Street and looked up at the unassuming brick townhome. So this was where Charles lived. The townhome and its neighbors sat in a neat row lining a cobblestone street. Emma pondered why she had never seen where Charles lived before this. He travelled often, and when he was in town, he always visited at her house. She had always assumed he rented apartments in one of the fashionable buildings which catered to bachelors. The door to Charles' home was made of elaborately carved wood with an intricate iron gate in front. Emma questioned the need for extra security as she spied a bell pull and gave it a tug.

A dour faced butler opened the door. "I am here to see Mr. Whittingham."

"Whom may I ask is calling?"

"I am Miss Emma Whittingham, his niece." Bushy eyebrows rose high, then the butler quickly showed her into a small front parlor.

"Please wait here," he intoned.

The well-appointed room featured heavy and ornate furnishings and plush carpet. She turned slowly in a circle, taking in the beautiful artwork, vases, and trinkets set around the room. A room clearly meant to showcase the wealth of its owner. Emma's temper rose. Her house was practically bare as she had slowly sold off anything of value to provide for her family. She sucked in a calming breath. Perhaps it was just this one room that he richly decorated to impress guests. She crossed to the door, determined to look around.

Emma's jaw clenched tighter and tighter as she headed down the corridor with its silk-covered walls and paintings hung every few feet. She opened the first door on the left and found a maid cleaning the fireplace in a beautiful library. The walls were lined with books; deep comfortable couches covered in a dark burgundy velvet dominated the room. She closed the door and moved across the hallway to the next door. This room was a dining room. A large polished wood table gleamed, and a regal sideboard held silver trays and china stacked neatly behind its glass front doors. *Unbelievable!*

Next, she climbed the staircase to the first floor, where she found another row of doors. Down the hallway, in the space between each door, stood heavy wood pedestals about waist high. Each held a graceful marble sculpture. As Emma fumed at the extravagance of Charles' home, the man himself came out of a room a couple doors down. Charles stopped short when he saw her standing in his hallway.

"My dear, I was not expecting you today. I thought you would contact me by letter when you arrived back from the country."

"I needed to see you in person, to discuss your plan. I grew tired of waiting downstairs." Emma crossed her arms in front of her chest.

"Come into my study then. We may have some privacy in here." Charles ushered her into a bright sunny room. The walls were covered in green silk, and more bookshelves lined one side of the room, behind a lovely oak desk. By the fireplace sat two comfortable leather chairs to which Charles motioned her over.

"Uncle, I must speak plainly. I cannot be a part of what you suggested in your letter. I cannot steal from those I love."

"Love? Aren't you being a bit dramatic? You may have become involved with the duke, but the most you could mean to him is a quick affair, perhaps a few months as his mistress."

Emma gasped at the insult. Her uncle raised his hands up in defense.

"Now, I am not judging. Good for you for taking advantage of his attraction for you. We must all grab at good opportunities when they arise. But, my dear, it will end, and then what? Let us use the connection to our advantage while we can." He leaned back in his chair, his elbows resting on the arms of the chair, his fingers intertwined.

Emma needed a minute to compose herself. *Remember the plan.*

"It's not like that at all. The duke and his family are friends of ours. They sponsored Lucy during her season, and they have extended to us their friendship. I cannot steal from them." She shook her head for emphasis. Then looking up, she purposely let all her anger show through. "Why don't you just take the necklace yourself? They keep all the heirloom pieces in a safe in the library, underneath the table which holds the family Bible." She stood up to leave.

"No. Why should I put myself in a position to be compromised when you are in the perfect situation to acquire the necklace?" He grabbed her arm and roughly shoved her back into the chair. "You want to keep hold of your lover? Do not doubt I will leak the information about who is the real thief. Don't think I care a wit for the family name. What will poor Lucy's chances be then with her earl?"

"But I have told you where the necklace is…I can't be involved!" Emma looked down at her hands.

"Listen, we will make you the victim," he offered. His tone softened. "No one has to guess you are involved. All you have to do is convince your lover to lend you the necklace for an evening out at the opera. That shouldn't be so difficult. Men of his station love to shower their mistresses with expensive baubles. Let him know the necklace has caught your eye. Then I will rob you en route to the opera. You hand over the necklace. When you arrive at the opera, act the victim." He settled back in the chair, pleased with his plan.

Emma counted to twenty slowly in her head. She looked up at her uncle with a look of resignation. "All right, Uncle, I will do this, for my family. Unlike you, I do care about preserving our family name. Max and William will inherit at least that, even if I can't give them any sort of fortune to go along with the title. I can see now you don't care for all of us like I thought you did." She let tears swim in her eyes. It wasn't hard to bring them forth; her uncle's words sliced to ribbons everything she believed about their relationship.

"That's not true." Charles looked genuinely hurt. "Didn't I stay and help you when Henry died? Haven't I looked out for you, brought by presents? But life is hard, Emma, and sentimentality will only hold you back."

"I know only too well life is hard, Uncle. That's

why I will try to shield the rest of them from this truth. Know that this will be the last time I will work for you. Our relationship is at an end." She stood up, not needing to fake her shaking hands. Her plan depended on her uncle believing she felt all alone and out of options.

Charles' expression hardened. "We shall see about that. I will send you a note about where our rendezvous point will be. Friday evening is the next performance. And Sunday evening is the auction. You will see, the necklace will garner us a hefty sum."

Charles showed Emma downstairs to the front door. He reached out and kissed her hand before letting her go. "Until Friday, my dear."

When Emma stepped outside, she took a deep breath of cold air. She couldn't believe how stupid she had been to blindly believe Charles had her best interests at heart. Learning the truth of his manipulations should hurt more. But although his betrayal of her trust made her angry, it did not touch her heart the way such betrayals had in the past.

Her heart was too full of hope to waste time on bitterness. Because of Andrew she'd discovered what it was like to be truly loved. What it felt like to have someone put her first, to support her no matter what. By week's end she would close this chapter of her life. She walked briskly down the street toward her future.

****

By Thursday evening, Emma could not bear being apart from Andrew any longer. They hadn't had a chance to be alone at all since coming back from the country. Tuesday afternoon they had taken the children out for a picnic in Hyde Park. Being in public and surrounded by six children had not allowed them even the slightest touch or briefest kiss. Her stomach was in knots about tomorrow evening. Emma ached to have his arms, strong and reassuring, around her. Throwing back the covers, she got out of bed and quickly changed into her men's clothing.

Once at Gilchrest House, Emma climbed the wisteria vines that led to his balcony. She slid silently into his room. Turning, she closed the glass-paneled door and reached up to slide the velvet curtains closed. She jumped like a startled cat when Andrew spoke.

"I wondered when you would finally come see me." His deep voice was husky. The scratch of a match came from over by the bed. The candelabra on the bedside table came to life. Andrew sat on the edge of the bed naked, except for the sheet across his lap. He opened his arms to her, and Emma rushed over to fling herself against his broad chest. He kissed her, nipping at her bottom lip. All her worries flew out of her head as she sank against him, drinking in his spicy scent.

Andrew's hands began undoing the buttons along the front of her shirt. After the first three buttons, he became impatient, and with a rip he tore the shirt open. Her buttons hit the floor in a series of soft pings. She broke their kiss to laugh out loud. Andrew didn't look the least bit sheepish. His long fingers moved to cup her breasts. Emma let out a small sound of pleasure as his tongue flicked against one of her nipples, sending a flash of heat directly to her core. She threaded her fingers in his hair as he nipped at and sucked her sensitive flesh. Before she knew it, her pants were down around her ankles, and Andrew flipped her onto the bed.

Again, she let a delighted bubble of laughter release from deep in her belly. This was what she needed, to lose herself in the passion between them. He yanked the pants all the way off and moved over her like a predatory lion. She spread her legs to accommodate him, and in one swift move he was inside her to the hilt. She threw her head back and lifted her hips to celebrate the feel of him filling her, hot and hard. Their coupling was wild and furious, each of them frantic to thrust, to touch, to become one with each other. Andrew wrapped one arm under her shoulder, lifting and exposing her neck to his hungry mouth while he pumped his hips in and out, pushing her to the razor's edge of pleasure. Then he bit her neck, and Emma fell off the edge into a bright burst of sensations, her mind blank except for the feel and the heat of the man in her arms. She held on tight until the tremors of pleasure subsided.

"Am I crushing you?" Andrew mumbled against her throat. He made a move to push himself up, but Emma tightened her hold, banding her arms around him.

"No, don't move just yet. I like the weight of you." She wrapped one leg around his thigh and gave a squeeze of her intimate muscles, eliciting a groan of pleasure from Andrew.

"You minx." He nibbled again at her throat. Then he did push up, and grabbing her around the waist, he rolled them so she lay on top of him, her head pillowed on his chest. She listened to his heartbeat as it slowed to its normal steady rhythm.

"Tell me more about what happened when you saw your uncle. You didn't have a chance to tell me any details."

Emma propped her chin on one forearm. "His house looks modest from the outside, but inside it rivals the home of any peer of the realm. It was richly furnished, with artwork and sculpture placed around the rooms and down the hallways. The dining room curio held fine china and silver. I became incensed walking around his home. No wonder Charles always visited us. He needed to keep his wealth a secret. He didn't want me asking questions as to my cut of the proceeds. He didn't even make any excuses. He just sat there in his luxurious townhome and lectured me on how hard life was." She pressed her lips together in a frown.

Emma sighed and told Andrew the worst of it. "He said someone like you could only be interested in me as sport for the short term, a mistress at best. He said I should be thinking of what I will do after you tire of me."

Andrew leaned up cupping her face gently. "You know that is all untrue, don't you? Pure manipulation."

Emma let her expression soften. Some of the anger drained from her at his sweet assurance. "Yes, I believe you." She turned her head and placed a kiss in his palm. "There was a time, not too long past, I thought all those things and worse. But I meant what I said. I trust in your love. He thinks I am all alone, but I know I am not."

Andrew leaned in, pressing his lips against hers in a quick kiss. "I have something to show you." He rolled her to the side, and sliding out of bed, he crossed the room.

He opened a drawer in the bureau and returned with a large flat velvet box. Emma sat up, curious.

Andrew opened the box and pulled out the ruby and diamond necklace. He held it up. And she watched it sparkle as it reflected the firelight.

"Come over here." Andrew held out one hand. He led her over to stand in front of a tall free-standing mirror next to the washstand.

He turned her so she was facing the mirror, and then from behind, Andrew placed the necklace around her throat. The rubies felt inexplicably warm against her skin. It was incredibly erotic to see herself naked in the mirror, the necklace glowing like fire in the candlelight against her pale skin. Andrew's strong hands rested on her shoulders. This was far better than her original fantasy of trying on the necklace.

"So, thief, can you tell if this is real?" Andrew questioned.

"It's not the real one?" Emma's hand flew to her throat. She stepped closer to the mirror, running her fingers along the stones and peering at the necklace more closely.

Andrew chuckled. "Just teasing, this is the real one. I'm hoping the copy will be finished by tomorrow morning. I was assured by the jeweler it could be done." Andrew snaked a hand around her waist and pulled her back against him. He ran a finger across the rubies and then trailed his finger sensually down around the curve of her breast. "I would never give you anything counterfeit to wear around this lovely neck." He bent to place a kiss in the hollow between her neck and shoulder, giving it a slow suck. Emma closed her eyes, leaning her head back against his chest.

"No, love. Open your eyes. Look in the mirror while I worship your beautiful body." He cupped both breasts with his hands. "These beautiful breasts keep me up at night when I'm alone. I yearn to taste them, to feel the delicious weight of them in my hands." He brushed his thumbs across her nipples, making them stand erect. Emma moaned out his name. "And the smooth expanse of your soft skin, heated and flushed with wanting, drives me crazy." His hands slowly slid down her stomach and across to her hips, pulling her bottom tight up against his already-hard cock. "Can you feel how much I desire you, love?"

Emma's eyes were wide as she looked at his face in the mirror. She saw the desire smoldering in his eyes. She wanted to turn and kiss him, but he held her firmly in place.

"Now, darling, watch while I make you come. Look and see the fire in your eyes that I see every time you fall apart in my arms. It is breathtaking." His hand slipped lower, his fingers sliding into the curls of her mons. He found that wonderful spot, that nub of pleasure, and began to rub and to tease. Then he came around in front of her. He slowly knelt, replacing his fingers with his tongue on her sensitive flesh. She gripped his shoulders as he devoured her, his fingers sliding in and out of her slick core. She cried out his name as she came and saw reflected in the mirror her flushed cheeks, her eyes half closed in the ecstasy of the moment. She looked beautiful. Andrew made her feel that way. He looked up at her with a wide grin, and getting up, he slowly backed her toward the bed. His intent was clear in those sultry blue eyes.

"Oh no, now it's my turn to drive you slowly mad." She shimmied out of his grasp. Changing positions, she backed him up against the side of the bed.

"Hmm…where shall I start? Hands at your sides, sir." Emma ordered him. She was gratified when he complied immediately. She began at her favorite spot. Leaning up, she nibbled at his earlobe. He smelled so good there, and she knew he loved her hot breath on his ear.

"You are at my mercy." She kissed him slowly down his throat, nipping gently along the way. His Adam's apple bobbed up and down at each bite. She scraped her nails down the front of his chest, down his tight abdomen, stopping just below his navel. His sharp intake of breath told her his control was slipping. She gazed up at his heavy-lidded eyes staring down at her. His fingers were clenched into fists at his sides. How far could she play before he snapped?

"I wonder if your nipples are as sensitive as mine." She licked one hard flat nipple, never taking her eyes off his face. His eyes closed, and he groaned. "Very interesting." She moved over to the next one. Her hand had a mind of its own, and it wandered down to run one finger along the hard length of his cock. The skin was so soft. What would it taste like?

****

Andrew thought he would lose his mind when Emma got onto her knees in front of him. Her tongue flicked out and licked him right on the head of his cock. She looked up at him as if to gauge his reaction. "Don't stop, love. Explore all you want."

Then Emma took his length into her mouth, and he threw back his head, the pleasure of feeling her hot wet mouth around him pushing him past reasonable thought. At first, she was hesitant, but the moans he could not hold back seemed to embolden her. She put a hand around the base of his cock, and her sucking started in earnest. His balls tightening, he grabbed her hair, pulling her gently away from him. “Darling, I am about to explode. Please, have mercy.”

At his labored words, Emma stood up and gave him a push on his chest, forcing him onto his back. Then she climbed on top of him, taking him inside her in one fluid movement. With a toss of her hair, she began to ride him. The ruby necklace gleamed against her soft skin, but her eyes shone brighter than any jewels as she met his gaze. Her hips rolled up and down, and she arched her back with her breasts thrust out. She cried out his name as she wrung every ounce of her pleasure from his body. She was breathtaking. His orgasm rushed up from the base of his spine. He sat up, grabbing her around the waist, and he took her mouth prisoner as he spilled his seed into her, his cock pulsing again and again.

Later, Andrew ran his fingers slowly up and down the length of Emma’s back as she lay on him. He had never known a more uninhibited or generous lover than she. The hard edges of the precious stones from the necklace dug into his chest, reminding him what a vulnerable position she was in. He reached up to undo the clasp, then gently pulled the necklace from in between them. Kissing her brow, he made a silent promise to keep her safe, not just tomorrow evening but for the rest of her life.

Chapter 31

Friday morning, Emma received two deliveries. One was from the jeweler. She and Lucy ooh'd and aah'd over the counterfeit necklace Andrew had commissioned. It was just as beautiful as the real one.

"I am amazed. How do they make it so real?" Lucy asked, running a finger across the stones.

"The stones are made from a leaded glass and then polished and cut to shine like a real diamond. There is red foil applied to the back to give the stones the right color to pass as rubies. It's only if you look closely you can tell there is no depth to the color of the stone. It is just reflecting the foil. You would be surprised how many women of the ton wear paste or glass jewelry," Emma replied.

"Will it fool Uncle Charles?"

"Well, it will be dark, so it should be hard for him to tell the difference until he gets it home and under proper light. Once he figures out it is a fake, it will throw him into a panic about the auction. He will either have to try to sell the fake, and most likely get caught doing so by some very bad people. Or he will have to come after the real one at Gilchrest House. That's what we are betting on."

"What if he comes here after you?" Lucy's eyes were wide with apprehension. "I remember all too clearly the angry way Charles shook me when he lost his temper that day."

"The duke has insisted we all stay at Gilchrest House tonight. And for once I am inclined to go along with his idea, even if it will cause gossip. Mrs. Fenway will walk the children over after we leave in the carriage, just in case Charles is watching the house."

Lucy's eyes widened at the thought Charles could be watching them.

Emma gave her sister a reassuring hug. "I'm sorry. I'm the cause for this mess. But I promise I am trying to fix my mistakes."

"Emma, everyone deserves a second chance. You were led down the wrong path by Charles. He took advantage of you when you were most vulnerable after Father's death. It will be all right. We're here to help."

Emma's eyes filled with tears at the forgiveness which Lucy gave out so freely. Lucy had grown into a wise young woman over the past four years, and Emma had only just noticed. She gave her sister another hug.

"Now, what could be in this second package? The box is enormous." Lucy said.

They opened the lid, and Emma gasped in delight as she lifted out a beautiful cream silk evening gown. She held it up by the shoulders. The top of the bodice was trimmed in red ribbon, and it had a velvet overskirt richly embroidered with red roses.

"How exquisite!" Lucy exclaimed. Emma folded the dress back into the box. She picked up a card tucked inside.

I think this will go lovely with the necklace.

Love, Andrew

"It's from His Grace. He thinks of everything."

Later that evening, Emma put on the gorgeous

dress. It fit perfectly. How he managed it she didn't know. Red ribbons crisscrossed the bodice and tied in a bow, making her feel like a present waiting to be unwrapped. Emma's face heated at the thought. She wondered if that was why Andrew chose the dress. She slipped on a pair of ruby-colored slippers and finally the necklace. It lay against her collarbone, a glittery reminder of the purpose for the evening. Squaring her shoulders, she went in search of her sister.

****

The Duchess of Gilchrest met with her eldest son after dinner in her private sitting room. He was dressed for the opera in a midnight blue jacket and pants. A sapphire cravat pin winked against its snowy white background. There was a nervous edge to his posture tonight, and she wondered what he had come to see her about.

"Thank you, Mother, for agreeing to have the Whittingham family stay with us. Their guardian has become very hostile and increasingly erratic of late. I am concerned about them living in the house alone with so little protection."

"My dear, you hardly have to ask me for permission. This is your household. But I do appreciate that you are so considerate of my feelings. Why don't you marry the girl already, and then she and her family would be under your protection."

She studied her son, her first born, so tall and handsome standing in front of her, his hands clasped behind his back just like when he was a boy. She wondered why he wasn't seizing at happiness with this girl. It was obvious he loved her. "I know your first marriage wasn't a happy one, but that is no reason not to try again, especially now you are free to marry for love."

Andrew let out a short laugh and looked up at the ceiling. "It's not that I am afraid, Mother. I swear. I have asked her to marry me twice! And she has turned me down twice."

"What! That's preposterous."

"I think she loves me. I believe she has started to put her trust in me. I am helping her with this situation with her uncle, and then maybe she will finally feel free to accept my offer."

"Well, if she doesn't, you just let me have a talk with her. I will straighten her out." She huffed indignantly. The girl was a fool!

"Thank you, Mother, for being such a fierce protector. Not everyone is as lucky as I. I love you." He bent down and gave her a kiss on the cheek.

"I love you too." She patted his cheek. "Now go on and have fun at the opera tonight. I will organize where to put all the children when they arrive."

"Oh, and one more thing. Fergus will be arriving with the children."

"Fergus?"

"Miss Whittingham's Irish wolfhound."

"Her what?" She put a hand to her heart. Did he just say wolfhound?

"Wherever Emma goes so does Fergus." He shrugged his shoulders. "Just wanted to give you fair warning."

****

Emma sat with Lucy in the hired hack. She gripped the edge of her seat and watched the street corners roll by. Charles' note had arrived that afternoon. It instructed Emma to rent a hack and said he would intercept it at some point en route to the opera to take possession of the necklace. Lucy insisted on coming with her; she refused to let Emma face Charles alone.

Both ladies had to grip the seat edges as the carriage came to a sudden halt. Loud male voices could be heard shouting. Then a great thump came from above where the driver sat. A moment later, the door swung open, and Charles stepped to the top step, dressed all in black.

"Good evening." His smile turned to a frown. "I did not expect to see you, Lucy."

Lucy didn't reply. She reached out and took Emma's hand in hers.

"What did you do to our driver, Uncle? We heard a commotion from the box," Emma asked.

"He was quite angry when I ran out in front of his carriage. I tried to bribe him to turn a deaf ear, but he became quite adamant about not letting me get near his passengers. An unusually protective man, it seems. I was forced to knock him out." Charles gave his heavy walking stick a small jiggle. "Let's make this quick before anyone comes walking by. Hand over the necklace."

Emma reached up and unclasped the necklace with shaking hands. She hoped Charles wouldn't examine the necklace too closely. Handing it over to him, she held her breath. She needn't have worried. Charles stuffed the necklace into his coat pocket without even giving it a second glance. He tilted his head, considering her. Then like a snake striking, he dealt her a backhanded blow. Pain exploded in her cheek as her head snapped back. She could taste blood from her lip where his ring had made contact. Lucy cried out and scooted back into the far corner.

"That is for all the trouble you have caused me." Then reaching out, he took hold of the sleeve of her dress and yanked, ripping the material. "We must make it look like a real robbery. Now run along to your duke. I'm sure he will be appalled at the crime in the city, tut, tut."

"How are we supposed to get there now that you have knocked out our driver?" Emma spat out. It took all her self-control not to launch herself at him in a fit of fury.

"Walk, of course, the opera house is only about a half a mile south of here." He pointed his cane to the right. He stepped down and disappeared into the night.

"Oh my God, Emma, how badly did he hurt you?" Lucy slid next to her and, taking her chin, gently tilted her head to look at her cheek.

"I'll be all right," Emma said, brushing her sister's hand away. She tore off her glove and gently probed the corner of her mouth. Emma was incensed she had let Charles hurt her again. Her sister handed her a handkerchief. At least he hadn't tried to hurt Lucy. She would make sure he was locked up if it was the last thing she did. "Let's get walking. It will likely take us at least twenty minutes, and Andrew will be worried that we are late."

****

Andrew was indeed worried. He waited restlessly inside their box at the opera house. They should have arrived by now, unless something had gone wrong. Andrew tapped Jack on the shoulder and nodded to the exit. Jack returned his nod and settled back to watch the performance with Vivian and Caroline on either side of him. Andrew quickly made his way outside to the front of the theatre and was pacing up and down when he saw Emma and Lucy turn the corner.

He hurried toward them. "Why are you on foot? Where is your carriage?" He wrapped an arm around each lady and escorted them back to the front of the opera house. "Where are your wraps?"

Emma and Lucy exchanged a look of surprise, as though they hadn't even noticed they weren't wearing their wraps.

"I guess we left them in the carriage. Andrew, I can't go inside like this. Please take me home." Emma's voice wavered.

It was then, in the brighter light spilling from the theatre's entrance, Andrew took in Emma's torn dress and her face. Dear God, her lip was cut and swollen. He reached out tenderly with two fingers to grasp her chin and get a better look. Even in the dim light, he could see a bruise forming on her cheek. Fury rose in his throat, and he choked out, "Oh, love, what did he do?"

Emma just shook her head, her eyes shone with unshed tears, then she buried herself against his chest. Andrew looked over her head and saw Davenport was bounding down the stairs toward them. Ethan immediately grasped something had gone badly with the plan.

Turning to Lucy, he asked, "Are you all right? Did he hurt you?"

Lucy shook her head. "No, he wasn't happy to see me there, but he only hurt Emma." She hiccupped. She looked as if she were struggling not to cry. "He said he needed to make the robbery look believable. He knocked out our driver."

He and Davenport exchanged a look of mutual disgust. Andrew asked, "Can you call for my carriage to be brought around? And have a note sent up to my brother telling him we had to take the ladies home."

Ethan looked at Emma curled up in his embrace and then over at Lucy, who gave him a wobbly half smile. "I'll be right back," he said.

When the four of them arrived back at Gilchrest house, his mother was just coming down the main staircase. She took in their grim faces and Emma's swollen lip in one sweeping glance.

"What happened?" She rushed over to Emma and examined her face. Emma tried to look away, embarrassed, but his mother had none of that. Her eyes rose to his. They flashed with anger. "Is this because of the uncle?"

"Yes," Andrew replied. Emma's head snapped up. He met her gaze. "I told my mother that your guardian had become erratic and angry of late. That's why I am having you all stay with me." He leaned down to say quietly in her ear, "You should get used to it, people taking care of you, I mean."

"Let me show you to your rooms, and we will clean up that cut." His mother took Emma's hand and motioned for Lucy to follow her up the stairs. Emma's fingers slid from his. It was difficult to let her go. He wanted to be the one to tend to her hurts.

He reined in his impulse to grab her back from his mother.

Andrew turned to Davenport. "Let's have a drink, shall we?"

Chapter 32

"This is a fake." Mr. Dorling lowered his magnifying glasses to the counter.

"What! Impossible!" Charles Whittingham snatched up the necklace to look it over carefully.

"It's paste, quite well done, but paste nevertheless."

"I can't believe it." Charles shook his head.

"Many women of the ton have paste jewelry made. It is quite real to the untrained eye." Mr. Dorling sneered.

"I know a fake when I see one." Charles glared at the man. Dorling raised one eyebrow mockingly. "I didn't look closely at it last night. I trusted my thief. I have never had any reason to doubt he would deliver."

"Perhaps he thought this was real?"

Charles frowned. Had Emma betrayed him? Did she have the audacity to try and trick him when there was so much for her to lose? And where would she get a counterfeit made in such short notice? He knew he had been tough on her recently, but she needed to know who was in charge of their agreement. She needed him, and they both knew it. She must not have realized it was a counterfeit. Her duke obviously didn't trust her with the real one.

"Listen, Whittingham, I have buyers coming tomorrow evening who are expecting to bid on a ruby necklace. You have disappointed me terribly, and you know I do not like to be disappointed." Dorling snapped his fingers. Two men appeared from the back room. Their burly physiques seem to fill the room. They stood to either side of the door, waiting for instructions from their boss.

Charles swallowed, then cleared his throat. "Dorling, you know I would never want to jeopardize our working relationship. I can get the real necklace tonight. I know where the lockbox is in the ducal mansion. I will go in myself and see it done."

Dorling nodded. "Bring me the necklace by morning, or you will be receiving a very unpleasant visit from my friends." He gestured toward the thugs. "Remember, I know all your hidey holes, so don't try and disappear on me."

Charles slipped back into his bravado as easily as an eel sliding into the river. No one knew all of his hiding places. "Don't you worry, I will procure the necklace and save the auction. You can be certain of that." He tipped his cane against the brim of his hat. He turned to walk out the front only to be faced with a wall of muscle. He turned back to Dorling, one eyebrow raised. Dorling gave a nod, and the pair parted to allow Charles to exit the shop into the freedom of the freezing cold afternoon.

He walked briskly down the street, putting as much distance between him and the shop as possible. He laughed a bit at the idea that Dorling thought he knew all the places Charles kept throughout the city. He could disappear anytime he wanted. But for now, what he wanted was the proceeds the necklace would bring at the auction. He wanted that money. He would deal with

Emma later.

He had thought to grab her last night from the carriage. Take her and the necklace on the run. They would be a brilliant pair on the Continent. Emma had so much potential. But that simpering chit Lucy had been with her; she would have raised the alarm for sure. He had a lot of planning to do if he was going to break into the ducal mansion tonight. He would have a visit with his niece after the auction and have a nice chat about the difference between real and counterfeit stones.

****

Saturday turned into a bit of a blur for Emma. The boys, ecstatic to have the opportunity to play with their friends, were happily being entertained in the nursery. The girls were in love with the splendor of the house, and in no small part with Andrew and his brother. At breakfast, Margie and Abby sighed dramatically when Andrew rose to kiss Emma's hand before he escorted her to her seat. The girls kept staring at both men over their eggs and toast. When Jack gave them a saucy wink across the table, they had burst into giggles, trying to hide their laughter behind their napkins. Emma sighed. She really needed to be stricter about which reading material the girls were allowed.

Anxious feelings gnawed at her stomach all day about what Charles' next move would be once he figured out the necklace was paste. She sat in the library with a book, pretending to read, but really, she agonized over the inevitable confrontation with Charles. Fergus, sensing her mood, had stayed glued to her side all day.

Around four in the afternoon, Lucy and the children barreled into the room and asked her to read them a story. She was reading *Robinson Crusoe* aloud, the children all sitting in a semicircle in front of her on the rug, when Andrew entered the library.

“Excuse me, may I borrow Miss Whittingham for a few minutes?” Andrew asked the children.

“But, Father, this is the most exciting part!” Grayson complained.

“Perhaps Lucy won’t mind continuing in my stead?” Emma suggested.

“Of course not.” Lucy took the book from Emma.

“Can you do good pirate voices, Miss Lucy?”

“I can,” said a voice from the doorway. Vivian swept into the room. She took Emma’s spot on the sofa next to Lucy. Tyler immediately climbed up into her lap.

“She knows what pirates sound like ’cause her father is a pirate.” He looked up at Vivian adoringly while the other children all gasped in delight. Their afternoon had just gotten far more interesting.

Andrew took Emma’s hand and guided her from the room. “Jack has some information to share with us. He is in my study.”

Jack stood as Emma entered the room. “Emma, I’m glad Andrew found you. Have a seat. Let me tell you what my source told me this afternoon.”

He sat down in one of the wingback chairs, and Emma and Andrew settled themselves on the sofa. The fire roared, but it couldn’t warm the chill Emma had felt all day.

Jack continued, “I think we have pinpointed the fence your uncle works with, a man named Dorling. He owns a watch shop as his front. He has been in the business for twenty-odd years. You said your uncle had been using him for a long time, right?"

"Yes, but how can you be sure? How did you find out who this Dorling is? My uncle refused to tell me anything about his fence. He said it was safer for me that way."

"I have several friends within the Home Office who work intimately with the underbelly of crime in London. Believe it or not, among thieves, your uncle is fairly well known for his exploits, although most think he is dead. He had several alternate identities he used when he was thieving, and apparently this Dorling was well known as being his fence. In addition, my source found out the auction is set up for Sunday at eight in the evening. But the location is a secret. It will only be revealed to the buyers the morning of."

"Why an auction?" Andrew asked.

"To garner the best price, having people in the same room bidding on the necklace makes it competitive. He will get a quicker return than if he takes the necklace apart and sells the rubies separately."

"So do you think Charles will show up tonight?" Andrew asked.

"I think unless they have already killed him for bringing in a counterfeit, he will have to show up and try to steal the real thing," Jack replied.

"He will have talked his way out of being killed. He has a silver tongue," Emma said. She knew in her gut he would be coming for the necklace tonight. She thought of all the things that silver tongue could say to get himself out of trouble. Her shoulders sagged. This was never going to work. She was sure to be exposed as his accomplice.

"All right, tonight we hope to catch Whittingham

red-handed as he tries to break into the lockbox. You made sure he knew the location, right?" Jack turned to Emma, and she nodded. "I've the name of a trusted constable we will call in to come and arrest him. This Constable Woolsey has been working on burglary cases his whole career."

Emma twisted her hands together in her lap. *Remember to trust. Andrew and Jack want to help.* She voiced her concern. "What if Charles tells them all about the jobs I have done? Once he is caught, I am sure he will try to blame it all on me." Too afraid to meet Andrew's eye, she focused on the pattern on her skirt.

"And what do you think the magistrate will believe? That Miss Emma Whittingham, a viscount's daughter, is really a thief? That she climbs through windows at night to relieve the rich of their baubles? More likely they will think he is a raving madman who will spin any wild tale to get out of going to prison. Your uncle's own precautions make it very difficult for him to pin anything on you. The fence, any informants, none have ever met you, correct?" Andrew tipped Emma's chin back up. She nodded. Then he gave her a quick kiss. "Don't worry, you are under my protection now."

That amazing warmth of being protected stayed with Emma and eradicated her nervousness over the inevitable confrontation with Charles. Much later, after they had tucked the children into bed, Emma and Andrew sat on the floor of the dark library. They leaned against the back of the sofa and waited for the thief to arrive. Andrew had initially ordered her to wait in the next room with Jack and Constable Woolsey, but

Emma was having none of his high-handedness tonight. Charles was her problem. She would have to deal with him personally.

She glanced over at Andrew. He looked quite stiff and proper in his snowy white cravat, dinner jacket, and polished shoes. He sat cross-legged with his back ramrod straight, on alert for any sounds indicating Charles had arrived. Emma, on the other hand, had changed from the gown she'd worn to dinner into a simple cotton house dress of dark blue. She had a knobby wool shawl around her shoulders to ward off the chill in the empty room. She would have preferred to be wearing her pants for a night of sitting on the floor but could not be seen by the constable in such a get-up. She must play the perfect lady tonight.

"You are dressed rather formally for a night of waiting on the floor, my lord," she teased him.

"This is what I wore to dinner. Should I have changed again in order to catch a thief?" Andrew looked affronted.

Emma giggled at his expression. "I'm sorry. You look every inch the Duke of Gilchrest, as usual. I guess I prefer the man underneath, that's all." Scooting closer, she reached out and untied his cravat, exposing the tanned hollow of his neck. Then she leaned forward and placed a kiss right in that spot. His spicy scent ignited a fire in her blood. She ran her hands under his jacket, enjoying his sharp intake of breath. Emma slipped the jacket off his shoulders and helped him out of it. Setting the jacket and cravat aside, she sat back on her haunches to assess him.

"Hmm, one more thing. I think." Unbuttoning the cuffs of his shirt, she rolled each up, revealing his strong forearms. "Yes, much better. Now you look like you're ready to catch a thief." Emma grinned.

****

"I believe the last time I caught a thief in my house, I was wearing considerably less." Andrew reached out to pull her into his lap. He nuzzled her neck and kissed the spot right behind her ear which always made her sigh.

"Andrew, we shouldn't get distracted," Emma murmured as she ran a hand through his hair.

"You started it, minx." Andrew kissed his way over to her mouth, silencing her protest. This woman was a revelation. Her humor, her sensuality. Life would never be boring with Emma in his arms. He pulled back slightly and almost proposed marriage yet again. But he held the words back. There was still a small part of him that wasn't sure she was ready to say yes, and his heart could not suffer another no. Besides, sitting on the floor of the darkened library hardly seemed advantageous to a decent proposal of marriage.

He saw Emma's eyes widen. He stopped thinking and started listening. Sure enough, there was a clicking sound from the french doors which led out to the garden. The sound of the lock turning, and then a cold breeze rippled across the room, sending goose bumps along his bare forearms. Light footsteps tapped across the wood floor. The lockbox sat tucked underneath a table across the room from where they were hiding. Andrew and Emma exchanged a silent look.

They had decided they would wait for Charles to have the box open before coming out to confront him. Andrew leaned around the end of the sofa. Whittingham was still working the locks. His lockbox had three key locks, one visible and two hidden behind secret doors. Whittingham had none of the keys. He sat back grinning, satisfied that breaking into his box was most impossible. They could hear soft curses uttered and then the snick of a lock opening. A few moments later, a rasp of metal sliding over metal and then a third rattle as the last lock opened.

"I can't believe it took him so little effort to break in," Andrew muttered under his breath, peering around the edge of the sofa again. The rustling of Emma's skirts caught his attention. He cursed as she stood up suddenly.

"Found what you are looking for, Uncle?"

Andrew stood in time to see Whittingham whirl around in surprise. The man's eyes narrowed as he spotted Emma. Andrew instinctively stepped partially in front of her.

Whittingham slipped the necklace into his jacket pocket. "I didn't want to believe you would betray me. But now I see you have set a trap. You." Charles pointed at Andrew. "You have ruined her, filled her head with promises I know you won't keep. She belongs with me!"

"So you may continue to put her in danger, to use her for your own gain?" Andrew snorted as he moved out from behind the couch. He stalked slowly toward Charles.

"Uncle, it's over. You're caught." Emma's voice rang out.

Charles whipped out a small pistol from his jacket pocket. "It's a good thing I think everything could be a trap." Cocking the trigger, he pointed it at Andrew's chest.

Andrew froze in place. He looked back at Emma and motioned with one hand for her to get down.

"Uncle, no! Put the gun down! I beg you," Emma cried out.

At that, the connecting door burst open. Jack and Woolsey burst into the room. They stopped in their tracks as they spotted the pistol pointed at him. Andrew knew they were too far away to stop Whittingham before he could get a shot off. He locked eyes with his brother. Andrew motioned with his head in Emma's direction, trying to indicate to Jack to protect her. Understanding, Jack took a step toward Emma. Before he could get to her, she stepped out from behind the sofa and began walking toward her uncle.

Andrew reached for her as she passed by him. "Emma, no!"

But she shook his hand off and continued toward Whittingham.

"Charles, don't add murder to your list of crimes tonight. Let's leave together. That's what you want, isn't it?"

He recoiled in horror as she smiled and extended her hand to her uncle. Whittingham's attention transferred to her, although he still had the pistol trained on Andrew.

Jack's footsteps advanced slowly from his left. He knew his brother would do anything to prevent Whittingham from shooting him, including jumping in front of him like some damned hero.

"Don't come any nearer, or I will shoot him!" Charles cried when he noticed Jack's approach. Andrew noted Whittingham's hand with the gun remained steady despite his outburst. He had no doubt that her uncle wouldn't hesitate to fire the gun.

Andrew raised his hand up in a command for his brother to freeze. Jack held up both hands and nodded.

"Charles," Emma soothed. "We can leave now, and after the auction tomorrow we will have the means to travel wherever you want. There are plenty of rich nobs in Paris or Brussels."

"You would come with me?" Whittingham eyed her skeptically. "I though you cared too much about preserving the family name."

"Let Lucy and her earl take care of the children. I am so weary of trying to be good all the time." Emma reached out and touched Whittingham's cheek lightly with her fingers. "We could have so much fun together."

The words made Andrew's stomach turn.

Whittingham snaked a hand around her waist, turning her so her back was tucked tightly against him. Emma's gaze collided with Andrew's. Her eyes were wide with apprehension. But she continued with her act.

"Come on, Uncle, we have an auction to prepare for. Think how lovely this necklace will look showcased around my neck. The buyers will be scrambling to pay top price."

"Well, it looks like I am getting everything I want tonight after all." Whittingham smiled at Andrew in triumph. He waved his pistol. "You may live."

Andrew's vision went red. He would rip the man to shreds. He stepped forward, fists clenched. But Jack grabbed both his arms from behind, firmly keeping him place. Charles lowered the gun. With a smirk, he grabbed Emma's hand, and they disappeared out the open door into the cold night.

Chapter 33

"Damn it, Jack. Let go of me!" Andrew struggled for several precious minutes to get out of his brother's grasp. "He is getting away!"

Jack finally released him, taking a step back, his face grim. "He had the gun trained on your heart. I couldn't let you get yourself killed."

Andrew raced out the doors after them. Whittingham dragged Emma across the lawn. Andrew froze, his heart beating wildly in his chest. They were almost to the back wall. Beyond it loomed the dark outline of the top of a carriage. If they made it through the gate, Whittingham would disappear with her.

Emma turned her head back, and the look of alarm on her face galvanized Andrew's brain into action. He gave an ear-piercing whistle, praying the dog was nearby. A moment later, out of the darkness, a large shadow raced across the lawn. A deep growl rang out in warning. In one powerful leap, Fergus tackled Charles, knocking him to the ground.

Andrew, his brother, and Constable Woolsey raced toward them. Whittingham lay face down in the grass, the dog's front paws on his back. Fergus growled in low menacing tones, his great jaws inches from the man's throat. Andrew pulled Emma into his arms. She buried herself against his chest. Her heart beat a rapid rhythm that matched his own.

He bent his head to bury his face in her hair. “Never do that again. What were you thinking going with him?”

Her head snapped up. “He was going to shoot you. It was the only way I could think of to distract him.”

“*I am* supposed to protect *you*!”

She laid a hand to his cheek. “Don’t be silly, we are supposed to take care of each other. You taught me that. I trusted you would come after me.”

Somewhat mollified, he leaned in to place a swift kiss on her lips. “Just promise me you won’t take risks like this in the future. My heart can’t take it.”

“Emma,” Jack interrupted, “perhaps you can call off your dog? We can handle it from here.”

They turned to look down at her uncle.

He lay very still, but his voice fumed. “Get this animal off of me!”

“Fergus, come here, boy,” Emma commanded. The dog’s head turned to her, one ear cocked up as though to say, “Are you sure?” “It’s all right, come,” Emma repeated.

Fergus stepped off of Whittingham and walked to her. She crouched down to give him a hug. “You were so brave. What a good boy.” The dog licked her face enthusiastically. She laughed and pushed up to her feet. Fergus sat next to her; Emma’s hand lay atop his head.

Constable Woolsey pulled Whittingham on his feet. He tied a length of rope around his wrists. Jack spied the pistol a few feet away and went to retrieve it. Woolsey turned to Andrew.

“Your Grace, I will have my men take him to the gaol. Is the lady willing to give a statement? If she is too overwrought, I can come back in the morning.”

Emma stiffened next to him. He looked down at her. She nodded her head, her eyes sparkling with anger. She looked more than ready to make sure her uncle was put away. He glanced over at Whittingham's furious expression. The man needed to be reminded how precarious his situation was.

"Yes, we will give a statement tonight. I will need a few minutes alone with Whittingham."

The constable cleared his throat. "That's highly irregular, Your Grace."

"Nevertheless, I will have a word with him privately." The constable, not foolish enough to keep arguing with a peer, nodded his assent. "Jack, would you please escort Miss Whittingham inside?"

Emma's expression was indignant. "Trust me?" he murmured. She still looked suspicious but allowed Jack to take her arm and lead her back inside the house.

He turned to Whittingham. "Come, Uncle, let's talk over here." He gave Whittingham a shove, directing the man to the low wall which circled the veranda. Far enough to ensure privacy, but still within sight of Constable Woolsey.

He got right to the point. "You cannot use her any longer, Whittingham. She is mine now to protect."

Whittingham's lip turned up in a sneer. "She was going to come with me tonight."

"She left with you to protect me from getting shot." He let the truth of that sink in for a moment. "Listen closely. I can make this go very badly for you. You were caught red-handed stealing from my house, threatened a peer of realm with a loaded pistol, kidnapped a lady." Andrew ticked the charges off on his fingers.

Whittingham's face paled as the seriousness of the charges sank in. Andrew continued. "If you breathe a word of Emma's involvement in your schemes, you will sound like a madman. A viscount's daughter working as a jewel thief? Preposterous."

Whittingham opened his mouth, but Andrew held up one hand to stop him from speaking. "My proposition is this: if you lead the constables to the auction and to your fence, then the magistrate will never know about the Ghost or any of your other identities from me. If you make any further trouble for Emma or any of her family, I will use the information I gathered to hammer the last nail into the coffin of a very long sentence. I can be an ally or your worst enemy."

He watched Emma's uncle consider the possibilities. The man let out a dejected sigh. "I was trying to help her, you know. She looked up at me that day in the solicitor's office with her tear-filled eyes. For the first time in my life, I felt compelled to step in and try and help. She's a brilliant thief."

"She would be brilliant at anything she put her mind to. I've never met a more resourceful, determined woman. She is amazing."

"You love her." Whittingham sounded astonished.

"Yes. She is going to be my duchess, if I can finally convince her to marry me." Andrew glanced back at the house. The light from his study spilled out into the darkness. He needed to get back inside and make sure she wasn't too shaken by the night's events.

When he turned his gaze back to Whittingham, he found the man staring at him, his expression inscrutable. Considering his options, no doubt.

Whittingham's next comment surprised him.

"I agree to your terms. I hate that bloody bastard Dorling anyway."

Andrew entered back into his study. Jack and Emma sat by the fireplace. Emma was sipping a glass of wine.

"I have convinced your uncle to turn in his fence and lead the constables to the auction tomorrow in return for me advocating a more lenient sentence for him. Woolsey is taking his statement now." He sat down next to Emma on the sofa. He ran a hand over his face. What a night.

"Will he tell about me, though?" She gnawed on her bottom lip.

"No, I think he knows he will just end up looking crazy if he tries to blame anything on you. As much as it pains me to say this, I think he has genuine affection for you, in his own warped way. I believe the threats in his letter were a bluff to get you to continue to work for him."

Emma sat back and took another sip of her wine. She closed her eyes. "It's not entirely his fault. I allowed him to take advantage of me. I could have looked harder at what money we made, asked to have a larger share. The truth was I was scared to go at it alone. He offered me an easy way to support the children, and I took it without regard for the consequences to others."

"You did what you had to, to take care of your family. There is no shame in that. You never used anyone the way he used you." Andrew was concerned about her defeated expression. He reached out, but she abruptly stood up.

"I think I am too tired to give my statement tonight after all. Please tell the constable to come back tomorrow." She downed the wine in her glass and handed it to him. "Goodnight."

Andrew watched her leave the room; a strange tightening around his heart made him rub the spot with his hand.

Jack leaned forward. "She'll be all right after a good sleep. She had a tough night."

****

Later in the night, Emma woke feeling safe and warm. Through a thick fog of exhaustion, she realized Andrew was in the bed with her, his long limbs wrapped around her from behind. His soft, even breathing soothed her. She snuggled closer and fell back to sleep.

When she woke again, sunlight streamed through the window. She was alone in her bed. The only indication Andrew slept there was the indent in the pillow next to her. Last night, when she had tumbled into bed, all the drama of her life had felt like a great ache in her chest. Now that the threat of her uncle telling her secret was lifted, she needed to figure out how she could break the cycle of her poor choices.

She reached over and grabbed the pillow, hugging it close. It still held Andrew's scent of bergamot and lemon. Thinking about him invigorated her. Today was a new day. She was no longer a thief, or a dutiful daughter, or that innocent girl of her youth. Today she was a wiser, stronger woman, and she would forge forward into a new future.

Chapter 34

The knock on her door came just as Francine finished fastening the buttons up the back of Emma's dress. She hurried over to the door, her heart in her throat. But when she opened the door, it was not Andrew. Instead, Lucy and Caroline came bustling into the room in a flurry of peach and pale blue skirts. Their arms linked, identical smiles wreathed their faces.

"Emma, you must come help us hang decorations. All of the fresh pine boughs that Mother ordered have arrived."

"Decorations for what?" Emma asked.

"Christmas, silly! It's at the end of this week," Caroline admonished.

"What? It can't be!" She looked from Caroline to Lucy. "How could I have not realized it was almost Christmas?"

Lucy reached out for her hand, giving it a squeeze. "It has been a rough month, with you going to take care of Mama's ill friend." She gave her a pointed look. "It's no wonder you haven't thought about the holiday."

"Oh dear, we better gather the children and head home this morning. We have baking and shopping to accomplish."

"No!" both ladies cried out, startling her.

They exchanged an odd look before Caroline continued, "Emma, you all must join us for Christmas. I want to invite Davenport as well. We haven't had a proper celebration of Lucy's and his engagement. We'll have a special Christmas dinner, just the family."

Lucy's head bobbed in agreement. "Davenport has no other family besides a few distant cousins. I do so want to see him for Christmas."

"I insist," Caroline said.

"Well…" Emma warmed to the idea. Christmas with Andrew and his boys. A proper celebration for Lucy and Davenport. "All right, I accept. If you're sure this is acceptable to your family? I don't want us to intrude."

"Andrew will be so pleased, I'm sure." Caroline gave her a hug. "Now come down and help us with the decorating. All the children are already downstairs. We'll have you taken home after teatime."

Emma allowed herself to be led downstairs. As they descended the stairs, the smell of pine filled her nose. There were a dozen servants rushing around in the entrance hall. Some were twining lengths of ribbon through the staircase railings; some were hanging long boughs above the great front doors. Many more were gathering fragrant boughs and wreaths and heading off to different sections of the house.

"The family always decorates the main drawing room ourselves. It's tradition." Caroline gestured for them to follow her.

When they entered through the door to the drawing room, a cacophony of cheerful sounds assailed them. Margie was playing "While Shepherds Watch Their Flocks" rather poorly but enthusiastically on the pianoforte. The sounds of children talking and singing mixed with the occasional bark and howl from one of the dogs. Indeed, the whole family was in attendance.

Max ran over to hug Emma around the legs. His brown eyes danced with excitement. "I am helping with the popcorn chain! And we can eat some while we work. Miss Vivian said it was all right."

"It looks like fun." She ran a hand over his soft mop of hair and grinned. "Get back to work."

Something bumped against her leg, and she automatically reached down to give Fergus a scratch behind his ears. "Have you been keeping watch on all the chaos, boy?"

Caroline led them over to a table. "Let's begin by cutting lengths of ribbons for making bows. And I'll explain the method to our madness."

Vivian already sat at the table, frowning down at a sea of red and gold ribbon. She looked up as they approached, relief etching her face. "Thank goodness you are here. Caroline, you know I am utterly hopeless at making bows. How I got assigned this task I do not know!"

They joined her around the table. "Here, you be in charge of cutting." Caroline handed Vivian a pair of scissors.

"I volunteer to help with cutting also. I have no earthly idea how to make a decent bow." Emma gave Vivian a wink.

"All right. Lucy, can you help me with bows?"

Lucy nodded her head. "Certainly."

Chatter around the table turned to what foods were favored for Christmas dinner. As the menu was discussed, Emma observed the room. Her eyes immediately found Andrew, standing in front of the fireplace with his son sitting on his shoulders.

"A little higher on the left, right there. What do you think, Tyler?"

"I think it still looks crooked," the boy replied.

There was a groan from Jack, who was standing on a ladder adjusting the giant wreath. "You two are killing me," he said over his shoulder, as he adjusted the wreath a bit to the right.

"Yes, perfect," Andrew proclaimed. He hefted Tyler down, giving the boy a kiss before setting his son on the floor. Then he turned, and his gaze met hers. He gave her a wide smile. Her heart fluttered in response. Looking down, she cut another length of red ribbon. This man loved so easily. A kiss to his son, teasing banter with his brother. Even after years of unhappiness and betrayal, the death of his wife, the struggle to get sober, he still wasn't afraid to love.

"Isn't that true, Emma?" Lucy interrupted her thoughts.

Emma shifted her attention to her sister. "Sorry, I missed that."

"I said we always hang stockings by the fire."

"Uh yes, the children love it," she said. Her eyes drifted back to Andrew.

He walked over to a table set with refreshments. He poured a glass of lemonade and brought it over to his mother. The duchess sat in an armchair, stringing popcorn and dried cranberries. Around her, most of the children had gathered on the floor, making their own strands. They listened to her tell a story about how in Germany St. Nicholas filled children's shoes with treats. Sunlight poured in to the room today, pooling around the group. Lady Gilchrest occasionally reached down to help the smaller boys push the needle through a particularly hard berry or gently admonish the girls for eating too much popcorn.

The duchess accepted the lemonade from Andrew, patting her son's hand affectionately. Then she reached into a basket next to her chair. She pulled out a round ball of mistletoe and pointed across the room.

"I think over in front of the entrance. Hang it from the ceiling. The nail should still be there from last year."

"Yes, ma'am." Andrew gave a small bow before he leaned in to buss her cheek.

Emma's scissors froze in mid snip. Her mind scrambled to catch up to what her heart already knew. This man was not going to hurt her or leave her. He had invited her to be part of his circle of loved ones, repeatedly. Why was she still afraid to take a chance and say yes?

A sense of calm settled over her, and she set her scissors down. She knew the answer. She wasn't afraid anymore. She rose to her feet. The other ladies looked up quizzically, but she ignored them. All she could see was Andrew.

****

Andrew hung the ball of mistletoe from the ceiling. Giving it a small tug, he was satisfied that it wouldn't fall off. A rustle of skirts caused him to glance down. Emma stood at the base of the ladder, her beautiful face upturned and very serious.

"Emma, you look lovely this morning. Are you wanting a kiss under the mistletoe?" he teased her. "I'm happy to oblige."

Emma shook her head. "No."

"No?" He began to climb down the ladder.

"No. I want so much more."

He froze, one foot still on the second rung. Around them, shouting from the boys rang out. Lord Pettigrew raced by at full speed with a chain of popcorn in his mouth. The children all got to their feet to join in pursuit. Then the other dogs, wanting to get into the game, barked and raced by the ladder as well.

Emma didn't move, never broke eye contact with him. It was as though the whole world shrank down to just the two of them. All the chaos in the room became a blur.

Her chest rose and fell as she took in a deep breath. "Andrew, your love has changed everything for me. The courage with which you love despite your battered heart amazes me. I didn't think I was worthy of it." Her eyes grew watery. He quickly stepped to the floor and took hold of one of her hands, bringing it to his lips. Overwhelmed, he shook his head in denial. It was he who was floored by her courage to continue on after the abuses she had endured.

Her shoulders straightened. "I want more than what I thought I deserved. I want to be your wife. I want to wake up next to you each morning for the rest of my life. I want to dance with you, and laugh with you, and raise all these children together, and maybe a few more. It's been difficult to have the courage to trust in love. For me to take a chance with my heart. But I am finished with being afraid to reach for happiness." She took a step closer and placed her hand over his heart. "I love you. You make me indescribably happy. Andrew Blakely Langdon, will you marry me?"

Her words washed over him, rushed into that small corner of his heart where he'd still believed maybe he had been mistaken about her feelings for him.

"Yes." He pressed his lips to hers. His arms slid around her to bring her close, trapping her hand against the beat of his heart.

She pulled back her head slightly, a line of worry creasing her brow. "Are you sure? An uncle in prison, four more children, and don't forget all the dogs…"

Andrew interrupted her with another swift kiss. "Yes," he murmured against her mouth. "My answer is yes."

He knew this woman would need reassurance she had made the right decision to trust in him. He was happy to oblige her every day for the rest of their lives. He spoke softly, his forehead resting against hers as he stared into her golden-brown eyes.

"For much of the last year, I was mired in anger and guilt. Then you climbed through my window. I knew from that moment my life would never be the same. I had resigned myself to a life of duty, taking care of my sons, taking care of my estates. You and your family have brought vitality and laughter back into my life…into our lives," he corrected. "I've realized my boys need me to be more than just present. They need me to show them how to live life after tragedy. We welcome all the chaos, energy, the love you all bring. I love you, Emma Whittingham. I vow to love and care for you, your siblings, and all the crazy dogs you wish to have, for as long as I live."

Her eyes shone with unshed tears as he captured her trembling lips. No amount of words could express his feelings of happiness at this moment. He could only let them pour out into that kiss. Emma's eyes fluttered closed, and her whole body melted against him. He finally managed to capture her trust and with it her elusive heart.

Epilogue

"Ooh, look—they've trimmed the front door with holly," Abby exclaimed. Her nose pressed against the window of the carriage as they rolled up the drive to Gilchrest House.

As the carriage came to a stop, Emma saw Andrew emerge from the house. He stood tall and handsome as ever, snowflakes falling to dust his shoulders. A welcoming smile graced his face, and he lifted a hand to wave as he descended the stone steps.

Emma had not seen him in several days. There had been far too much to do in preparation for Christmas. Purchasing Christmas presents for the children, preparing Boxing Day gifts for Mrs. Fenway and Francine, mending and pressing their best clothes for Christmas dinner with the Langdons. The last few nights, Emma had fallen exhausted into bed.

She flung open the carriage door, nearly knocking the poor footman senseless. Not caring about propriety, she flew across the short distance between them and threw herself into his waiting arms. Feeling those strong arms band tightly around her, she buried her nose into his neck, drinking in the scent which was uniquely Andrew. The fur collar of her cape tickled her ears along with his warm breath.

"Hello, my love. Miss me?" He laughed at her enthusiastic greeting.

But Emma didn't mind. "Yes, indeed I did, Your Grace," she mumbled against his throat.

Fergus' paws landed against them, and his large wet nose snuffled against her cheek. They broke their embrace, laughing. Excited voices rang out as her family tumbled from the carriages. Last to exit was Lucy, who step elegantly down. Her eyes scanned from Emma and Andrew across to the front door, and a smile bloomed on her face. Davenport stood on the top step, a large black umbrella open above him. The look exchanged between him and her sister proved Emma wasn't the only one who had missed her beau.

"Let's get everyone inside," Andrew said.

In the drawing room a fire was roaring. Caroline greeted them with a warm smile. "Welcome. Happy Christmas! Can you believe the snowflakes outside? Normally we have to be at Stoneleigh for any hope of a white Christmas."

"It is a lovely surprise," Emma agreed. Then she made her way over to Andrew's mother. "Happy Christmas, Your Grace."

The duchess gave her a kiss on the cheek. "Happy Christmas, my dear. We are so glad your family could join us for dinner."

Two footmen came through with trays of hot apple cider. Emma wrapped her hands around the mug, grateful for the warmth it gave off. A tray of gingerbread squares set on a low table caught the attention of the children. They devoured the fragrant biscuits while they sipped their cider.

The duchess clapped her hands. "Let's give out some gifts before dinner, shall we?"

A chorus of yesses rang out. Emma stood back

behind the sofa as the children gathered on the rug to open gifts. The happiness and excitement of their faces warmed her heart. This strange feeling replaced her usual knot of worry and regret in the center of her chest. She rubbed the spot with her fingers as she realized the feeling was hope.

Max and William would be raised as gentlemen. They would be able to attend the right schools and stand with their peers as equals. The girls would be able to make proper matches, with gentlemen that they chose. It had been sheer luck Lucy had met Davenport. Her sister could have just as easily ended up marrying the wrong man simply for financial security.

Emma watched Lucy open a gift from her betrothed, who sat next to her. She pulled out a velvet scarf in a vibrant blue hue. Lucy rubbed the soft fabric across her cheek. Davenport took the scarf from her hands and gently wrapped it around her neck. The smile they exchanged was intimate and full of love.

Emma startled as a hand stole around her waist from behind. Andrew turned her to face him, his hand still settled on her waist.

"You wore the dress I bought you." His other hand was behind his back.

"Francine mended the shoulder for me. I though the red flowers were just right for Christmas."

"You look beautiful." He brought his arm out from behind his back and held out a beautifully wrapped present. "I have a gift for you."

"You shouldn't have. I haven't anything in return." She'd barely had time to shop for gifts for the children. Distressed, she eyed the package with its elaborate gold bow on top.

“Open it,” he commanded. Then he smiled and gave her a cheeky wink.

She snatched the gift from his hands, quickly untying the bow. Unwrapping the beautiful paper with care, underneath she found a flat velvet box. Her head snapped up. Andrew stood there looking supremely pleased with himself, his hands clasped behind his back. Emma slowly lifted the lid, and she could not hold back a gasp as dozens of rubies winked at her from their dark velvet background.

“Turn around and let me place it around your neck.” Andrew’s eyes glowed under hooded lids.

Emma knew exactly what he was thinking. She too remembered the last time she had worn these jewels in Andrew’s bedroom, and all that happened between them that night. She shook her head to break the spell the memory wove around them.

“I couldn’t. These are your mother’s.”

“Who do you think gave them to me? She wants you to have them.” Andrew gently turned her away from him. Picking up the necklace from the case in her hands, he drew the necklace around her throat. The ruby flowers and gold filigree vines wound down her collarbone, and the large ruby pendant hung right above her cleavage.

She looked across to where the duchess sat, catching her eye. Emma lowered into a curtsy. The older woman smiled and gave a graceful nod of her head. Emma leaned her head back against Andrew’s shoulder. She drank in the cheer and chatter from the family gathered. Feeling Andrew’s strong chest behind her and his arm about her waist, she allowed herself to believe that this could actually be her future.

Emma ran her fingers along the red gemstones at her throat. This necklace would always be her most-prized possession. Not because of the value it held, but because it had brought her to Andrew. She had planned to steal a small fortune in rubies, but instead she had stolen his heart and gained a sense of hope in love and what the future could hold.

Check out the following preview from

Book Three
in the
Hearts of Stoneleigh Manor Series

Unmask My Heart

featuring Caroline Langdon.

And if you missed Jack and Vivian's story, you can find it in
Book One, *Captain of My Heart.*

Happy Reading!

Sounds of laughter and the strains of Brahms spilled from the open doorways of the ballroom. From this distance, everything looked bright and shiny. Small knots of guests congregated on the veranda, and the glowing ends of cheroots flared like fireflies. There were no torches placed along the garden paths, and the darkness felt cool and damp where he sat in the wisteria-covered arbor. Silently a shadow approached, the soft crunch of pebbles barely audible. Cage stood to his full height and waited for the man to enter the privacy of the arbor.

"Winters." He nodded to his superior at the Foreign Office.

"Morgan. It's nice to see you dressed appropriately for once."

Cage ran his hands down the lapels of his formal jacket and smiled. "You said to look pretty, so here I am trussed up like a pig to market. What's the job?"

"I don't believe pretty was the term I used." Winters chuckled. "Regardless, I need you to blend in with that crowd in there, so whatever makes you feel pretty…" He smirked.

Cage had the uneasy feeling his joke was about to turn on him. Winters expression settled into grim lines. He sat heavily onto the curved bench. Cage settled next to him. Setting one ankle across his knee, he waited. Winters never spoke without full deliberation.

"Madame du Barry runs an exclusive brothel in

Convent Garden. She was the darling in the French court before the revolution, said to have been a favorite of Louis. Then she managed to return to Paris as a close friend of Campeau. Last year during The Peace, she turned up like a bad penny here in London. I know that she caters to Knightsbridge, Watson, and Gaylord. Knightsbridge came to me, practically on his knees, to confess she was blackmailing him. Threatening to let his particular sexual proclivities be made public if he didn't pass on the exact locations where we've erected blockades. Damn fool."

Cage snorted in agreement. *What a mess*. He had a pretty clear picture already of why Winters needed him. Not exactly the action he had been expecting, but it would keep him in England, and for that he was grateful. He had his own mystery to solve, one on which he couldn't afford to lose focus.

"He had enough sense to placate her with false information. But she is far from done with him. I can't let him hang in the wind. We need his vote. Everyone is tiring of Addington, and many say Pitt is next in line for Prime Minister." Winters ran a hand over the back of his neck.

"Can't you just arrest her now? Certainly Knightsbridge's testimony would be enough to have her hanged for treason."

"Not yet. I need you to get in there and find out what other secrets she has ferreted away. I don't want any surprises. You need to be invited by a current client. No outsiders allowed without a reference. So get inside and make some friends, Lord Wrotham."

His head snapped up at the name. "No. Not like that." He be damned if he'd use that bastard's name.

"Morgan, we can't concoct a name this time. It's too risky. She will do her research for any new client. We need the title to be recognized immediately. The mysterious heir reappears into society. That's your entre. Besides, according to your invitation, you are Wrotham." His expression brooked no further argument.

Cage reluctantly took the card held out to him. "You are a real bastard, you know."

"Think of it as just another alias. No more than another skin you've slipped on. See you inside, Lord Wrotham." Winters disappeared into the night as silently as he had arrived. Cage slipped the invitation into his pocket and stood. All of a sudden, his perfectly tied cravat felt as though it was strangling him. Damn it, why did it have to be Wrotham?

He had over the years taken on the role of a cast of different characters: wealthy lord, innkeeper, highwayman, footpad, sailor, horse breeder. He could copy any accent, any demeanor—his ability for mimicry discovered by his lieutenant by accident one night. Cage had been entertaining his fellow soldiers with an impression of the French commander Napoleon. His value as an undercover agent was immediately recognized.

Cage strolled down the pebbled path, walking parallel to the long stone veranda. The din from the ballroom lessened as he made his way to the far corner of the house. The invitation with Wrotham's name burned against his chest like a hot coal. The name only brought with it regret. Grace. He wanted to throw back his head and yell her name into the night. Not that it would help him find her. Pinching the bridge of his nose, he closed his eyes, hoping to find some inner calm. A soft thud echoed in his ears as something whacked him in the head. He looked down to find a mask, its jewels winking at him from the grass.

He bent down to retrieve the mask, and when he straightened, he looked around for the owner. Stepping out of the shadows, he looked up at the veranda lit by torches. A woman stood at the balustrade, her face tipped to the sky, her eyes closed. Mahogany hair framed an oval face, with a small pointed nose and high cheekbones. Dark lashes lay against luminescent skin. An emerald green gown encased her lush figure. Torchlight created flickering shadows across her face, giving the illusion of a tortured expression. Drawn to her, he stepped forward.

"I believe this belongs to you."

The woman startled. Her eyes flew open. He came closer, into a circle of light that spilled onto the lawn. Giving his most charming smile, he held up the mask. She frowned, assessing him. Her gaze fell onto the mask, and the frown deepened.

"You may keep the dratted thing."

"It's not really my style." Cage laid the mask on the balustrade. She sighed, and a delicate fingertip traced the edge of the mask. "Miss, are you all right?"

"Have you ever wanted to run away? Go somewhere no one knows who you are and start over."

"Yes." He had been running his whole damned life.

"Did you? Run I mean."

"Yes."

"Did it work? Can you outrun who you are?" She gazed down at him with wide sad eyes.

He thought of the name on the invitation in his

pocket. “No. No, you can’t.”

She straightened at his response. Wiping her cheeks with the back of one hand, she appeared to gather her emotions. “What you must think of me standing here feeling sorry for myself when I have so much. A wonderful family, all the pretty things I could ever want.” She took in a deep breath. “I’m sorry you were witness to my display of self-pity. Perhaps you could forget this entire conversation?”

“As you wish, my lady.” He gave a bow. He knew all too well that money was not always a buffer to suffering. He wondered what she wanted to run from.

“I best get back inside before someone notices I am missing.” She gave a small curtsy and rushed off down the veranda, leaving the glittering mask behind.

A word about the author...

From the time she read fairy tales as a child, Karla was hooked on stories that ended in Happily Ever After. She was fourteen when she read her first romance and discovered there was a whole genre that celebrated the HEA. Karla writes sexy historical romance with strong, spirited heroines and flawed heroes with hearts of gold.

When she is not reading or writing, she is cheering on, applauding, or chauffeuring around her two talented kids. She lives in Northern Virginia with her husband, her children, and two adorable pups.

http://www.karlakratovil.com

Thank you for purchasing
this publication of The Wild Rose Press, Inc.

For questions or more information
contact us at
info@thewildrosepress.com.

The Wild Rose Press, Inc.
www.thewildrosepress.com